THE LAST SECRET

Cover designed by Regina Wamba/Mae I Design.
Interior formatting by Key of Heart Design.
Interior graphics © Dover Publications, Inc.

Published by Snowy Wings Publishing
Turner, OR
www.snowywingspublishing.com

ISBN: 978-1-948661-27-0
eBook ISBN: 978-1-948661-26-3

Third Edition.

PRAISE FOR HEARTS OUT OF WATER

THE LAST SECRET

HEARTS OUT OF WATER · BOOK THREE

ANNIE COSBY

Snowy Wings
PUBLISHING

TO MOM

my life is better for being your mini-me

Is maith an scéalaí an aimsir.
Time is a good storyteller.
(Time will tell.)

- IRISH PROVERB

An t-am ar Fad
ALL ALONG

MY ARMS SHOOK. HE WAS GONE. AIDAN WAS gone. The wind lashed at those of us left on shore as we scrabbled around the rocks in confusion and terror.

"Oh my God," Rosie muttered. "Oh my God. He didn't … Oh my God."

"Roz, be quiet," I said as gently as possible, glancing at Rory, who sat down on the side of a decrepit boat, his knees jiggling and his head in his hands.

"Be quiet? Be quiet?" Rosie roared at me, her hands in her wet, tangled hair. "A guy just turned into a seal, and you want me to be *quiet*?"

I looked nervously around us, but there was no one within hearing distance. The rain was letting up now, but it had fortunately been heavy enough to keep most morning walkers away. I pulled the soaked long sleeves of the dress I'd borrowed from Rosie the night before over my hands.

"We have to go to the cops," Rosie said, her voice shrill. "Now!"

"Are you kidding?" Rory snapped, his face contorted in anger. "We can't go to the freaking cops!"

"Your brother just disappeared!" Rosie shouted at him. "And you're not going to report it?"

"What are they going to do?" Rory yelled, launching to his feet. "He won't be found! He can't be found! It would raise more questions than we can answer without being sent to an institution!"

"Well—"

"He's right, Roz," I interrupted softly, putting a hand on her arm. It was cold and clammy through the sopping sleeve of her dress. She hadn't changed out of her previous night's outfit, either. "At the very least, we'd waste the cops' time looking for someone who can't be found, while people actually missing are still lost and alone out there."

Rosie gulped, wrapped her arms tighter around herself, and recommenced her mantra: "Oh my God. Oh my God. Oh my God."

"Besides, he sent that letter to my parents," Rory murmured. "They'll know he's not missing. They won't know the right reason, but…"

"You have to tell them the truth!" Rosie snapped.

"Oh, please do counsel me on how to tell my adoptive parents that my birth parents are mythical creatures!" Rory nearly screamed at her. "You, who haven't known hardship a day in your life!"

Heat raced up my neck. Last summer, Rory and I had gone through so much trying to overcome the differences in our upbringings. But I couldn't dwell on that now. No, now we had a much bigger problem.

I glanced around again. There were still no eavesdroppers, but my heart tripped around in my chest all the same. There in the water behind us was the boat Rory and I had sneaked onto the night he told me I'd broken his heart. And across the river was the Spanish Arch, where a bird had shit on my head and it had somehow seemed enticing to a dog. And over there was the beach where I'd lost my shoes to the tide and where Rory had later given me a Claddagh ring. How far away all those things felt. It seemed we had stepped through a break in time the second Aidan had disappeared.

"Y-you can't let your parents think he's traipsing around Europe," Rosie stammered, "when … when … "

My eyes flashed to the water. The mouth of the river opened up to Galway Bay, which, much farther out, met up with the great Atlantic Ocean. And out there, somewhere, were two O'Learys now. "Where …where do you think he went?" I whispered, more of a rhetorical question than anything.

"I don't know!" Rory wailed, his head in his hands again as he paced the beach. His hair was wet and plastered to his forehead, and I could see he was shaking. "God, what are Mum and Dad going to think? Eventually, I mean? That he just disappeared on his little trip to Germany to find our birth mother? They'll be horrified."

"Maybe it won't come to that," I said. "When is he coming back?"

"I don't know, Cora!" Rory bellowed.

"Thirty years!" Rosie yelled. "He talked about coming back in thirty years!"

"Okay, not helping," I hissed at her.

"Y-you gotta go to that guy," she stammered, unperturbed, "that old guy. Your dad. That's the only thing to do. If we can't go to the cops—"

"That man," Rory said through clenched teeth, "is not my father."

"What does it freaking matter?" Rosie yelled. "Your brother, your flesh and blood, just transformed his flesh and blood into a freaking animal!"

"We don't know that for sure," I said, as if that would help the situation. I glanced desperately at Aidan's discarded clothes. "Maybe he's out there swimming, ended up farther down the shoreline after … after failing." Failing to transform, to accomplish this unfathomable plan he put into action. Looking from Rory's face to Rosie's, I could tell nobody was really listening. "We should go back to the apartment and wait," I finished lamely. "He might be on his way back now."

Silence descended upon our little corner of the boat graveyard. It had never felt so much like a graveyard, either. Cold and silent, the boats rose like gloomy specters from the rocky shore. Only the sound of the seagulls broke the silence as I imagined Mrs. O'Leary here, listening to this conversation, reading Aidan's note. As much as I wanted to believe this was all a dream, I knew it wasn't. Aidan had come out here with his sealskin to try what Rory wouldn't dare. My mother's grief-stricken face rose in my mind, or what I imagined it would look like, years younger, having just lost her first daughter. Her face was followed swiftly by Mrs. O'Leary's.

Oh, Aidan. What have you done? His brother paced relentlessly, and I couldn't bring myself to imagine how Mrs. O'Brien would react when she received that letter. I wanted to reach for Rory, hug him, comfort him, but all of a sudden, he stopped.

And crumpled inward.

He looked so delicate I didn't dare touch him.

"This is my fault," he finally said, and there was so much water in his chocolate-brown eyes, tears filled my own.

"No, it's not," I said quickly, rushing toward him, the tennis shoes I'd thrown on in my haste this morning squishing beneath my toes.

Rory waved me off before I could reach him. But his eyes never met my face. "I should have told him. A long time ago."

Before I could even comprehend what that meant, Rosie turned like a flash. "Told him what?" she asked, suspicion lacing her voice.

"He wouldn't have made this brash decision if he'd known all along."

Something prickly climbed up my spine. "What do you mean?"

Rory merely sniffed.

"Rory?" I said, willing him to look at me.

He wouldn't.

Suddenly my soaked shoes felt like they contained an ocean. Like my feet couldn't find solid ground. I was slipping and sliding. Drowning.

After a long hesitation, Rory finally said, "I knew." It was nearly a whisper, his eyes still on the perfect stones of the shore, worn smooth by years, decades—centuries—of saltwater waves. "I've known for years."

My blood ran cold. "Known what?"

"All of it."

All of …

"Who Mrs. O'Leary was, Seamus, the selkie thing…everything. I started figuring it out on my own shortly after Seamus left, and once I started asking questions, Mr. Hall came clean."

No.

My mind was whirling, stuck in a relentless tornado. This whole year I'd spent in turmoil—to tell him or not to tell him, grappling with reality and the surreal turn my life had taken—and he'd known all along?

"I asked Mr. Hall not to tell Aidan. He was just a kid, and he had such a hard childhood, with the illness and everything. And Mr. Hall agreed. He didn't think Aidan needed to know. He said he wouldn't even have told me if I hadn't started snooping around. And Aidan's shy, it wasn't hard to keep him away from Mrs. O'Leary's. He never learned enough to question any of it."

Is that why Mrs. O'Leary had never recognized Aidan as her second son? Rory had endeavored—successfully—to keep his own brother from their birth mother?

The absurdity, the underhandedness, the deception of it, made my already freezing bones ache with a cold quite unrelated to the temperature.

Rory had found out about his true past and then spent years lying to people about it. Not least of whom, his own brother.

"Why?" The whisper was out before I registered that it was from my own mouth.

A single tear slid down Rory's cheek. There was no more rain to disguise it. And it surprised me that I felt no urge to wipe it away. No urge to comfort him.

"I was scared, Cora," he said. "I didn't want to believe, but there was a seemingly trusted adult telling me everything I'd ever suspected, all the pieces that seemed to fit together really did make up this giant puzzle that explained the entirety of my life! Was I supposed to just dump that on my little brother? I was scared."

That, at least, I could relate to. I'd been scared for the last ten months. Not a day had gone by that I didn't worry about whether or not I should tell Rory O'Brien what I'd found out last summer. But I was scared. Alone.

And as much as I wanted to understand that same fear of his, there was another, stronger emotion coursing through me.

Anger.

"You lied."

Rory shook his head desperately. "I—"

"When we got here," I said. "When we got to Ireland…you…you pretended not to know!"

"I played along," Rory said, his shoulder lifting in a helpless shrug, his face the picture of despair. "I'm sorry! I didn't know how to tell him I'd kept this secret from him. I was afraid if I did, he'd do something drastic! Something ... something like this." He gestured weakly at the sea. "And I really…really believed Seamus would stay hidden."

"You knew," I said, the ghosts of emotions long past filling me as I remembered how lonely and terrifying this last year had been. "You knew!"

"I know. I'm sorry, Cora. I'm so sorry you got caught in the middle of this."

Caught. That made it sound like it was all an accident. Like I hadn't stepped willingly into the fray. And that wasn't quite accurate.

But I could certainly step willingly out of it.

Cosc
BANNED

T HE APARTMENT FELT STIFLING. IT WAS IRELAND, but it might as well have been Missouri for the way I was sweating. Niamh and Niall were both at work, but Rex stood looking between the three of us as we sat in the sitting room, as still as the Oscar Wilde statue below the window.

"So … are we going to the cops?" Rosie finally piped up. She'd regained some of her composure and had stopped muttering, "Oh my God," every other breath, but I could tell she was still ruffled. Her usually perfect hair was still in morning disarray, and she hadn't looked in a mirror once yet today.

"No," Rory said, standing.

"Seriously, are we going through this again?" Rosie asked.

Without a word, Rory left the room, his sneakers making soft squeaks on the tiles in the hall.

"Cora," Rosie said, turning to me immediately after the door closed. "I think we should leave."

I gulped. As much as I wanted to tell her I couldn't leave him now, I was angry. I didn't want to be, not with everything he was going through, but the emotion was there in my veins, as identifiable as anything. The sand in my clothes itched, making my skin crawl, and I pulled at the dress. We'd slept in these sandy clothes. The couch was probably covered in it, and it suddenly became very important to me to go check. To clean it. To do anything mundane and simple. Of this world.

"Cora," Rosie said, louder, prompting Rex to jump to his feet. "He lied to you. To everyone. About something preeeetty huge!"

I bit the inside of my lip. It would be so easy to leave now. Go with Rosie to the airport and slip back into our lives, where we'd pretend none of this had ever happened. Couldn't we? Maybe not. With my dad's lawsuit. With everything we knew now. Home wouldn't be the same.

But it would probably still be mundane. And simple. It would be so easy to leave.

Wouldn't it? I'd tried to do that once before. And I'd failed miserably. That's how I'd ended up here in Ireland.

"Our return tickets aren't for another week," I said.

Rosie rolled her eyes toward the ceiling. "This is bad, Cora, so bad, and it's only going to get worse. I think we should change our tickets and go home. Today."

My anger flared up, aggravated by new annoyance. "I suggested a week for this trip, Rosie. *You* were the one who wanted to 'make it two'! You told me to 'live a little'!"

"Yeah, well, I didn't exactly know we were going on this spooky, bizarre…what…seal hunt, now did I?" She looked at me pointedly. "Rory's not the only one who was keeping secrets, was he?"

Rex growled low in his throat, the tension clearly making him nervous.

Rosie was right. I had not told her the real reason behind this trip. She hadn't known what she was stepping into. Yes, there was plenty of subterfuge and guilt to go around. And maybe that's why I couldn't leave just yet.

"I have to stay," I said, twisting the Claddagh ring that was so new to my hand it felt like a foreign body, hanging there on my finger. Back and forth, back and forth, my left hand twisted it. "He's … my boyfriend." It was the first time I'd ever used the word, and I saw Rosie's eyes widen almost imperceptibly, but there was no other word for what Rory meant to me. "He's all alone now. But you can go—"

"I can't leave you here!" Rosie snapped, looking appalled that I would suggest such a thing.

The door opened again, and Rory stood there, looking nervous, his brown hair ruffled as though he'd been running his hands through it. "I think you're right. We should go to Seamus."

Rosie and I just looked at him.

"I-I probably have between one and three weeks before my parents find out," Rory went on. "Before that letter arrives, if Aidan really did send one. I have to figure out what to do before then… And I don't know who else to go to."

It was as good a plan as any.

"Cora and I were just discussing—"

"I agree," I said quickly. "Let's go to Seamus. See what he told Aidan."

Rory looked relieved, and I sent Rosie a pointed look. If she thought I could walk away now when we were so deep in this, she didn't know me at all.

"Three tickets to Inis Mór…because my friend has no backbone and I, apparently, don't either," Rosie said in a mockingly placid voice.

The man behind the counter chuckled. I recognized him from the first time we'd been here in Rossaveal—he was the man who'd bought Aran Ferry from Seamus. "Ye sure ye don't wanna try Inis Oírr? Just as fascinating a place, I can promise that. And Inis Mór's fierce crowded today."

Rory opened his mouth, but Rosie interrupted him. "We have … business … on Inis Mór," she said curtly.

"Tha's not somethin' I hear every day," the ferryman said with a chuckle. "Very well. Coming right up." He turned to an ancient laptop perched on the counter. "Where ye from?"

"The U.S.," Rosie said.

"I could tell that righ' enough," the friendly man said with a laugh.

"St. Louis," I clarified when it was apparent Rory wasn't going to partake in pleasantries. He'd been particularly quiet on the bus ride here, and now he'd wandered off to study a giant poster about one of the Aran Islands hanging on the wall of the trailer.

"Ohhh!" the ticket man said. "The one with the … " As I looked up at him, he drew an arch shape in the air. "Hang on." He squinted through his glasses. "You're the pair who was here with them American lads looking for Seamus O'Leary." He glanced from me and Rosie to Rory at the back of the room.

I looked over my shoulder at Rory, whose ears reddened, but he didn't turn, leaving me to stare helplessly at his backpack. As much as my heart wanted to go grab his hand and comfort him, face this whole mess together, there was a bitter part of me that couldn't stop the refrain:

He knew. All along, he knew.

"Yeah," I said quietly, turning back to the ferryman.

"So now, did ye find him?" he asked conversationally.

It took me a moment to remember who he was talking about.

"Yeah," Rory said darkly, turning back to us. "He's living on the island. And he's a—"

"Expecting us," I interrupted quickly. No doubt he was going to end that sentence with a word like "prick" or "life-ruining bastard" or maybe some new insult he'd learned living in Ireland.

"You know him well," I said to the man, attempting to cover up the awkward exchange, "don't you?"

The man shrugged. "Well enough. We were acquaintances back in the day, and I spent some time with 'im learning the ropes—literally—before I bought the boats off 'im." The man chuckled again. "He's a strange enough fellow."

"What do you mean?" Rory asked, eyes narrowing.

"Oh, he keeps to himself mostly. In a small place like this, that's a bit frowned on. Leave a man to his own devices, I say, but the rest … they'll gossip."

It reminded me of what Mr. Hall had told me Oyster Beach had done to Mrs. O'Leary when she was young and new to town. I wondered if Mr. O'Leary liked the same treatment. Bitterness rose inside me. I didn't want to dislike Seamus already, but I was predisposed to blame him. He had left his whole family because of a mistake he'd made—falling in love with a selkie woman.

"Let me get ye booked," the ferryman said pleasantly, oblivious to Rory's bad mood or my roiling emotions. He turned back to the computer. "Names?"

"Rosario Balducci," Rosie said before nodding at me.

"Cora Manchester."

"Rory O'Brien."

"Could you spell that Italian one?"

Rosie did, and after a moment, the computer made a *bling* sound that I associated with error boxes popping up.

"Arah, here," the man snapped at the computer, frowning.

"What? You don't get a lot of Italians over here?" Rosie asked.

The man shook his head, clicked the mouse a few times, and started typing again. "B-a-l-d-u-c-c-i," he whispered to himself.

The computer dinged again.

"To be honest, it's saying you two are on our no-sail list."

Oh my God.

Rosie's cheeks reddened, and I slapped a hand to my forehead.

"That can't be," Rosie said, recovering smoothly.

"Well," the man said, and his voice had lost its friendly luster, "luckily I always have my staff add a note when they ban a customer, and this says you tackled one of our hands."

In all the drama of the past few days, I'd completely forgotten that Rosie had jumped on top of an employee of the ferry company in order to convince them to wait for Aidan and Rory. And really, I hadn't expected to be returning to the island any time soon. Or ever.

"We … I … " Rosie looked desperately at Rory, who's face had turned an ominous shade of red, and then me.

I shrugged helplessly. "You're the one who tackled the guy! I was going to let them leave Aidan."

The man behind the counter crossed his arms over his chest, all pleasantries having evaporated completely.

"Look, we didn't mean to," Rosie said sweetly. "Well, I mean, I *did* mean to tackle him, but … "

"Do I have to call my security man?" the ferryman asked.

"There's security out here?" Rosie said incredulously.

"Okay, I think we should go," I said, grabbing Rosie's arm.

"Oh, let 'em on, Paddy!"

All three of us whirled around at the newcomer's lilting voice. A young woman stood there, a load of shopping bags in her arms.

"Now, Lorna, you stay out of it. They're on the no-sail list," the supposed Paddy said firmly.

"So's half the island, ya big brute!" Lorna winked at us. "Now give 'em their tickets and then get me two. Deirdre's waitin' outside, and we want to go home."

The ferry pitched violently to the right, and I felt my stomach go with it. Maybe it would have been better if the mysterious Lorna hadn't come to our rescue after all.

"Thanks for getting us on," I said anyway as Lorna shuffled into a row behind us in the covered part of the boat. I sat beside Rory, our arms carefully not touching, and Rosie sat a few seats away from us, sprawled across several of them.

"Oh, it was nothing," the woman said, shifting her many shopping bags, which lay around her feet. "Paddy's an ogre when it comes to his boats."

"Get anything good?" Rosie asked, in a considerably better mood after defeating Paddy the Ferryman.

"Oh, this and that," Lorna said with a bright smile.

"It looks like you bought an entire store," Rosie said.

"We don't make it into Galway much, so when we do, I stock up on everything," she explained. "My friend Deirdre's up at the snack counter." The ferry did indeed have a counter where they sold small bottles of water and bags of chips. At first I'd found it strange, but now that I realized how often the islanders must have to go to the mainland, it seemed convenient.

"Isn't there anywhere to shop on the island?" Rosie asked.

By this point, my stomach was roiling as angrily as the waves outside, but I tried to follow the small talk for the sake of manners.

"Ah, no," Lorna said. "Not for clothes or anything besides the essentials. Wouldn't be enough business in the winter to keep them going."

Just like Oyster Beach. During a heated argument last summer,

Rory had reminded me that none of the kids in the big houses knew what Oyster Beach looked like in the winter. So it appeared that in the end, Mr. O'Leary had left one Oyster Beach for another. A glance at Rory's face didn't reveal whether he was even listening, his eyes on the waves outside the window. But the movement made my head whirl, and I had to look away.

"So there aren't any tourists in the winter?" Rosie asked our newfound friend.

"There'd be some, but not like the summer, and none of 'em wanting to rent a bike when the wind's fierce howlin'. The bike shop, that's where Deirdre here works." She reached out to take a miniature bottle of water from the woman walking toward her and added, "Thanks, love."

Just as the new woman's face registered in my slow, nausea-addled brain, Rosie chirped, "You work for that Kevin Browne guy!" and Rory whipped around.

"Kieran," I corrected, hoping the action of opening my mouth wouldn't invite vomiting.

"Oh, that's right, Kieran Browne," Rosie repeated.

Sure enough, it was Deirdre. The woman we'd encountered working behind the counter in Kieran Browne's bike shop. And her face had gone stark white.

"I was just telling these Yanks a bit about the island," Lorna said, motioning for Deirdre to sit beside her. Deirdre did, slowly, depositing her own shopping bags on the floor as her glance flew between Rosie, Rory, and I, her face looking increasingly frantic.

"We were there last week," Rosie said, also noticing the woman's strange reaction. "You gave us bikes to go meet up with Kieran?"

But remembering us wasn't the problem. Deirdre nodded, her lips pressed tightly together, her gaze lingering on Rory, who looked just as uncomfortable as she did.

Rosie looked at me to exchange a look, but I was teetering on the edge of total humiliation and could do nothing but stare at the floor and hope my stomach didn't embarrass me.

"Ye've met then?" Lorna asked, surprised.

"Briefly," Deirdre said. "They came into the shop." An awkward silence descended, one in which even Lorna seemed concerned about her friend's reticence.

"So you work for Kevin Browne," Rosie finally said with the air of someone struggling to maintain an impossible conversation.

"Kieran," Deirdre corrected again, so I didn't have to. I heard a touch of ice in her voice. "My father-in-law."

I felt bile in my throat and lurched forward, but it was a false alarm. Rosie and Lorna glanced at me like I was deranged, but Rory touched my arm gently. I shook my head, trying to tell him I was fine—a total lie, but some sort of automatic defense mechanism.

"What are you doing out here again?" Deirdre asked, her eyes still on me under a furrowed brow. Though the question was friendly enough, her tone implied otherwise.

"I was wonderin' too," Lorna said cheerfully. "What's out here that could possibly entertain young folks like yourselves so soon again?"

"We're here to see Seamus O'Leary," Rosie babbled on. Rory threw her a dark look, and I thought to stop her there—was she really going to reveal our reason for wanting to see him?—but another surge in my gut prevented me from daring to open my mouth.

"What could ye want with him again?" Deirdre asked carefully.

"Well," Rosie said, looking around us, as if to verify that the Spanish tourists behind us weren't listening in. "He was involved in some messed up business years and years ago, and we're here to get some questions answered."

Rory was glaring at her. But she wouldn't meet his eye—either on purpose or because new people to converse with were more interesting.

Deirdre's face was a mask, but I couldn't help but wonder: did she find it suspicious that we were back so soon? She probably thought we were up to no good. "How … how could ye possibly be involved in sordid business from long ago?" she asked. She was sitting so still it was noticeable, but I thought that could have been because of the contrast to the rest of us rocking helplessly with the boat.

"We weren't, but those boys we were with"—Rosie jabbed a thumb over her shoulder at Rory, like he wasn't even there—"they're Seamus's long-lost—"

"Rosie!" Rory snapped.

The boat tipped to the left, and I leapt to my feet. God would have to shut Rosie up, because I needed a bathroom—now.

"Cora?" she called after me. But the hand clutched over my mouth prevented me from replying.

To my dismay, the little red "occupied" signs above the two tiny ferry bathrooms were alight, so I dashed right on past them toward the stairs at the back of the boat. I took the stairs two at a time and rammed open the door to the deck. A gust of warmth hit me in the face, making my clammy skin crawl. My gut hit the railing just as I lost control and my stomach emptied over the side of the boat. Again and again. I heard people walking and muttering behind me, but I was so far past caring how I appeared right now.

Aidan was gone. Rory was a liar. And we were on my way to confront Mr. O'Leary about this impossible situation. And this damn boat was tossing and turning like a sleepless old man. *Oh God, this really is the lowest I've felt in ages.*

The breeze from the sea was chilly, but the air was still warm somehow. The cold of yesterday had given way once again to a warm day, and for once, I wished it could stay cold and miserable so I could curl up in a blanket and feel some semblance of comfort. My stomach clenched, and I bent over the railing again.

I felt my hair lift off the back of my neck, but on the precipice of puking, I didn't dare turn. It was surely Rosie, being an obedient friend. If there was one thing she'd learned in college, it was probably how to comfort a vomiting girl.

Bile surged up my throat, and I lost it again.

A hand twisted my hair into a knot on the back of my head, and another started rubbing my back. "There, there," a voice said near my ear, but it was a heavily accented one.

Wiping my mouth with the back of my hand, I turned just a fraction. Deirdre stood beside me with a tight smile on her face.

"The crossing gets to many tourists," she said.

I wasn't exactly a tourist. In fact, I'd had no wish to return to Inis Mór for sightseeing purposes. But I wasn't in a position to correct her.

"In fact," she said, her hand still rubbing my back, "I'd like you to go and gather your things. We'll be docking momentarily, and you'll feel much better on land. Then I want you to take your friends and go to Supermac's, which is Ireland's answer to McDonald's, so you'll really feel quite at home. And I want you to wait there until the next ferry, which I want you to get on and return to the mainland. And then I want you to never return to Inis Mór."

A creeping sensation crawled through my veins. I glanced to the side as my hair fell back over my neck. Deirdre smiled a tight-lipped smile at me, held my gaze for only a moment, then turned, her short, sensible heels clacking on the deck, and disappeared back inside.

Míle Fáilte
A THOUSAND WELCOMES

S HE SAID WHAT?" ROSIE ASKED FOR THE THIRD time.

"She knows!" I hissed, nervously twisting my Claddagh ring around my finger. "I mean, she knows *something*, but I don't know what!"

"But even if she knew something, why would she care?" Rory asked.

"I don't know, but she does," I said.

We stood on the pier on Inis Mór, watching the tourists pour off the boat. Deirdre had been the first to disembark, without another word to us. Lorna had lingered to say good-bye and wish us well, but then she'd run to catch up with her friend. In the distance, we saw them make their way toward the bike shop, their forms weighed down with their plethora of shopping bags.

"Well, what are we going to do?" Rosie asked.

Two red Irish setters came running toward us. They'd

apparently been waiting for the boat, and they kept running down the pier to escort tourists to the town, like we were sheep that needed herding. And since we didn't exactly have a plan here, we could use some leading. The dogs ran right up to us, the last remaining lost sheep. They both ran circles around Rory, excitedly nipping at his heels, obviously wanting him to follow them to Kilronan, the biggest town on the island—and the only one, by normal standards.

Rory shrugged. "There's only one way to find Seamus—the bike shop. We don't know where he lives."

The bigger of the two dogs nudged my hand.

"Could we have just a moment?" Rosie said to Rory before dragging me a few feet away—not nearly far enough for a private conversation—and then grasping both my shoulders. "Cora, we are in over our heads. We're obviously poking at something that shouldn't be poked. Let's go back to Galway, wait for our flight home, and then *go*…back to that glorious landlocked state where nothing ever happens and everything makes sense."

The smaller setter finally left Rory to bound up to us, and I used it as an opportunity to get away from Rosie's frantic gaze. Kneeling, I pulled the dog's tags around. "He's called 'Peewee,'" I said. The bigger dog pushed in front of me, eager for attention. "This one's 'Storm.'"

"Cora!" Rosie said, stomping her foot like an actual toddler, and both dogs skittered backward, startled.

"Rosie, I couldn't get back on that boat right now if I wanted to," I said, standing. "Unless you want to be wearing the rest of my breakfast, we need to stay put. Let's just go to the bike shop. She was probably just messing with us."

Rosie made a strangled groan. "And if we're getting into some hocus pocus we shouldn't be getting into?"

I shrugged again. "Then it was nice knowing ya. At least we'll go out together."

Without waiting for her argument, I turned back to Rory, who, by the look on his face, had heard the whole exchange. The two setters bolted off toward town, turning back to us every so often as if to say, *This way! This way please!*

The bike shop was bustling with customers, and I recognized the man out front from the last time we were there—Deirdre had called him Patrick that day. Today, there was a little girl with him wearing a matching shirt and talking enthusiastically to visitors who appeared to be charmed by her knowledge of bikes.

The dogs got distracted by all the people, but Rory and I marched right past them into the familiar shop, where a line had formed at the counter. There was nothing for it but to wait obediently. Rosie caught up to us, mumbling angrily, but when the woman in front of us stepped aside, I was glad to have any support I could. Deirdre positively glared at me.

"What part of my instructions did you not understand?" she hissed, leaning over the counter.

"Unfortunately, we don't like fast food," Rosie said sarcastically. "It's bad for you."

That was a lie—I could down a burger in record-breaking time— but I appreciated the backup.

"We need to see Seamus, so just tell us where to find him, and we won't come back here," Rory said reasonably, gesturing around at the shop.

"Look, I know what…*sordid* business you're here about," Deirdre said, glancing behind us to make sure no customers were listening, "and I'm only going to tell you one more time to leave us be."

"Who made you the police?"

"Actually, there is only one policeman on the island," Deirdre said, her eyes narrowing. "And he's often away."

"Is that a *threat?*" Rosie squawked.

"Shh!" I hissed at her. "Stop. We're not here to make trouble, Deirdre. We just need to talk to Seamus."

"And I'm telling you to leave an old man alone," Deirdre snapped.

"Seamus is expecting us," Rory assured her. "He knows we're coming, and he *wants* to talk to us."

"That's not the old man I'm talking about," Deirdre said.

All three of us blinked at her. "You're worried about Kieran?" Rory finally asked. "What does he care if we talk to Seamus?"

"Seamus isn't even here," Deirdre said, folding her arms across her chest. "He's on the mainland."

"Then we'll wait," Rosie said, crossing her arms. "If you're even telling the truth."

"Look," Deirdre said, changing tactics. Her tone changed something near wheedling. "I'm sure you're nice kids, and I know this is an intriguing situation, but you're in one of the most beautiful countries in the world, with the run of the place. Go explore, be tourists, enjoy the pubs. There's nothing for you here."

"This is ridiculous!" Rosie snapped.

"It is," Deirdre said with finality. "And if you don't leave now, I'm going to have to call someone in here to escort you to the ferry."

Rosie scoffed. "This is a free country—"

Deirdre's eyes flashed, and she planted her hands on the counter, dislodging a stack of brochures. "This is a tiny island off the coast of another tiny island. Do you really want to find out how free it is?"

Rosie grumbled, but Rory and I exchanged a look. That was a definite *no*.

"Why do you think she cares so much?" I asked as we trudged toward the small shop down the road. Our next step was the uncreative approach of asking random strangers if they knew where Seamus O'Leary lived. It wasn't exactly a detective-worthy plan, but we were on an island of, like, 900, so we felt good about our chances.

"Isn't it obvious?" Rory asked, surprising me with his enthusiasm.

"Uh…" My steps faltered as I looked at him.

"Cora," Rosie said, as if I were the slowest person on the planet. Apparently I was the slowest person on this road. "They *killed* a man. That night of the storm. Seamus pushed that guy overboard, and these other two guys witnessed it. They would be in trouble, too, if that came to light."

Rory looked at me, eyebrows raised, as if Rosie having to explain something to me was embarrassing. "But it was an accident," I said, more defensively than necessary.

"Was it?" Rory asked, his eyebrows still near his hairline.

I don't know. None of us did. Seamus had pushed his friend—James

Cassidy—overboard for attempting to kill Aidan. And James had drowned. Perhaps Seamus had done it simply in the defense of his son. But maybe it had gone beyond that. He didn't have to push him *overboard.* He could have subdued him another way. Maybe it was an accident. But maybe it wasn't.

It suddenly seemed that the only two things I knew for sure about Seamus O'Leary were that he left Mrs. O'Leary to wither away alone in Oyster Beach and was responsible for a man's death.

Meeting him was looking less and less appealing.

"So you think Deirdre knows about all this, and she's afraid we're going to dig all this up and report it to the cops and get her father-in-law in trouble?" I asked, looking between the two of them. Rory was reluctant to continue the conversation, but Rosie was enjoying the scheming. "What could the cops do now, years and years later?"

Rosie shrugged. "I don't know, but I do know that if *I'd* witnessed a murder and hushed it up for a friend, I'd be scared to death of being discovered for the rest of my life."

"Stop calling it a murder," I snapped.

"It was murder, Cora!" Rosie yelled.

We were squabbling beside the shop door now, and the woman who exited next looked at us in alarm.

"A murder of crows," I said quickly. "Yep, that's what it's called."

Rosie rolled her eyes at me and pushed inside the shop. Rubbing a hand over his face, Rory followed.

It was hot and sticky inside, probably due to a lack of air conditioning, and I considered going over to the refrigerated section just to cool down before starting this conversation. But Rosie had already marched over to the counter.

A young guy stood behind it, and he greeted Rosie enthusiastically. Because she's Rosie.

"Hi," she said, oblivious to the guy's interest. "I'm not actually here to buy anything, we were wondering if you know Seamus O'Leary."

The boy smiled. "Sure, it's not tha' big a place," he said easily, running his hand through his auburn hair. "And Seamus is…quite the character."

"Could you tell us how to find him?" Rosie asked.

"He works down in the bike shop. If you just—"

"Yeah, could you tell us how *else* to find him?" Rosie interrupted.

The guy looked perplexed but smiled again. This time, he held Rosie's gaze for a few moments. "What do a couple of Yanks want with a craggy old fella like Seamus O'Leary?"

Rosie huffed. "It'd be great if people could stop calling us 'Yanks.' And as a matter of fact, it's none of your business what we want with him."

The poor guy grinned. "Fair enough. Well, he lives over near the colony."

The what now? Did we stumble upon some weird cult?

"I can show ye in…a few minutes. Don't know that he'll be home. But I'm off in a bit, I can walk ye over."

"That would be splendid," Rosie said. She gave him a bit of a wave and moved aside to let another tourist purchase what appeared to be a bag of prawn cocktail-flavored chips. Ew. "We'll just be waiting outside," she added.

The guy watched dreamily after her as we trooped out behind her.

Poor kid. Constantly having tourists stream through here must've been annoying. It was probably slim pickings in a population of 900. And any nice girl you happened to meet in the summer would be away just as quickly as she arrived.

Like Oyster Beach, I thought. Except Rory hadn't been confined to any unsatisfactory pickings. The blonde Jenn reared beautiful and sun-kissed in my memory, and I wondered, for the first time since that summer, how she was. Had the pain of losing her brother softened? Did the pain of losing someone to the sea subside after a while, or did you carry it with you for the rest of your life?

My mother still carried it. Afraid of going down that mental path, I shook my head and tuned back in to the conversation happening in front of me.

"Don't lean against that. Those are generations old."

Rosie harrumphed and leaned against the wall anyway. "There's not exactly a plethora of resting places, and I'm tired."

"These things are constructed by master builders who train in the art of dry-stone-wall building," Rory snapped. He had to step right up against said wall to let a horse and buggy pass on this tiny road. The low stone walls bordered everything on the island, crisscrossing the fields in the distance to create a vast, gray spiderweb.

"Hey," Rosie snarled over the roar of the sea and wind. "I didn't ask to come on this little 'adventure.'" She even used air quotes. "Find me a bench—or better yet, a foot massage—and I'll leave your precious wall alone."

Something cold and wet pressed against my hand, and I yelped.

The little Irish setter wagged his tail, staring happily up at me, before bounding over to Rory and weaving through his legs. "Peewee," I breathed in relief.

"Geez, Cora," Rosie grumbled. "Overreact much?"

I bit my tongue because I knew everyone was in a tenuous mood, myself included.

Storm, the bigger dog, was a few feet down the road, watching us carefully. When I looked at him, he barked.

Peewee's little tail went ballistic, and he lunged into a run to catch up with his friend.

"Don't let him boss you around!" Rosie yelled after the little dog.

But Storm was still looking at us. He barked again.

"I think he wants *us*," I said, a genuine smile gracing my face for the first time in too long.

Storm took a few steps toward us then spun in a circle and darted away a few steps. He stopped again to look at us.

I glanced at Rory, and the ghost of a small smile was playing across his lips, too. Despite still feeling betrayed by him, at my very core, I wanted that smile to grow bigger.

I took a step toward the dogs. "We have nothing better to do!" The setters' tails moved with ever-increasing excitement.

"What? No!" Rosie snapped. "No way! We are not following a pair of *dogs*. Are you kidding me?"

"Hey, where's your sense of adventure?" I shouted over my shoulder. "You're the one who told me to 'live a little'!"

"That was before I knew the truth about what a weirdo you are, Manchester."

Okay, that was very true. But we were too far down the rabbit hole now. "C'mon!" I yelled at her, walking backward. Rory shrugged and jogged to catch up with me. The dogs ran back to lick his hands, then bounded ahead of us again, continuing their pattern: run—pause—check that we're still following—run. Within two seconds, I heard Rosie's frustrated roar and then her footsteps on the gravelly road behind me.

We walked in silence, moving to the side of the tiny road every so often to make room for hordes of bikes, tiny vans packed with tourists, and the occasional horse and buggy, also packed with tourists and always manned by a wrinkled older man. They were as weathered and worn as the rocks here but also firm and rugged in a way I wasn't accustomed to seeing in older people.

We passed house after house on one side of the road, their faces turned toward our left, where the ocean glittered like sapphires, attacking the craggy shore with such violence it was a wonder this tiny island hadn't been washed away. The road we walked was just yards from the water, and the field separating us from the waves was so rocky you wouldn't be able to grow a thing in it.

After a while, Storm and Peewee hopped up onto the wall, the little dog copying the big dog's every move.

"Oh, so it's okay for *them* to climb on it?" Rosie grumbled.

Then Storm plopped down into the rocky grass on the other side and darted across the field, toward the water. He stopped once to see if we were following, which we obviously weren't, and barked at us.

"Great," Rosie grumbled. "He wants us to go swimming. Great idea to follow the dogs, guys."

I approached the low wall to gaze out at the bay, across which I could see the yellow-tinted shore of County Galway, where we'd set sail. It was strange to be so close to the mainland yet so terribly cut off from it.

That's when my attention was grabbed by something down on the shore. A mass of thick, dark bodies was laid out on an outcropping of rock that jutted into the waves.

"The colony!" I cried.

"Huh?" Rosie followed my riveted gaze. "What? What are those?"

"Seals," Rory breathed.

"It's a haul-out," I said, glancing at Rory. I couldn't help it. The first time I'd seen a group of seals like this was one magical night in Oyster Beach, long before I knew much about this boy but certainly after I'd fallen for him. Fallen like a tumble of stones into the sea. Long gone.

It was the first night we'd kissed. My cheeks felt warm, and my heart sped up a little.

The bark of a seal pulled me out of the perfect memory. Searching the shore, I found the source of the sound: a lone seal moving along the edge of the rock. Several heads popped up out of the water around it, but none of its napping companions moved a muscle.

"I wonder how many of those are human," Rosie hissed at me, bobbing her eyebrows up and down.

I gulped but didn't answer. I'd been wondering the same thing.

"If that's the seal colony..." Rosie said then, whirling around. "One of these houses must be Seamus's!"

But my eyes had found Rory, and his eyes didn't leave the seals. I tried to remember what it had felt like—kissing this boy for the first time—but it felt so natural, so familiar, so *right* now, that I couldn't remember. The newness had worn off my crush, and it looked different now. Not lesser or smaller…just different.

Down at the far end of the field, the dogs had paused, still a fair distance from the seals, as if they knew they weren't supposed to go any closer. But Storm kept looking back at us, perturbed that we hadn't followed. What disobedient sheep we'd turned out to be.

I glanced over my shoulder at the houses nearest us here, all small, squat things with little decoration or distinction. Seamus lived behind the windows of one of those houses, each one gazing down on a colony of seals.

"What are the odds?" Rory mumbled, voicing my thoughts exactly. Except maybe it wasn't a coincidence, Seamus living so close to a seal haul-out. "Kilronan," he said.

Ronan. Little seal. "Something little seal?" I asked.

"Church," Rory said quietly. "'Kil' means church. But I think the town's actually named after the saint, not these guys." He nodded toward the haul-out.

"Guys, come on!" Rosie called, obviously far beyond being impressed by something as mundane to Irish island life as a group of seals.

Behind us, she was trudging down the road. "Where are you going?" I asked.

"It's gotta be one of these houses." She was already climbing up a short slope to a small white house, facing the sea like all the rest. The land sloped upward from there, the highest point of the island being right in the center.

The first house had a rusty blue van in the yard, but nobody answered Rosie's incessant knocking. She finally shrugged and nodded toward the next house, several hundred yards away.

There was a goat in the rocky garden beside the house, and he lifted his head to stare at us as we paused at the end of the walk. A miniature house, about the size of a Barbie dreamhouse, sat to the side of the door.

"What the heck is that?" Rosie half-laughed.

"For the faeries," Rory said. I glanced at him, but his face was dead serious.

The goat watched us walk to the door, his jaw chewing away at something. The hiss of the ocean was behind us, ever present, ever pressing. I suddenly wished Aidan would step out of the waves and run to join us. And handle this. And support Rory as he faced their father.

Rosie knocked on the door.

It opened almost immediately.

The old man standing there squinted at us, and I recognized Seamus immediately from that day in the bike shop. Not to mention the pictures from his youth that I'd seen in Mrs. O'Leary's little yellow house nearly a year ago. Only his face wasn't friendly and innocent any longer. He looked from me, to Rosie, to Rory, to the empty walk behind us.

He cleared his throat and asked, "Fionn?"

Finally, after all this time, I was going to be able to confront the man who had been so elusive while still causing so much trouble and turmoil in the life of the boy I loved. And I didn't know what to say.

"Aidan," Rory said firmly. "He's…gone." His bitterness was tart in the air, which was understandable—this man had been the one to give the sealskin to Aidan. Maybe he'd even encouraged him to go.

The old man nodded his head once. He wasn't surprised.

And, I mean, while we're talking blame, wasn't it true that if this man had never fallen for Lia O'Leary in the first place, we wouldn't be in this mess? But then again, Rory wouldn't exist either.

Mr. O'Leary sighed and stepped back. "Ye'd better come in."

Insíonn Seamus a Thaobh
SEAMUS TELLS HIS SIDE

HIS HOUSE WAS BRIGHT AND CHILLY, AND IT smelled like the sea. Every window was thrown open, and the salty breeze blew things around—the curtains on the windows, the doily on the old upright piano, and a stack of papers on a side table.

"I wasn't expecting ye…so soon," Seamus said, glancing over his shoulder as he led us down the hall.

"Aidan left yesterday," Rory said.

The kitchen was big, and Seamus gestured toward the table, which was surrounded by five chairs. I wondered if that table was ever full, if Seamus ever entertained. Imagining him at a festivity like those in the big houses in Oyster Beach wasn't easy, but maybe a gathering like the O'Briens' Lúnasa party. After all, that boy working in the shop had implied everyone knew everyone here. Of course, he'd also called Seamus a "craggy old fella" and "quite the character." It was something I might've said about Mrs. O'Leary once upon a time. And it reminded me of the way people in Oyster Beach whispered about Mrs. O'Leary. Maybe the past did haunt Seamus like it had Mrs. O'Leary…

Rosie plopped down in one of the stiff wooden chairs, and I followed suit. Rory stood awkwardly behind, as if sitting down would be some sort of forfeit. And he was glowering.

Seamus moved to the counter and flipped the switch on something that looked like an electric coffee pot. Then he turned and leaned back against the counter, crossing his arms across his chest. He had the challenging confidence of a much younger man. I was reminded immediately of the pictures of him I'd seen in Mrs. O'Leary's house. Seamus had been thirty years younger in them, but his self-assurance was unmistakable, and his eyes were as green as the sea across the road from his house.

"So what have ye come for?" he finally asked.

That's certainly not what I'd been expecting. Hadn't Aidan said in his letter that Seamus was expecting us? Well, Rory anyway. Was that a lie? Not that it mattered. Not really. We still wanted answers. To start with,

"Why did you give Aidan his sealskin after all these years?"

Rory and Rosie both looked at me, and I realized I'd shouted it rather abruptly. But, really. I'd spent this whole year thinking badly of the man who'd left Mrs. O'Leary to rot in Oyster Beach, and he was really living up to it at the moment.

"Aidan told me you were quite close to Mrs. O'Leary at the end," Seamus said to me—carefully avoiding my question. "Seems odd for a young girl to strike up a friendship with a lonely old woman."

The way he called her that—*Mrs. O'Leary*—seemed cold and unfeeling, but I realized it could've just been a characteristic of earlier times. But admitting that he knew she was lonely? That was altogether cruel. "She was a great woman," I said firmly. "With a lot to teach anyone who would listen."

Seamus stared at me, the ghost of a smile on his lips.

"Why did you give Aidan his sealskin after all these years?" I repeated.

"Fionn," Seamus said on a sigh. "The boy was sick. It seemed barbaric to deny him the one thing he wanted."

"The way you denied it to Mrs. O'Leary?" I asked.

The water in the contraption on the counter behind him was bubbling and frothing angrily, and maybe that's why I'd felt bold in that moment, or maybe it was because Mrs. O'Leary couldn't speak up for herself anymore.

Seamus shook his head slowly. "There were more things at play than you can understand."

"Then explain them to me," I said. Glancing quickly at Rory, I took in his tense stance, his gaze on his clasped hands. "To us."

The machine behind Seamus clicked off in the ensuing silence.

Finally, he sighed and wiped a hand down his face. "We'd best have a cuppa then. How do ye take it?" His accent was softer than the others we'd met on the island, but I remembered Mrs. O'Leary saying he was from Doolin, a place south of Galway. Maybe he was an outsider here on the island, too.

When we all just stared at him blankly—except Rory, who still glared at his own hands—Seamus prompted, "Tea."

"Uh, lots of sugar," Rosie piped up. We didn't exactly have a certain way we took tea. Because we didn't actually drink tea. But at that moment I was going to pretend I was a connoisseur.

"A little milk," I said stiffly.

Seamus turned and took two mugs from a cabinet, then two more. I couldn't see what he was doing, but he busied himself with the contraption—an electric kettle, apparently—and much clanking of a spoon against ceramic. "And you, lad?" he asked without turning.

"None," Rory grunted.

"Very well," Seamus continued. "So, ask me what you've come here to find out."

Rory's lips were in such a tight line, I wasn't sure words could get out if they tried. Of course, who could judge him? I certainly had never confronted my estranged father who'd posed as my neighbor for most of my life in order to hide a magical secret. So I didn't begrudge Rory his anger, but…I was still a little miffed at him for lying. And wasn't that exactly what he was mad at Seamus for?

Rosie gave me a helpless shrug, so I turned back toward Seamus— or his back.

Of course there were a million things I wanted to ask Mr. O'Leary, and they were all clamoring to get out. So I stopped holding them in. What won first was: "Why did you leave her there, waiting for you to come back, all those years?"

Seamus stopped what he was doing and turned to face us. "She wasn't waiting for me," he said.

"Of course she was—"

"She was waiting for Fionn."

My eyebrows scrunched together. "But he was there…all that time. He was in Oyster Beach. Practically next door."

Seamus turned back to the tea and resumed the soft clinking of the spoon. "Aye, but she didn't know that," he said simply.

"But how could she not?" I pressed. "She knew who Rory was." As I said the words, I realized this was an argument not just for Seamus—Rory, too, had gone to great lengths to keep the secret from her, from Aidan. My eyes found him involuntarily, and I saw the embarrassment that flashed there before the stony look of anger returned.

But I wanted answers Rory couldn't give. Yes, he'd endeavored to keep his little brother from this terrifying truth, but how had it happened? How had the two of them come to be living with the O'Brien family in the first place?

Seamus brought two steaming mugs to the table and placed one in front of me, one in front of Rosie. Then he turned back for the third cup. "One brother was outgoing, constantly seeking out the company of neighbors. The other was shy, a homebody, only too happy to avoid an acquaintance. Are you surprised, then, that things turned out the way they did?" He placed his cup on the table, pulled out a chair to sit, and looked me in the eye. "Fate hands us the cards we need to play this game of chance."

I stared at him. He talked in riddles as confusing as Mrs. O'Leary's.

After a moment, he asked, "What's your name, child?"

"Cora," I said, finding my voice again. "A-and this is Rosie."

Then Seamus's eyes went to Rory, the real elephant in the room. The silent elephant.

"And Ronan," Seamus said.

"Don't call me that," Rory said, his lips barely moving.

"You let her call you that," Seamus said.

Her. Nobody needed to elaborate. Mrs. O'Leary hovered on the edges of our minds, the ghost we followed.

"She stayed," Rory said simply.

Seamus heaved a great, world-weary sigh. "Well, Cora, Rosie…Rory… I think we best start at the beginning."

Finally. Finally, after the longest year of my life, I was going to hear it all.

"I'd been in America nearly two years when we met. It was fairly normal for Irish lads to live abroad for a bit, see what the world had to offer. After two years, though, I'd notions of returning home, taking up the mantle of the family business—fishing, it was—but then I met her… We married rather quickly after meeting, or so was the opinion of people around town, but we were…enchanted. I remember my father, God rest his soul, was less than pleased when I wrote him of my plans. He'd expected me, his only son, home. But sometimes life gets in the way of the best-laid plans…"

Like Mrs. O'Leary's. For years, she'd never returned home, either. She'd told me as much in one of our very first conversations. And Seamus had done his part, in hiding her coat, to keep it that way for a long time.

He cleared his throat, as though finding his train of thought again, and barreled on more confidently. "We both wanted children. Ronan was born March 16, 1962."

Rosie choked on a mouthful of tea and looked at me, her eyes bulging. *1962?* she mouthed. I looked to Rory. His eyes were on the floor, but his nostrils were flared, and I could hear his deep breaths from here.

"I remember it clearly," Seamus went on, "because I was holding out hope for a St. Paddy's Day baby." The smile on his face spoke of happier times, and the warmth in his voice melted the ice in my attitude toward him just a bit. His face had softened as he remembered the birth of his first son, and I could only imagine the happiness both he and Mrs. O'Leary must have felt at Rory's birth.

Seamus stood then and disappeared down the hall, and Rosie and I exchanged glances, thinking maybe our luck had already run out. He was gone so long I started to stand, but he returned then with a small wooden box. Sitting again, he set it on the table and opened it. A puff of dust rose up, and inside I saw papers covered in sand and a handful of seashells. Seamus picked up the top paper, dusted it off, and handed it to me.

It was an old photo. Of a tiny baby.

Ronan.

The photo was faded and torn around the edges. Tentatively I turned and held the photo out toward Rory. The muscle in his jaw ticked once, and then he reached out and carefully took it by the edges, as though it might bite him. Behind me, Rosie gave a little "aw," as Seamus pulled another photo out of his box. This was a larger print of a young, beautiful couple. He had his arm around her middle, and the love between them was palpable.

"When did you learn…what she was?" I asked.

Seamus let out a deep sigh. "She told me the day we met." He shook his head. "I didn't believe her at first, of course. I found her on the beach, nearly naked she was, wrapped in that…that *skin*, and I thought she was just a young, lost girl. Definitely a girl with an imagination the size of Ireland."

"You are skeptical, like my Seamus was in the beginning," Mrs. O'Leary had said to me once, and I hadn't realized the implications of it. The gravity of it. Until now.

"Yet you married her?" I asked. "A woman who thought she was a selkie?"

Seamus looked up from his mug of tea to stare me in the eye, his own eyes narrowed. "Love doesn't discriminate, child." His gaze fell back to the table. "I played along with her games. I hid that-that thing—she called it her coat. I hid it. She told me I had to. I didn't know what it really was, but…well, I knew the legend. And maybe I worried, yes. Maybe I suspected, on some level. But…then Ronan was born, just perfect—ten fingers, ten toes, as healthy and hearty as a baby boy could be, and I was sure that no matter what the truth was, everything would be alright. I told myself it didn't matter if maybe she was a bit confused, in her mind, d'you know, because I loved her all the same. I always loved her."

I somehow doubted that, given the way he'd left her in Oyster Beach, but I didn't say anything. Provoking him now might result in an end to this conversation.

After a long moment, Seamus stood and walked back to the hall.

His broad shoulders were curved inward, and I thought maybe this conversation had cost him more strength than he was letting on. "There's something I think you should have," he said when he returned moments later holding a book, which he passed to Rory.

It was covered in tattered red fabric, and as Rory handed it off to me, wearing a look of indifference that had to be feigned given what we were learning here in this kitchen, I felt how weak and broken the spine was. Pieces of the binding stuck out of each end. "What is it?" I asked.

"Mrs. O'Leary kept a diary for many years. Irish was her native tongue, d'you know. My mother was a native Irish speaker, and that's why I was the only one of the lads who could speak to her when we met. But it was difficult for her, and I taught her English. How to read and write, as well."

My fingers brushed against the cover of the diary. "She told me once she couldn't read."

"Those later years..." Seamus blinked a few times in quick succession. "In those later years, she was a different person. Shut up in the house with only her memories and her...herself, she...regressed. But this is from the good years." He scoffed. "'Good' being a relative term."

The comment burned, and I had to think for a moment to figure out why. "She spoke of you with nothing but admiration," I finally said. "Even after all those years. So how can you sit here and pretend you were never happy?"

"I'm not pretending anything of the sort," he said, and when I glanced at his face, I saw the tears in his eyes. "It happened when

Ronan was three months old," Seamus nearly whispered.

The baby photo of Rory fluttered to the table next to me, and when I turned to look at Rory, he was floating away to another corner of the room, his back to us.

"It was June," Seamus went on. "I was out on the boat with Colm. When we came back, we saw Lia down on the jetty, where she liked to go and sit sometimes. But her arms were empty. At first, I was furious. I thought she'd left the baby home alone. I went tearing down the boardwalk to the house."

Seamus rubbed his eyes with his big, weathered hands, and his fingers came away wet. "But it was empty. Colm walked her back to the house, and I rounded on her. She was all wet, but she was…ecstatic. And wild. She told me immediately what she'd done.

"I was furious, of course. I ran back to the jetty. But I couldn't find him. I started yelling at her, and she just turned and started yelling at the waves. When I looked… When I looked, I saw two seals just yards away. She never denied what she'd done."

The quiet that fell over the kitchen felt heavy, and I knew that if the silence reigned much longer, it might win altogether. I opened my mouth to prod him on, but it wasn't me who broke the silence.

"What did she do?" Rory asked.

The rest of us looked at his broad back, shocked into silence as he turned, staring firmly, unwaveringly, at Mr. O'Leary. He walked slowly to the table, picked up the photo of a young Mr. and Mrs. O'Leary, and set it beside his baby photo. They looked, for all the world, like a happy, beautiful young family.

"What did she do?" Rory repeated, his fingers brushing over the photo of his biological mother and father.

Finally, Seamus drew in a shaky breath. "She told me she'd sent you home." Even in the telling, some fifty years later, the words made me shiver. "She said she'd sent you to the sea, and you'd transformed and joined her family—your family."

There was another long silence.

Then Rory breathed, "Family," shaking his head.

"Son, I—"

There was a great crash from the front of the house. Seamus started, and the dull roar of the sea grew louder, as though someone had let the waves right into the house.

"Seamus!" The angry shout was followed by the heavy footsteps of someone in the hall. "What the hell are you doing, Seamus?"

Kieran Browne appeared in the doorway, his face twisted in anger. He stood, panting, as he looked from Mr. O'Leary, to Rory, to Rosie, to me. His gaze landed on the photos on the table.

"Kieran," Mr. O'Leary said in surprise. "What are you doing here?"

The answer came in the form of Deirdre, jogging down the hall behind her father-in-law. She stepped into the kitchen and looked to Seamus, avoiding my gaze. "Kieran—"

"What are you telling these children?" Kieran demanded, ignoring her.

"Nothing that concerns you, Kieran," Seamus said evenly.

That's not exactly true, I thought. After all, we all knew how this story progressed. Kieran was tangled up in the night of Great Storm.

"I don't believe that for a second!" Kieran bellowed. He looked at me and Rosie and, finally, Rory. His nostrils flared. "Go on now! Get out of here! You're not needed nor wanted!"

Rory took a step back, as though slapped. Knowing the story of his biological parents all these years, and hiding it away inside himself, how many times had he thought those things to himself? Heard them whispered in his subconscious as he lay in bed awaiting sleep? I wanted to reach out and grab his hand, but I was surprised and embarrassed, too. Rosie looked confused but followed my lead as I stood quickly, clutching Mrs. O'Leary's diary tightly to my chest. However, Rosie wasn't the type to take abuse without putting forth a few words of her own. "We weren't doing any—"

"I said you're not wanted here!" Kieran shouted over her.

Rosie squawked indignantly.

"Now, Kieran, lower your voice!" Seamus shouted. "You're scaring the poor children!"

"As well they should be!" Kieran thundered, advancing on Seamus. Rosie and I backed away across the room as Rory took a tentative step forward, and Deirdre pulled on her father-in-law's sleeve.

"Leave it be, Kieran," she said, "you're only making things worse."

"What's making things worse is that old bastard digging up skeletons!"

Rosie and I exchanged a look. Was he afraid of our knowing what happened the night of the Great Storm? He didn't need to yell at Seamus for that; it was Colm Vesey who needed the earful.

"They're not skeletons—"

A slap across Seamus's face prevented him from finishing that sentence.

"Kieran!" Deirdre shrieked, dragging on his sleeve, but he was stronger than he looked.

"You say another word to those Yanks…" The end of Kieran's threat was a whisper in Seamus's ear that I couldn't hear from my spot in the corner. And then Rosie was dragging on my own sleeve.

"Cora, let's get out of here," she hissed, tugging me toward the hallway.

"Rory!" I said, snatching at his sleeve but getting all air. He looked over his shoulder at me but was mesmerized by the fight.

"You're a damn fool!" Seamus was yelling at Kieran, one hand massaging his own bristly white cheek, which had turned bright red.

Kieran pulled his fist back and shouted something unintelligible at Seamus—it might have been Irish.

"Rory!" I shouted again. I was so afraid of Kieran Browne's seeming affinity for violence, I let Rosie drag me down the hall, and none of the adults in the kitchen took notice of our leave, even when Rory took one last look, gulped, and came after us. We slipped out the front door, and the first sight to meet our eyes was the sleepy colony of seals that lived just a stone's throw from Seamus's doorstep.

Stoirm Mhór Eile
ANOTHER GREAT STORM

W HAT THE HELL WAS THAT ABOUT?" ROSIE screeched as we dashed for the relative safety of the deserted road.

"I don't know," I said, nervously glancing back at the house. The goat eyed us suspiciously, but the little faerie house sat perfectly peaceful, as though it was normal as anything and *we* were the mad ones. "I guess he was freaked out that Seamus might tell us about James Cassidy drowning."

Rory wiped his hands down his face, but nobody could get a word in when Rosie was spooked. "But why did that woman care?" she yelled. "His daughter or whatever? She's deranged! They're all flipping deranged!"

"You said it yourself—they probably think we'll report it and get them in trouble," I said, glancing at Rory as he paced away from us.

"Isn't there a freaking statute of limitations on that

kind of thing?" Rosie snapped.

"I don't think—"

"Jesus Christ, I thought he was gonna hit us!" She wiped a hand across her face, and I noticed then that she was shaking.

"Roz—"

"That was effed up, Cora. This whole thing is really effed up!" She threw a pointed look at Rory.

"I know," I said, reaching a hand out to soothe her, but she stepped away from me.

"We should sue them or…or something!"

"Stop being ridiculous," I murmured.

"Oh, *I'm* being ridiculous?" she nearly screeched. "I'm not the one in love with a shapeshifter! You dragged me into this mess without my consent! I didn't ask for this, Cora!"

"Well neither did I!" I shouted right back. As soon as I said it, my eyes flashed to Rory. He was staring at me, his mouth open just a fraction. It was genuine shock.

Rosie didn't notice. "That doesn't mean it's not your fault! *I* wouldn't have gone off making friends with some creepy old lady!"

And even after all this, the insult still hurt. I still felt a protective sympathy for Mrs. O'Leary, though it wasn't so one-sided anymore. Already, I could sense that much. Seamus's story had made one thing clear to me: back then, he'd been a bit lost and confused, too. And maybe that was the problem with love. It was a confusing, messy business.

I'd never understood that fact as much as in that moment, when Rory finally swallowed and tore his gaze away from me.

"I know you wouldn't have," I told Rosie quietly. "I guess that's what makes us different."

"I guess so," Rosie said evenly. "I want—"

"Get out of here!"

The bellow came from Seamus's front stoop, and all three of us flinched and skittered like scared dogs. Kieran stood on the small hill, face red and wild. He came lumbering down the walk then, and the three of us bolted in the direction of Kilronan. Luckily the island was small enough that we could see the little town in the distance.

But Kieran Browne was old and slow enough that we could watch over our shoulders as he trundled into the street, shaking his fists like a raging cartoon. Deirdre was flying out of the house by then, too, but Kieran's gaze caught on something down by the shore.

The seal colony. He heaved a stone from the field in front of him, and before I could even worry that he was going to aim for us, he hurled it toward the shore. It didn't come anywhere near the seals, but it shocked me nonetheless, and his yelling startled the sleepy seals.

"What's he doing?" Rosie gasped.

"*Fág! Gach duine! Go hIfreann libh!*" He grabbed another rock, this one larger, and hurled it toward the haul-out. This time, it clattered upon stone, and I gasped as it just missed several seals resting nearby. They shuffled quickly away and slipped into the water.

"Stop!" Rory yelled, taking a step toward him.

Rosie looked at Rory in shock, but I knew he'd just had the same thought I had: Galway wasn't far—by water. What if Aidan…

"Stop him!" Rory shouted, running back toward the old man.

Deirdre had reached Kieran, but he was climbing over the squat stone wall, and the man was less than frail. He procured another handful of rocks before she could catch him in the field, and lobbed them at the seals, causing a flurry of movement as they tried to escape their attacker.

"*Fág muid le suaimhneas! Mallacht ort!*" Kieran's Irish was faint below the thrashing of the waves. "*Níl muid thú ag iarradh anseo!*"

The haul-out was empty now, the waves crashing violently against it. Rory stopped walking toward Kieran, paused a moment, and turned back toward us.

A crack of thunder made me flinch and Rory look up. It was then that I noticed how confusion and sadness had contorted his features.

"Let's get of here," he said, more to the sky than anyone else. "We shouldn't have come."

We stood huddled out of the wind, up against a building on the pier, waiting for the ferry. The sea had turned a slate-gray color, and waves were crashing furiously against the pier, sending a chilly spray at us again and again. But there was nowhere to escape them. No matter where you were on this island, you were never far from the sea.

There was still an hour before the next ferry left, and we'd fallen into silence after a dead-end conversation of repeated exclamations akin to, "What the *hell* was that about?" We even talked briefly about finding that one police officer Deirdre had mentioned. But what exactly would we tell them? That an old man wanted us to leave the island for no discernable reason? And on an island this size, he was sure to be well acquainted with Kieran. Surely the cop wouldn't side with us. Meanwhile, the sky continued to darken ominously.

I was still holding Mrs. O'Leary's worn diary, and though I'd flipped through the pages, I felt it wasn't my place to be the first to dive in. That right belonged to Rory and Aidan. But Aidan wasn't exactly available, and when I looked at Rory, his eyebrows were slanted over his eyes, behind which roiled thoughts certainly more churning than the sea. I didn't dare bring it up right now. And maybe I didn't want to. As much as I tried to quash the feeling, I still felt just a little bit angry that Rory had known this secret for years, and had kept it from *me* for one of those years.

I wasn't ready to confront that, so I avoided any topic that might lead us there. That could wait for the warmth of Rory's apartment back in Galway. Still, I couldn't deny that I was grateful to Mr. O'Leary for handing the diary over so easily, and though Kieran Browne was obviously afraid of us knowing too much, it appeared that Seamus O'Leary was not.

If only he'd shown a little more restraint in the things he'd shown—and given—Aidan.

How on earth were we going to find Aidan?

When the first raindrop fell, pulling me out of my thoughts, my very first reaction was to get the diary out of danger. I'd never forgive myself if this, Rory's last lifeline to his mother, was ruined in my care. So I stowed it carefully in my bag.

"Oh, great," Rosie muttered, looking up at the sky.

Rory and I both followed her gaze, as though we hadn't realized what the heavens were brewing. Maybe Rory hadn't. He looked wrapped up enough in his own thoughts to have missed anything out here in the rest of the world.

Dark clouds had rolled in some time ago, but they'd mostly brought wind. Now the first round of raindrops was quickly giving way to a steady patter. Glancing back toward Kilronan, I saw people at the bike shop hurriedly wheeling bikes inside. I recognized Deirdre, and the man—Patrick—and the little girl standing helplessly in the doorway. That's also when I saw the two setters running down the pier toward us, as happy in the rain as I was out of it. After greeting Rory first, Peewee nuzzled my hand and then turned and ran a few steps back toward town, glancing back to see if we were following.

"We're going the other way now," I told him. He cocked his head and looked between me and his bigger friend, who was darting toward the ferry, where a lone worker was doing something with the ropes mooring the boat to the pier. "Storm," I murmured.

"What?" Rosie snapped.

"The bigger dog. His name is Storm," I said in a quiet voice. "That's ironic."

Rosie glared at me. Rory didn't even look my way.

A great gust of wind blew Rosie sideways, and she looked quite ridiculous trying to regain her balance. Storm came trotting over to us and then darted after Peewee, again glancing back over his shoulder at us.

"I think they want us to follow them," I said.

"Right, because that worked out for us so well last time," Rosie retorted. "The only thing I'll follow is that man"—she nodded toward the ferry worker—"back to the mainland."

But her savior had other ideas.

Within five minutes, a few other groups of tourists had gathered around our nearly sheltered spot, and a few more Aran Ferry workers were consulting with the first. After a few moments of consultation, an older gentleman walked toward us and shouted,

"We've just been informed that dangerous weather has formed nearby, and all further crossings today have been cancelled. Please seek accommodation in Kilronan, as we won't be able to sail until tomorrow, at the earliest."

A collective groan went up.

"Are you kidding me?" Rosie squawked. I groaned, too, but Rory's mouth only fell into a thin line.

"If you need assistance," the man shouted over the hubbub, "please see an Aran Ferry attendant, and we will do our best to help."

And this wasn't in the forecast? I wondered.

"What do we do now?" Rosie wailed.

"We do what the guy said," Rory replied gruffly.

"Um, okay, yeah, let's return to the town where a murderous old man wants us gone," Rosie spat.

"Don't be melodramatic," I murmured.

"You're right. Let's just go back to the bike shop and ask old Kieran to put us up. He may or may not attempt to murder us in our sleep, but, hey, worth the risk, huh?"

"Or we could try the hostel," I said sarcastically.

Rosie rolled her eyes and stomped off down the pier, which was full of other disgruntled tourists making their way back to town. Turns out we all had the same idea, too.

The hostel was a small, squat building currently advertising "no vacancies." But as we crammed into the entrance hall, a woman behind the counter was yelling over everyone's heads.

"We'll find accommodation for everyone, do not worry!" I recognized her voice immediately. It was Lorna—Deirdre's friend from the boat. "Some of you may be referred to the hotel or a B&B, but we will find a place for everyone to sleep tonight."

In the end, Lorna and her workers sent most of the older people to various B&Bs and kept the younger crowd at the hostel. And so we found ourselves in a room with six other travelers from around the world. There was a pair of quiet Brazilian girls, and a lone German boy who looked downright spooked by the situation. Can't say I blamed him.

Rosie plopped down on one of the beds we'd been assigned, staking her claim on a bottom bunk. The bed creaked noisily, but not as loud as her sigh. "I need a drink," she proclaimed. After slinging his wet backpack on the floor, Rory climbed into the top bunk of another bed and collapsed on the plain sheets. "And a nap. And a nice, long bath."

"This isn't quite the Four Seasons," I said, watching Rory roll onto his side to face the wall.

Rosie eyed the bunk beds around the room and the strangers pretending not to listen to our conversation—or maybe they really weren't, who knows? "Trust me, I've noticed."

But she did condescend to suffer through a shower down the hall in the floor's shared bathroom. I was standing in front of the mirror along the row of sinks when she finished and stepped out in a towel.

Self-consciousness was an alien concept to Rosario Balducci.

To my surprise, she was smiling as she joined me in front of the mirror. "That was divine," she said.

I glanced at the small tiled cubicle in the corner. "Really? I didn't think you had it in you, Roz."

"College changed me, Cora," she said matter-of-factly. Then she shuddered. "Today changed me, too. God, today was weird. A freak storm comes out of nowhere and strands us on this creepy, godforsaken island? It's weird, Cora. It's damn weird."

I agreed with her. But there was a tiny part of me that felt like I was missing something.

After a moment of running her fingers through her wet hair, she glanced at me in the mirror. I was just standing there, staring. Bedraggled and damp, I felt a bit like a wet dog and imagined I smelled as bad. I'd already rinsed out my mouth in lieu of a toothbrush and splashed water on my face, but I still lingered here in the cold bathroom, not wanting to go back to the room where Rory was either napping or staring at the wall. I didn't know what to say to him. I didn't know what he wanted me to say to him. And even if I did, I wasn't sure I would say it.

"You okay, Cora?" Rosie asked softly. At least, about as softly as Rosie is capable of being.

I had to clear my throat before answering her. Slowly, I turned away from my depressing reflection to face her. "I can't believe he *knew*." It was half sob, half accusation.

Rosie's face fell, indicating she hadn't expected such an honest answer. I'm normally queen of the "I'm fine" brigade, tamping down anything and everything. But isn't that what had created this whole mess in the first place? I mean the first first place. Seamus O'Leary and Lia and Rory and everyone. Tamping it down, hiding it. That didn't make it better.

"He *knew*," I repeated.

"I know," Rosie said. "It's nuts." She twisted her lips to the side. "But…"

My mouth fell open, and I glared at her as she twirled a wet tendril of hair around her finger. What had happened to her resolute opinion that we should leave immediately? That Rory had lied to me about something "pretty huge"? Those had been her exact words! "But *what?*"

"But, I mean, it is *his* life," Rosie said carefully. "It's not surprising that he knew, right? I've been thinking a lot about it. If all these old people were hanging around him his whole life, whispering behind his back and everything, it's not all that surprising that he figured it out. I mean, you figured it out after just one summer."

"Aidan didn't know," I pointed out.

Rosie shrugged. "His big brother was actively trying to prevent it."

The fact that she was making sense rankled me. "So what are you saying? I'm an idiot for being surprised? I should have told him everything I suspected last summer? I'm just a big—"

"Of course not," Rosie interrupted, rolling her eyes toward the ceiling. "But…"

"Please stop with the buts!"

Rosie shrugged again, turned away, and continued to speak while putting on her still-damp clothes. "I just think maybe you shouldn't hold this against him. I really have been thinking about this. I mean, what was he supposed to do? Tell the girl he had a crush on last summer that he thinks he's…well…a seal?"

The heaving breaths leaving my chest began to slow. She was right. So right. Completely and absolutely right.

Why was I *mad* at him? This was about his life, not mine. I'd just happened to stumble into it. That didn't completely stop the irritation rolling through me, but I could try.

"When did you become the smart one?" I murmured.

Rosie smiled. "Oh, Cora. I've always been the smart one. But it's great that you've finally realized it."

Cluichí agus Athmhuintearas
GAMES AND RECONCILIATION

NOT LONG AFTER WE RETURNED TO THE ROOM, there was a knock on the door. We all looked at each other—Brazilians, German, and Americans—unsure what the protocol here was. It's not like any of us knew anyone on the island. You know, besides the murderous octogenarians.

Whoever it was didn't wait for a reply, though. The door opened and the boy from the shop stepped in. Just as he said, "Welcome, everyone," his eyes lit on Rosie.

A half grin pulled up one corner of his mouth, but it looked more like a grimace to me. "Ah," he said. "The Yanks who stood me up."

Whoops.

"We found another tour guide," Rosie said easily from her bunk.

The boy raised his eyebrows.

"Peewee," she said with a smirk.

"Ah, ye've met the welcoming committee, then. They'll show you the island, sure enough. Did they happen to find Seamus?"

As Rosie nodded, I saw Rory roll over. So he wasn't asleep after all. Just avoiding us.

"How do you lot know him?" the boy asked.

Rosie and I both glanced to the top bunk. Carefully avoiding our eyes, Rory again rolled away from us, returning to his vigil over the wall. "He, uh, he's our friend's father," Rosie said. "They were estranged for a long time, but they recently reunited. We wanted to ask him some questions, so here we are."

It was a fairly safe answer, I was relieved to hear. "What about you?" Rosie went on. "Do you work here too?"

The boy chuckled. "Nah, just the shop. My aunt runs this place, so this's more a chore than a job. It's Evan, by the way." They shook hands, and then his eyes moved to me, which I guess made him realize they had an audience. He took in the rest of the room, the other kids watching the conversation with interest. "Anyway," Evan said, clearing his throat and then addressing the room at large, "I was just doing the rounds to invite everyone down to the lobby. We've got snacks and cards, and those intrepid enough to face the storm will find great craic at Watty's or the hotel."

The others in the room broke out into chatter in different languages, and Rosie looked at me, eyebrows raised expectantly, a smile creeping to her face. Nothing could appease her like a night out. Though I wasn't sure an island night out would be quite what she was used to.

"You're the one worried about the bloodthirsty old people," I pointed out.

"Ugh. You're right. We better stick to card games," she ceded, moving toward her clothes lying across the room's only radiator to dry.

My eyes darted to Rory. "Actually, I think I'll turn in early."

Rosie's face fell, but then she followed my gaze to Rory. "Ah," she said knowingly. "Good idea." She turned to the rest of the room and shouted, "Hey, guys, I'm Rosie! You should all join me in a card game down in the lobby! There's food and stuff!" As the Brazilians shrugged and headed for the door, Rosie turned and winked at me. It only took a bit of cajoling for her to convince the German to go, too.

As they left the room, I heard Evan ask her, "What's this about dangerous pensioners? Rough day on the island?"

"Oh, you have no idea," she groaned.

He laughed. "Seamus not a barrel of laughs then?"

"Oh, he's a barrel of something," she said, and the door clicked shut behind them.

My heart was hammering so much I was sure it was shaking the whole bunk. I don't know how long I sat there with Mrs. O'Leary's diary in my lap, but I started to worry the others would come back before I'd even summoned the courage. And then I'd have to take a *lot* of crap from Rosie. One deep breath was enough to launch me to my feet.

"Rory?" I asked gently, in case he was asleep. But his reply came too quick for that.

"Mm?"

"Can… Can I come up?"

He rolled over, looked at me for a brief second, and nodded.

I tucked the diary under my arm and went to the skinny ladder at the foot of the bunk. The rails were thin and cold and they hurt my feet, which were shaking unhelpfully, but I climbed the rickety ladder and slipped onto the end of his bed. He sat up and slid toward the pillow, as if to put space between us. Swinging my legs around, I sat hunched over at his feet, the top of my head brushing the dusty ceiling. I placed the worn red diary between us on the stiff blue hostel blanket.

We sat in silence for a moment, and I knew I had to steer this ship. Rory was adrift, and there was no point in me being here if I couldn't help him. So I finally squeaked out, "Strange day, huh?"

Okay, so that was the understatement of the century.

"A bit," he murmured. He was staring at the little white stitches in the blanket, which allowed me to study him unchecked. His dark hair was tousled, sticking up in the back and on the right side where he'd been lying on it. He was a bit paler than that first summer of ours— perhaps a result of living in Ireland. There were dark smudges beneath his eyes, too, and I wondered how long they'd been there.

But even so, he was just as beautiful as when I'd first spoken to him at Mrs. O'Leary's little yellow house.

"I wish you'd told me last summer," I finally said.

"I know," he whispered, more to the bed than me.

"Or when we first got to Ireland."

"I know."

I swallowed past a lump in my throat. "Why didn't you?"

He rubbed his eyebrow. "The more you tell a lie, the easier it gets.

And the harder it is to remember that it's a lie. I'd been pretending it away for half my life already."

I nodded, but he wasn't looking at me. "Okay," I said.

He looked at me then. "Okay?"

I nodded again. Gave a little shrug.

His big, beautiful brown eyes filled with water, and I couldn't stand to see him go under. The blanket scratched at my knees as I crawled to his end of the bed. When I turned to sit next to him, he pulled the blanket out from beneath me and helped me climb under. Then he slid beneath, too, and his arm looped around my shoulders as natural as anything. I curled into his side and took a deep breath, the smell of him, so inherently Rory, calming my pattering heart like a drug.

He pressed a kiss to the top of my head, and I knew everything was going to be okay. We were still learning, how to do, how to be, how to love. But that was enough.

"Cora?" he said softly.

"Hm?"

"I'm really glad your family came to Oyster Beach last summer."

I smiled against his shirt. "Me too."

His Adam's apple bobbed against my forehead as he gulped. "Are you?" he asked softly.

I pulled away just far enough to see his face—and the fear in his eyes. As if he was afraid of my answer. And then I realized my mistake. The effect my words had on this boy who was already so broken. Falling back against his side, I pressed a palm over his chest. "What I said earlier…about not choosing this. I did. I did choose this. I chose you."

He gulped again and found my hand. Instead of holding it, he touched my Claddagh ring. "*Fan liom.*"

Wait for me. I smiled. "I'm glad I don't have to wait anymore."

He didn't reply, and at first it made me nervous, but then I realized that we hadn't discussed, you know, the future. It wasn't abnormal for that to make him reticent. But then he whispered, "I'm scared. For Aidan."

"I know," I whispered back. "We'll figure this out, I promise."

As I shifted to curl against him, hold on to him a little tighter in the face of my thoughts, my foot brushed the diary, which had gotten pushed to the end of the bed and was in danger of falling. I pointed to it. "Do you want to…?"

He nodded reluctantly. "Sure. Will you read aloud?"

"Do I get to do the voices?" I asked, reaching for the book. "I do a cracking Irish accent." I said that last bit with the worst brogue known to man.

But it made Rory smile. I checked.

"Please don't," he murmured.

I opened the book to the first page. *Cordelia O'Leary* was scrawled on the inside cover, and a slanted script covered the opposite page. The letters were cramped and tentative, unsure.

"What does that say?" I pointed to the first line, a mix of numbers and jumbled letters with a line through them.

Rory followed my finger. "The twenty-fifth of Meán Fómhair, 1960."

Below that, another line. This one not crossed out. I snuggled deeper into Rory and read, "September 25, 1960. Dear book…"

Leabhar Beag
LITTLE BOOK

~~25 Meán Fómhair, 1960~~

25 September, 1960

Dear book,

Seamus says I'm to start ~~at~~ with a greeting ~~wen~~ when I ~~rite~~ write here. He says the only way to make E~~e~~nglish ~~nachn~~natural to me is to ~~rite~~ write ~~ich~~ each day. It was kind gift for him to give. You are a ~~beutiful~~ beautiful thing, leabhar beag. But I feel silly ~~riteing~~ writing to a book. What does a book want to ~~no~~ know?

26 September, 1960

Dear ~~diery~~ diary,

Seamus says a book like this is called a ~~diery~~ diary. But I didn't want to write to a book at all, so Seamus made a list of things to tell you, little book. He says to tell stories to you will help my

English so people don't tease. Three ~~monfs~~ months Seamus ~~teeched~~ has been teaching me, but other people still speak better. Why he wants me to write here. And I will, so I do not make Seamus ~~embaris~~ embarrassed.

Seamus helped me spell that and he reads this. He says he is not embarrassed and he loves me very much. Seamus. Seamus. Seamus. It is the first word I learned to write ~~becus~~ because it is in the jetty. Before I could write, Seamus wrote Seamus + Lia ~~with~~ ~~thing~~ knife he keeps in his pocket. Now it is in the jetty forever.

That was since three ~~monfs~~ months. It was still Bealtaine then. And that is when he ~~aksed~~ asked me to be his ~~wyfe~~ wife. I told him I don't know how to be a ~~wyfe~~ wife, but that I will love him always. He ~~sayed~~ said that is all it means to be a ~~wyfe~~ wife. And so he planned a wedding.

The first thing on his list for me to write about is how we meet. But I think I will do the second first. That is the story of a wedding. It is still so clear in mind. One week since. Anniversary is what we will call the day, Seamus says. And every 20 Meán Fomhair, we will count how ~~the~~ many years it is ~~to~~ since 1960. I count slow, but I will remember always. The day I joined Seamus forever.

He said our wedding ~~is~~ was small because people don't think love should be rushed. But he says he loves me and I love him, then it is not rushing. There is a small ~~chirch~~ church in ~~Oster~~ Oyster Beach and the man who is there is Father ~~Jorge~~ George. He is very nice. He speaks Irish little. Irish is what Seamus calls my ~~tong~~ tongue. ~~Gwaylgu~~. Gaeilge. Nobody in Oyster Beach can speak it so why I learn English.

~~Fillip~~ Phillip is Seamus's best man. ~~Fillip~~ Phillip Hall. Seamus's best friend. And his ~~wyfe~~ wife is ~~Martha~~ Martha. I have no friends in Oyster Beach, so ~~Martha~~ Martha is my maiden.

I ~~was wear~~ wore a white dress with ~~lase~~ lace sleeves Seamus brings home one day. ~~Martha~~ Martha ~~tells~~ told me it is a ~~bridesmayden~~ bridesmaid dress that I not *should wear it. She showed me pictures in magazines, and many weddings ~~has~~ have dresses that drag on the ground behind the woman. Mine did not touch ground at all. I like ~~Marthu~~ Martha is teaching me things, but I love Seamus and I would wear the dress he gave me. So I did, with my hair up on my head, and I put ~~theyr~~ there tiny seashells from the sand and small white buds of a flower Seamus calls Do Not Forget Me.*

Seamus ~~did wears~~ wore his best black pants and a shirt as white as the caps of waves in the sea. From ~~Fillip~~ Phillip he borrowed a tie as blue as home, and his hair was oiled back like men in magazines of ~~Marthu~~ Martha.

We ~~standed~~ stood on the ~~alter~~ altar with our best man and ~~mayden~~ maiden, and we ~~repeats~~ repeated everything Father ~~Jorge~~ George had us to say. Then Seamus kissed me, and Father ~~Jorge~~ George said we are husband and ~~wyfe~~ wife forever.

How ~~kik~~ quick forever happens.

Then we go to Doyle's Corner and ~~was~~ had the biggest meal ever. There ~~is~~ was more flounder and whiting than I could fit in my belly, and Seamus could not stop laughing. That is when he gave me you, little book. After, I asked him to go to the jetty with me. We ~~standed~~ stood there and kissed for long. Then we waited and ~~put our hands together~~ held hands. I think Seamus did not know why I want to stand there, but I hoped that Mamaí would be nearby. Maybe the others would see and know I am happy.

Seamus says the ~~yelo~~ yellow ~~hows~~ house is mine now, too. It is actually Mr. ~~Ak Acoo~~ Acone's, but Seamus says he will buy it, ~~peece~~ piece by ~~peece~~ piece. I never knew what owned is until now, but this little ~~hows~~ house ~~does starts~~ is starting to feel like mine. My home. I think wherever Seamus is ~~was~~ will feel like home.

He calls me Mrs. O'Leary now. It is strange not to be called Lia since. But Mrs. O'Leary is a fine name.

Now, I have told you of our wedding, little book. Seamus will see that I ~~do~~

~~writing~~ write very often and be proud. But there is too much sun outside and the sea calls to me. Later. Later he will show me everything I write ~~rong~~ wrong and I write to you ~~tomar~~ tomorrow ~~agin~~ again. Seamus says to practice writing my name. So I must sign at the end,

Mrs. Seamus O'Leary

30 September, 1960

Dear diary,

How the days escape! Every day, Seamus tells me to write. But he goes away in the boat, and I forget. We ~~eet~~ eat fresh fish and walk on the beach ~~in~~ on nights he is home. The wife of a ~~fishing man~~ fisherman! I never thought that to be so. But I never know I could be so happy. Not with a landsman or anyone.

Martha and Phillip come to call but not others. Seamus says they are ~~jel~~ jealous. That I am so pretty and others wish I was their wife. But I think it is not. Woman smile at Seamus and talk to him outside church on Sundays or on the street near the shop. But not me. I hear ladies talk quiet to the others when I am not looking. I know I am different, but I did not think they know. I have told no one but Seamus. I think he told Phillip, because Phillip is his best man, but no others. Do they know? How do they know?

I try so hard to be same. I do not swim or speak to waves. I sit in houses like all ladies and go to Father George mass and walk on boardwalk and listen to Seamus. So how can anyone know what I am?

How I wish other ladies would come to me and our house. Martha is nice, but she has many friends. I have Martha only.

And I have my house. I sit on the porch when Seamus is gone. ~~B~~because there I can look at the sea. It is too quiet when Seamus is gone. He plays his ~~whissle~~

whistle when he is home and the porch is full of ~~lafter~~ laughter. In the quiet nights I go to the jetty to see Mamaí and it is ~~silly~~ strange. To see her there and me here. Like this. On some days it makes me sad but I do not tell Seamus. Because he is sad already.

He tells me he writes to his father. He lives in a place called ~~Irlan~~ Ireland. That is where Seamus is from. He came to America two years ago. I'm happy every day that he ~~come~~ came here or we may not meet. I ask Seamus if we will go to ~~Irlan~~ Ireland, but he says it takes more money ~~then~~ than we do have. He had a letter from his father back, and that is when he ~~becomed~~ became sad. When I asked why, he said his father is upset. Seamus wrote to his father about coming to ~~Irlan~~ Ireland to live ~~yet~~ again. But that was before he ~~meeted~~ met me. His father wants him home. But Seamus will never leave me.

I wonder if this father hates me. I do not want a stranger to hate me. It is bad ~~yet~~ enough for the ladies on the street hate me. I do not want the father of Seamus to hate me too.

I wish you could tell me your thoughts, little book.

Love,

Mrs. O'Leary

10 October, 1960

Dear diary,

I not told you of when we met. That is on the list Seamus made ~~to~~ me. I saw him in the water, little book. I saw him when I was swimming and he sat on the old jetty. He is beautiful, my landsman, my Seamus. Dark hair and eyes green like the sea. He cried the first day I saw him. I wish it ~~so~~ was laughter. But for a selkie it is not so. His ~~teers~~ tears are what brought me. I don't know why he ~~cries~~ cried, but I

~~wach~~ watched him many times before I talked to Mamaí and made my ~~choise~~ choice. It is not a ~~choise~~ choice a selkie can make easy, but Mamaí loves me very much and agreed I follow ~~to~~ my heart.

I left in Bealtaine, May, the birth of the summer, when the sea is warm and wild and beach is fresh. Seamus found me, just like I planned. But he not alone. Phillip Hall and James ~~Kassady~~ Cassidy and ~~anoter~~ another man was with him. They drink and have fun on the beach many times, I knew, I see, and one of those times. I hid behind the rock, wait for Seamus to find me by himself only. But James ~~Kassady~~ Cassidy saw first and called to the others. He looked scared. He said something to me first but I could not ~~understood~~ understand.

I say, Cad a duirt tú?

They all looked funny at me. Only Seamus smiled.

The smile as ~~bryt~~ bright as the sun on the sea.

He said, An bhfuil tú inan Gaeilge a labhairt? Then he said something to the men in their tongue that I thought ~~sounds~~ sounded strange. The others grumbled and walked down the beach, but they looked again and again. Seamus asked me if I was hurt and when I said no, he touched my arm. I've never felt anything like it, leabhar beag. I shook from head to toe. He took me to his yellow house and gave me a shirt to wear and pants. They were too big for me, but I knew I could not wear my skin forever. It is not big enough for my new long legs.

I told him everything then. I told him where I come from and that he had to hide my skin or I would go back. I've heard stories—of selkies waking up back in the sea. I told him it was a ~~thing~~ force I could not ~~kuntrol~~ control. To hide it as best as he could. Little book, I don't think he believed me. Not at first.

He told me to sit and made me ~~tee~~ tea. And he talked, in his deep, soothing voice. He told me about Oyster Beach and where he ~~come~~ is from, the place called Ireland, and all of his friends and his fishing. And he asked me where I was from.

But I already told him.

I told him, again, and maybe he believed me then, because he didn't ask again. And he took my sealskin. He said I could stay at his house if I had nowhere ~~for~~ to go to. He didn't know I did have somewhere to go to. His little yellow house.

He hid my coat but still I worry. I worry every night I sleep that I ~~am waking~~ will wake up back in the waves. Would I be able to find Seamus again? Would he take me back after I disappeared from him? I do not know and I hope we to never find out.

He still teaches me English every day. He reads you, little book, to show me where my words are wrong. He reads others, too. He has books all around the little yellow house. My favorite is about some thing called an ashray. Seamus says they're called tales, stories that are not true, but he didn't think I was true. Not at first. So maybe true is not always what we think.

Seamus sits me down to practice writing, too. I learn so that I can tell him everything in my head, because I love him so. But I do not enjoy it. Sometimes he teach to write ghaeilge, for that tongue comes more natural. But English I not enjoy. It is ~~difi~~ difficult. Unlike Irish.

Like Seamus says just before he laughs,

Is fearr Gaeilge briste, ná Béarla clíste.

Love,

Mrs. O'Leary

Díoltóir Beag Bídeach
A TINY SALESGIRL

W HAT DOES THAT MEAN?" I ASKED SOFTLY, pausing at the bottom of the entry and attempting to work out the pronunciation. *"Is fear galguh bristy na bearla cleestuh?"*

When Rory didn't say anything, I looked down at him, afraid hearing these things was proving to be too hard for him. He'd slumped against me, his head resting on my shoulder, and his chest rose and fell in the perfect rhythm of sleep. I smiled, relieved, and closed the book gently. There was no way I would read on without him.

Sleep weighed heavy on my limbs, but my mind was too wired to actually succumb to it. And as difficult and long as this day had been for me, I couldn't imagine how it was for Rory. His face was so calm in sleep, I wanted to touch it. So I brushed the hair out of his eyes as soft as possible. We'd have a lot to do tomorrow—figuring out what to do about Aidan, what to say to all the O'Briens, whether to drag Mr. O'Leary into the mess. And that didn't even include what I'd tell my own parents, who were no doubt struggling with the news of the court case.

I sighed. All of that would come with the morning. But for right now, I just needed to sleep.

I considered crawling back down to my own bunk, but the thought only lasted a moment. Snuggling deeper under the covers, I gently tugged my own arm out from under Rory and then curled up on his pillow, our faces inches apart.

When I woke up, I was sprawled over the entirety of the bunk. Embarrassed and thinking Rory had moved in the middle of the night for comfort, I glanced down at the bottom bunk. It, too, was empty. In the next bunk over, Rosie snored peacefully. Most of the other beds still held sleeping forms, too. I checked the old analogue clock on the wall. 7:42. Way too early to get up. In normal times. But these weren't normal times.

As I climbed down the ladder as quietly as possible, the door to the room creaked open. Rory walked in, his face damp and his hair combed. He looked up, surprised, as I hopped to the ground. "Oh, hey," he said softly.

"Hi," I whispered, intensely aware of the awkwardness of this conversation with a room full of slumbering strangers.

"How'd you sleep?" he asked, his eyes darting nervously around the room.

"Fine," I said, bending to slip into my shoes. "Is it still storming out? We should get back to Galway. I'll wake Roz."

"Um, let her sleep a bit," Rory said, biting his lip. "I wanted to go talk to Seamus again."

"Oh. Okay." Did he want me to come? Did he want to talk to him privately? I paused, glancing everywhere but at his face. His eyes were like magnets to my own, though, and when my gaze finally did end up there, he was smiling gently.

"Will you come with me?"

My answering smile was automatic, and I nodded eagerly.

Outside, the craggy island glistened in a blanket of raindrops, but there was nothing falling from the gray sky anymore. The sea, that constant backdrop, was as steely and churning as ever, but people milled about cheerfully, and a few cars were inching through the town, which sat just below the hostel.

As we picked our way toward the road that led to Seamus's, Rory reached out and slipped his hand into mine. It felt so good and right and comforting, I wanted to squeal. I didn't. But it was a hard battle to win.

By the time we reached the seal colony, a soft spray was blowing in from the waves. There was a lone seal sleeping down on the rocks, and Rory stopped when he saw it. He stood, frozen, staring, for at least a full minute before I rested my cheek on his shoulder. He jolted, pulled from wherever he'd been—the depths of the ocean, probably—turned, and gave me a weak smile.

I wondered if he was thinking the same as me: *Aidan? Is that you?*

But I couldn't say that. Instead, I murmured, "It's pretty, isn't it?

The ocean?"

Rory squinted back out at the waves. "It's just the bay," he said. "Galway Bay. Nothing scary."

He sounded more like he was trying to convince himself than me. But he was a good swimmer. Where had the notion of the sea being dangerous come from? Was he just worrying about Aidan?

Perplexed, I let him guide me toward Seamus's house. Seamus's goat was nowhere to be seen, but the tiny fairy house was in its place, shining and wet. I tried to remember if Mrs. O'Leary had told me any stories about fairies, but it was so hard to conjure her here in this place where Seamus had run to after leaving her.

Rory freed my hand and knocked twice before huffing angrily.

"Maybe he's at the bike shop already," I suggested.

"Well, we can't go there," Rory said, running a hand through his damp hair. "Not after yesterday." I didn't argue. Running into Kieran Browne again didn't seem like the smartest idea.

Rory knocked again, harder this time.

"Was there something you wanted to talk to him about?" I asked.

Rory sighed. "I just… I feel more grounded today." He squeezed my hand, and it felt good to know maybe I'd played a part in that. "So I wanted to ask him some questions."

Twisting my lips to the side and nodding, I pretended to understand. But my curiosity got the best of me. "Anything in particular?"

He turned away from the door and looked down at the haul-out. There were two seals there now. A muscle in Rory's jaw ticked, and then his gaze found mine. "Yes," he said.

Okay. This was like drawing blood from a stone.

He started back down the walk, pausing only a moment, this time to gaze at the seals. "You know," he said, turning back toward Kilronan, "I was really scared yesterday."

"With Kieran? Yeah, me too. He's a lunatic."

"Not for me," Rory said, stuffing his hands in his pockets. I tried not to overanalyze why he didn't hold my hand again, but it smarted. "For Aidan."

My heart fell, and I stumbled over the rocks in the road. This whole goddamn island was made of rock.

"All I could think while Kieran was throwing those rocks was…what if Aidan was down there?"

"Me too," I murmured. I remembered Rory going toward Kieran while Rosie and I ran away. It was hard to imagine—how *real* the situation was for Rory. Aidan being…what he was now. Looking for all the world like…an animal.

And Rory's own body with the potential to do the same.

"I was so scared Kieran was going to bludgeon him before my eyes, and I wouldn't even know." Rory sniffed.

A cold chill spread through me, and I watched my feet, not trusting my coordination on the slick gravel.

"I was so, so scared. I couldn't… Not knowing…"

When he didn't say anything else, I knew he needed comfort. "He left from Galway," I said softly. "That's quite a bit away."

"Not by water."

The barking of a dog interrupted us, followed by the squawk of a kid. "Bikes! Bikes! Bikes!" It was a little girl. "Biiiiiiikes!"

Maybe it wasn't the best advertising slogan, but as we came toward one of the only intersections in the tiny town, she came darting up to us. It was the girl from Kieran Browne's bike shop, and she was closely followed by the welcoming committee. Peewee jumped up on Rory's leg, his tail wagging nonstop, and Storm ran circles around us, as if attempting to herd us together.

"D'ye wanna rent a bike?" the little girl asked, proffering glossy brochures that were bent from her fierce grip. "Or two bikes, I mean. Ye can't ride the same one!" She giggled, energy humming off of her as she danced from leg to leg. She looked no more than ten, and her long, dark hair was in two braids down her back.

"No thanks," I said as cheerfully as I could muster. "We're going to be leaving soon."

"Are you sure?" the little girl asked. Her accent was a little different from Rory's friends in Galway. More lilting and foreign, more prone to drawing out certain words. "Are you absolutely positive?" Just when I was about to assure her we had no need for bikes, she added, "It's spring tide. Ya'know what that means?"

Oh, boy, did I. Yet…that didn't quite make sense. "I thought that was yesterday," I said.

"Spring tide?" she said easily. "It lasts a few days. 'Round the full moon. And then again at the new. And guess what my mammy says? She says it's the best time for shells and seaweed. So ye can ride out to the other end of the island"—her eyebrows raised like a salesman offering up a rare deal—"and at low tide, it'll get real, real low, and there'll be seashells for miles. 'Specially after a storm like last night's."

"Thanks, but we—"

"Can I be honest?" she said dramatically, a hand going to her head like a careworn old woman. "I could really, really use the help."

I glanced at Rory, who only looked eager to get away from this ball of endless energy. "Oh yeah?"

"Yes, today's my first day on com…commission. *Dadó's*—er, Granddad—he's giving me a euro for every customer I bring in. Ye'd be *two* euros!"

Granddad. She spoke of her granddad as if he owned the bike shop. What were the odds her granddad was the murderous Kieran Browne? Swallowing, I glanced again at Rory. This time, he was biting his lip.

"I'm afraid we can't today," I said, "but good luck on your commission. I bet there will be a lot of people interested when the ferry gets in."

The girl's face fell, but she mustered up a smile. "Fair enough. C'mon, Peewee. Storm."

"Is Seamus working today?" Rory asked suddenly.

"He works every day," the little girl said glumly. "He's in the back working on the bikes." Suddenly her face broke into a smile. "Want to see him? I bet if ye come in and chat a while and *then* decide to rent a bike, I'll still get my euro."

"Uh, no, that's okay," Rory said. "We really do have to go."

The girl deflated, and I felt sorry for her as we walked away. Peewee and Storm tried to follow us, but the little girl snapped at them to stay, and they obeyed reluctantly, both watching Rory go with big, round brown eyes.

Glancing over my shoulder, I watched the little girl scope out other pedestrians, obviously weeding out the locals from strangers.

"Um, how about you go wake up Rosie?" Rory suggested, his hands back in his pockets. "I'll go by that little shop to grab us some breakfast, and then we can catch the first ferry back."

"Okay. But if it's not covered in sugar, Rosie won't eat it."

"Noted." With a small smile, he turned around and headed back toward the shop, his head bent but his stride quick. With a deep breath, I turned toward the hostel.

We had a lot ahead of us, and nobody was making any decisions. But I knew this was hard for Rory, so I couldn't blame him. What were we going to do back in Galway? He'd need to call his parents, and what about his brothers and sisters? Even his roommates were going to want to know where Aidan had disappeared to. There were many lies ahead, and lying was one thing I was *never* good at.

At the hostel, people were milling about and beginning the trek down to the pier. The first ferry of the morning would be leaving shortly. In our room, I found the Brazilian girls straggling, and Rosie, braiding her hair over her shoulder, and I put a hand to my own damp, tangled bird's nest. It was in severe need of a washing, but there were more important things to deal with at the moment.

"Where'd you two lovebirds go this morning?" Rosie asked, wrapping a hairband around one braid. She had the irritating ability to do her hair and makeup without a mirror. It made the rest of us—okay, me—feel inadequate. But I quickly shook the mundane thought. What did hair matter when Aidan was still missing? Though, could he really be called missing when we knew exactly where he'd gone?

"Rory wanted to talk to Seamus again," I said, climbing the ladder to the top bunk to make sure we hadn't left anything there. Not that we'd brought anything with us. Just Rory's backpack, which sat forlornly at the foot of the bed. I slipped it over my shoulder. It was light as a feather. Had he even brought anything?

"Well?" Rosie prompted. "Did the old man have anything more useful to tell you today?"

The diary! It was lodged beneath the pillow Rory and I had shared last night.

"Dunno," I said, crawling across the bed and grabbing the tiny book before jumping back to the floor. "We never found him."

"That Kieran guy probably murdered him," Rosie grumbled, standing and straightening her rumpled v-neck.

"Or he went to work," I suggested. "We were too scared to go looking at the bike shop."

"Good," Rosie said firmly. "Otherwise we'd probably never have found your bodies."

The Brazilian girls bustled out of the room without a backward glance.

"Where is he now?" Rosie asked. "The ferry's leaving soon."

"He went to grab breakfast."

"This is the second time an O'Brien boy has made us almost miss the ferry. And I don't intend to spend another night here. It's like *Groundhog Day* on this island. I'm beginning to think we'll die here." She groaned. "Aren't you sick of waiting on O'Brien boys?"

The answer was no, but I kept quiet. Best to let Rosie entertain herself while we waited.

And wait we did.

"Should we go find him?" Rosie asked fifteen minutes later, as I peeked out the little window that looked down toward the sea. All the stranded tourists on the island were moving down the concrete pier like a living, breathing wave.

"I dunno," I said, just as the door to our room opened.

He wasn't out of breath. He didn't even look like he'd been hurrying at all.

"Finally!" Rosie snapped. "We're gonna have to run, and I am *not* a runner."

"Here," I said, slipping the diary under my arm and unzipping the backpack, "put the food in…"

I noticed his hands were empty just as he reached out to take the backpack from me.

"Didn't you get breakfast?" I looked up at him, and he was biting his lip.

Misean Tarrthála
THE RESCUE MISSION

H E REACHED INTO HIS BACKPACK AND TOOK something out of it, leaving the canvas of his bag dangling from his hand, limp, empty.

"Where were you?" I asked. "If you weren't getting breakfast…"

In his other hand was… It was a plastic bag. He watched me look at it, the heavy, dark thing inside obscured by the translucent white of the bag.

"What…"

The question died on my lips as I read the look in his eyes. It was fear trying to masquerade as courage. The hair on the back of my neck stood on end. "No," I said, darting forward.

Rosie looked from him to me, confusion lacing her features.

"Cora," Rory said.

"No!" I interrupted him. I made to grab the plastic

bag, but he heaved it out of my reach, causing a hint of saltwater to hit my nostrils.

"Cora, I have to," Rory said, steadying my flailing arm with his free hand.

"No," I said. "I won't let you."

"We don't have any other options."

"Yes, we do! We can go to the cops. We can go to Seamus. We can tell your parents—"

"I just talked to Seamus."

"What?" *The old jerk had encouraged this?*

"We can't just sit here and twiddle our thumbs," Rory said.

"Guys, what's going on?" Rosie demanded, joining our powwow by the door.

Rory looked into my eyes as he answered her. "I'm going to go look for Aidan."

"Okay, good," Rosie said, still confused. "That's what we need to do, for sure. But why is that bag pissing Cora off so royally? And where's breakfast?"

Without breaking our gaze, Rory held the bag out to her. Rosie looked at me, hesitated, and then peered inside.

She blanched. "Oh."

"You're not doing this, Rory," I said, my voice shaking with fear and anger and a thousand emotions I couldn't name. "I swear to God, if you do this…"

He waited, but neither of us knew how I planned to finish that sentence.

"Cora, I have to," he said.

"Stop saying you have to!" I yelled, tears finally leaking from my eyes. My fingers curled around the worn leather of Mrs. O'Leary's journal. "You don't have to! You didn't have to lie to him for all those years! You didn't have to lie to me last summer! You could've just been honest and told the truth and we might not be in this mess! Now make up for it! Be honest and go to—"

"You're right, you're absolutely right," he interrupted, "and that's why I *have* to do this. For him. For Aido. For lying to him all those years!"

"But he *chose* to go, Rory!"

"I can't just let him go!" Rory roared. "Let him disappear like it doesn't even matter!"

"Why not?" I sounded like a petulant child. "He *chose* it!"

"He's my *brother*, Cora! My *brother*! You wouldn't understand!"

It was a punch to the gut. He couldn't have known that, but that didn't lessen the pain swirling outward from my stomach, radiating through my limbs.

"You're right," I said evenly, no longer yelling. "I wouldn't understand anything as complex as *loving* somebody because I don't have a sibling."

Rory's eyes widened in horror as he realized his mistake. "Cora—"

"I don't have a sister because my sister *drowned* before I was even born. So why would I, the one left behind, understand anything about *missing* someone? About what it's like to lose your sibling?"

We fell silent. At long last. But too late to save ourselves from the pain of the words that had already been said.

I turned away from him, walked to the little window, and looked down at the pier. The oblivious people clutched cups of coffee and backpacks as they ambled around the entrance to the boat, tourists desperate to get back to the mainland to enjoy their vacation despite the overcast day and the bite in the air.

"Cora, I'm sorry," Rory whispered at my back.

I wasn't sure whether he meant he was sorry for so callously bringing up siblings, or for not letting me in on the big secret last summer, or maybe for what he was about to do next.

"It's still spring tide," he said. "I have to go now if I'm going."

I heard the jingle of keys in the silence, and then Rosie murmured, "Thanks."

Rory whispered, "There's an email to my parents in my phone. Send it if they start calling, because that means they've gotten Aidan's letter."

"Okay," she said softly. "Bye, Rory."

His retreating footsteps, scuffing quietly on the linoleum, couldn't have felt louder in the silence had he been wearing tap-dancing shoes.

"Cora," he said, farther away now, and I could hear the waver in his voice. "If you could save your sister, now, after all these years, would you do it?"

I closed my eyes against the sight of a happy family posing at the edge of the pier, Peewee dancing in front of them. It was a question I hadn't pondered often. In fact, for most of my childhood, I'd spent more time resenting my overbearing mother than thinking about Gretel. But it had only taken one kind old woman and one summer at the beach to turn my world on its axis. Learning to swim had only been the beginning. The nightmares I'd been having over the past year had deluged me with thoughts of Gretel and adulthood and the pain of loss. Sure, I'd wondered before what it would be like to have a sister. But for the first time, I wondered what it would have been like to have

Gretel. What kind of person would she have been? Would we have been close? Would Mom have been different? Dad? Me?

Just because I hadn't been born yet didn't mean she hadn't been a real person with a real personality, a real soul. A soul I now imagined at the bottom of the ocean in a merman's cage, trapped forever, while I walked around up here in the world.

Not daring to turn around and see Rory's beautiful face, I admitted defeat. "Yes, of course I would try to save her."

The rustle of the bag was the only indication that he was leaving.

"Cora, let's get on the ferry," Rosie said gently, after giving me a solid three minutes of stunned silence. "There won't be another one until this afternoon."

I bit the inside of my lips. "I can't believe he just did that."

It was quiet for a moment. Finally Rosie said, "Can't you?"

My head whipped toward her.

"Well, I mean… We're kind of running out of options here."

"Rosie, in case you didn't hear, he's going down there to turn into a *seal!*"

"Yeah, yeah, I'm just as freaked as you are, but…"

I rolled my eyes. "Spit it out, Rosario."

"Well"—she shrugged—"we can't go to the cops, and he can't tell his parents. Or anyone, really. And he's scared to just wait around. I think it's brave, really."

The scope of my foolishness opened up before me then. Suddenly, I remembered how scared Rory had looked that night we were in his room and he'd first touched his sealskin. When Aidan had hidden it beneath his pillow. Rory had been so afraid to touch it. I'd never seen him look so frightened. He *was* brave.

"I can't let him do this alone!"

"Wait, what?" Rosie sputtered as I dashed for the door. "That's not what I meant! You can't—"

"Well, I can't go *with* him," I said, "but I shouldn't have left him to face this alone! Mad or not, I shouldn't have— God, what if it hurts? What if— We don't even know how it works! What happens! How it happens!" I nearly tripped down the hall, leaving the door wide open.

"Cora, no! We need to leave! This isn't what… Cora, wait up!" she wailed behind me, when it was clear I wasn't stopping. I didn't even slow down. Across the pebbly parking lot devoid of cars, down the little grassy hill the hostel perched upon, past the tourists heading to the pier—I didn't slow down.

There was a stretch of sandy beach just to the left of the pier, obscured from the tourists by a long, low building. I hopped down a low wall into the sand.

It was empty. My heartbeat hitched. *No no no no.*

Searching frantically, my eyes scanned the waves. *I must look just as mad as Mrs. O'Leary.* The realization hit me with such force, I tore my eyes away from the ocean and ran down the shoreline.

"Rory!" I called.

The beach ended in an outcropping of rock up ahead—a dead end.

"Maybe he didn't come here," Rosie panted. I hadn't even realized she'd caught up, Rory's backpack in hand. "This whole island is practically shoreline."

She was right. As she ambled toward the rocks, panting slightly, I looked over my shoulder at the curve of the shore as it ran along on the other side of the pier and disappeared behind a splash of buildings in the distance.

"Or, uh, maybe he did." The sadness in Rosie's voice made me turn to her at once.

Standing beside the rocks, she was holding a neatly folded pair of jeans with a damp t-shirt, boxers, and hoodie stacked on top, a pair of shoes on the rocks beside her.

My heart plummeted, and I turned back to the waves, desperate for a glimpse of him—whatever shape that glimpse might take. The possibilities made my blood run cold even as I hoped against hope for some proof that he was alright.

God, how could I have let him leave on that note? Angry and yelling?

"It's okay, Cora," Rosie said, and her arm slipped around my shoulders, which I only then realized were shaking. "Everything's going to be okay."

I shook like a leaf in her arms for a full minute before she murmured, "Let's get on the ferry. It's freezing out here."

Despite the fact that it was quite chilly and my clothes were still damp, I shook my head. "Can we stay here for a while?"

Rosie sighed, but I saw her nod in my peripheral vision and move to place Rory's shoes and clothes in his backpack. I sank to my knees on the sandy shore and stared out at the waves, choppy and slate-blue as the clouds blocked out the sun.

Fanacht
WAITING

SOMETIME AFTER THE FIRST FERRY LEFT, ROSIE disappeared, too, but she returned with sandwiches and two deep-red Aran sweaters. An old man had joined my silent vigil, too, quietly painting an old rowboat with chipping yellow paint several yards away, not the least bit interested in why a weepy girl sat on the rocks in slowly mildewing clothes. Maybe it was normal for people to come here to contemplate their sorrows. Or maybe I just looked a little disturbed and he was afraid to approach me. I sat there, barely feeling the chill, realizing that I finally, *finally* felt just a tiny little fraction of what Mrs. O'Leary must have felt. Angry and lonely and a bit heartbroken and bitter. She must have felt like this for years.

It was a thought both sobering and terrifying. Because the man Mrs. O'Leary had waited for had never come home.

"She wasn't waiting for me," Seamus had said. *"She was*

waiting for Fionn."

I still didn't understand. But I wanted to. So I opened the diary and began to read.

"Read aloud," Rosie said softly, nudging my knee with hers.

So I did. As much for her benefit as for the waves'.

Ag Bualadh le Landsman
TO MEET A LANDSMAN

15 October, 1960

Dear diary,

It is more warm than usual today, and I can't stop thinking of Seamus. He's away on the boat overnight now, but my mind won't leave one moment of a warm warm day when Seamus kissed me in publick for the very first time.

It was Meitheamh and hot, so Oyster Beach was crowded. And Seamus ~~liked~~ likes to hold my hand and take me down the boardwalk when it ~~was~~ is full of people. He says he ~~shows~~ is showing me off. He bought me so many clothes, but he does not know I will never wear them with as much comfort as my coat. He took me to a store ~~for~~ and let me pick out all the clothes I wanted, so I did. I thought that would make me less ~~diffrint~~ different. But still, on the boardwalk, other ladies stop to stare.

Phillip Hall always says they stare because I ~~lived~~ with Seamus. He said it was unnatural for me to live with someone who ~~be~~ is not my husband. He said it is not ~~onist~~ honest. He would say that many times to Seamus. He stopped saying it when we married, but maybe that's why the women stare as we walked down the boardwalk all those months since. It happened once, ~~write~~ right after I came here, after my first time at church. It's such an odd thing, Father George's mass. Everyone moves and speaks at the same time, like they have practiced and I watch them for when to stand, sit and when to go to my knees. This day an older woman stopped in front of the church to ask Seamus who am I. She said it in front of everyone who just come out of church. Phillip told us that very day ~~too~~ it was unnatural, not ~~write~~ right, the way we lived. He said people talked about it.

So what did Seamus do? He said, "Mrs. Buckley, this is my Lia, the prettiest girl in the world." And he turned to me, put his arm around my waist, and kissed me.

I didn't know touching someone could make me feel alive so. Everything tingled.

And the old woman gasped like a seatrout stranded on land and walked away.

I am so ~~lonely~~ terribly lonely when Seamus is gone but when he is here I am ~~more happy~~ happier than any creature can be. I remember that kiss like it is in a storybook Seamus has read to me many times, but I have lost count of all the rest since.

Love,

Mrs. O'Leary

18 October, 1960

Dear diary,

I had a bad dream last night. Seamus is away on the boat again, and I know Seamus likes to be on the boat because his friend James works with him and the others, but James is not very nice and I wish Seamus likes the boat a little less. Last night I take pillows from the closet in our room and I put them down the bed on his side. I do this always when he is gone, so it makes me less scared when I wake up in the middle of the night to a bed so empty.

But tonight I woke up choking. I was drowning. Little book, I did not know I could drown. I know that I am not the same as I was. That my body is different now. That I would have to swim different with this body. But I haven't been in the water since I came here so I did not know how it could be. I was choking and I could not breathe. My arms and legs thrashed, and the water felt different on them. Like it was dragging me down, not supporting me.

And I knew then that I chose it. That I chose to go back, to leave Seamus, but did not have my skin. The sea, my home, was punishing me because I did not have that part of me that tells people who I am, what I am. My skin.

Do not worry. It was a dream, little book. It was a dream only.

Shouting and crying, I woke up that time to real, and I was in our bed. The blankets were tangled around my long legs, and the pillows all on the floor. I not choose to go back, leabhar beag. I never will choose that. Seamus is me now.

But I do worry. I love Seamus, but.

There are such tales in the sea, and I can not easy forget them now, even as my naked feet press against the cold wood of our little yellow house. I am a selkie, in my blood and my bones. I know what selkie love is. I feel it every day of my life. But can I ever know what true human love is?

I do not know, little book. And I worry. And I am shamed of these words. I do not want Seamus to read them.

Love,

Mrs. O'Leary

22 October, 1960

Dear diary,

I do so forget to write when Seamus is here, little book. He tells me every day to, but after he puts on a sweater and I put on my big black coat and we walk down the boardwalk and it is near empty because everyone else is inside their houses. Or Seamus makes a ~~fyr~~ fire on the beach and we sit by it until our faces burning hot. Or we curl up beneath a blanket and Seamus reads to me and our little yellow house.

Sometimes we go to Doyle's Corner, the pub where Seamus and his friends like to be, and we have dinner, soups and potatoes and clams, and it feels so nice to ~~be food~~ eat among others, talking and laughing. I ~~not~~ can not believe how easy it ~~be~~ is to open clams with hands instead of teeth! Harold, the man who cooks at Doyle's Corner, lets me go into the kitchen and watch him cook so that I can learn to do the same for Seamus.

Whatever we do, I forget to write. Being near Seamus makes me forget. Forget everything but Seamus.

Love,

Mrs. O'Leary

25 October, 1960

Martha has been to see me again. I like her visits much, little book, she is my only friend, but today she said things quite cruel. Not things she says, but things others say. Others can be mean. I like Martha for telling me.

She says the others find me odd. Martha says I look different, ~~forein~~ foreign, she says, and the worst bit is I know it is true—Harold once told me he found me a "rare little bird" until he knew me when I am "delight."

Martha says people mention how I dress strange and act different from them. I know my English is not good but I do try. Martha says Elizabeth Nelson tries to talk like me, and everyone at their partys laugh. We are sometimes invited to the houses of others but Seamus says he does not like to go. I want to know if he does not go because he knows Elizabeth Nelson would be cruel to me. If that is right, I should tell him to go to the parties without me. I don't want to ~~embr~~ embarrass him.

Martha also says her friend Laura wants to marry Seamus since she first set her eyes on him. And Martha says many women in Oyster Beach love Seamus. He is handsome and kind and he speaks different from them, too, but they don't mind he is different. They like it, little book. So why do they not like when I speak different?

In the post office, where Laura works, I often see her staring at Seamus. But sometimes her brother Frank stares at me. Seamus says it's because I'm beautiful, with big, brown eyes, the better to see through the waves, but maybe Frank really stares because he has heard Elizabeth Nelson teasing me.

Martha also told me everyone says we only married because I'm with child. I am not with child, but I wish it was so. I think that is a lovely reason to get married. But Martha says it's not right. She says it's frowned on. She told me Kate Rogers said we had a shootgun wedding that would not last and that she would grab Seamus as soon as it is over. I don't think she is waiting. I saw her at the shop when Seamus and I went last week. She came over to us, put her hand on his arm, and said hello. You do not need to touch someone to say hello. And she didn't touch me or say hello to me. It made me angry, because I know what it's like to touch Seamus.

Oh, little book, when I touch him everything in me quivers and I feel so warm like fire and I could burst. Warmer than I've ever felt in the water. It's unlike anything else.

That's probably why Kate Rogers touched him.

But I want to be the only one.

Again and again I have the dream where I wake up in the water. Even when Seamus is home sometimes. And it makes me wonder, maybe Kate Rogers would be better for Seamus than me. Maybe I'm not meant for real human love.

Maybe it would have been better if Martha didn't tell me these things. She didn't seem to mind telling me, though they made me very upset. I did start to cry, and she left then.

I think I will not ask Seamus for help writing again. If he reads this, he might become sad. Seamus has lots of books, and there is a big book with all the words in it. I will use that to make my words spell ~~rite~~ right.

It is getting cold now, and it difficult to move. It is like the wind glues my bones together. Seamus says he likes the cold, it reminds him of Ireland. I am used to cold water, but the air is a different beast. It bites harder than the coldest waves.

But Seamus says I will learn to love the winters. And I think he is right. It does mean he spends much time with his arms around me.

Lia

1 November, 1960

Dear diary,

The most curious holiday was yesterday! Little children dress up in all sorts of costumes and knock on your door. Seamus bought lots of candy. Cinnamon Bears and Lemonheads and Banana Splits and candy buttons. So many I've never tasted. They hurt my teeth, but the children love them! We gave pieces to each child who came to our porch.

One was dressed as a lamb, with a mask over her face that looked just like the pictures in a book about a shepherd that Seamus brought home once. And there was a boy dressed as a king. Another was a shark, can you believe that? He had only a mask on his face that didn't much look like it, but Seamus laughed loudest at that.

James Cassidy came by with his sister and her husband and their two children. They were dressed as characters from a film I don't know. James told me my costume was wonderful, but I was not wearing a costume, little book. It was most strange. His sister laughed, but Seamus did not hear and so I did not know what to say.

After they left, when Seamus and I sat on the porch and just watched the people on the boardwalk, I told him how cute all the children were. And you'll never guess what he said. He said we should have our own one day. Oh, I'm so happy, little book! Children are a symbol of love, and I will finally know what true human love is. We'll be closer even than we are now, and I can't imagine it, but Seamus says it's true.

Yours,

Lia

12 November, 1960

Martha was over again today. She told me the strangest thing. She thinks Phillip is keeping a secret from her. I find that hard to believe. Phillip and Martha are inseparable. And they've been married much longer than we. But Martha was so distressed today, and she's usually quite calm. It make me wonder. And it make me think.

Does Seamus keep secrets from me?

I don't think so. But I wouldn't know, would I? That is the thing of a secret.

I can't imagine what Seamus might hide from me, apart from where he's hid my coat, and that is a secret I can not know because the dreams haunt me still.

But Martha says there are all sorts of things a husband keeps from his wife. Like if he falls in love with someone else. Or if he has bad habits like to drink too much or gambling. I asked Martha if she thinks one of those is the secret Phillip is keeping from her, and she started to cry. Then she yelled that I should be the one worried, with Seamus always gone off on the boat. That hurt my feelings, and I think maybe I shouldn't have said anything at all.

When she left, I sat on the porch and thought, but sometimes my thoughts go only in circles.

The sea is beautiful today, little book! I don't think I could be happy on land if I didn't live so close to the waves. I can see them and hear them and smell them and even taste them on the air. Seamus insists on closing the windows, because he says it's too cold to leave them open, but whenever he leaves, I open them all. He comes back to a cold house, and grumbles and scolds, but I'd rather have the cold than not be able to smell the sea.

Forever,

Lia

Stoirm Selkie
A SELKIE STORM

W HAT ARE YE READING?"

Rosie gasped, and a wet nose snuffled around the warped pages in my hands. I looked up. The little girl from the bike shop—Kieran Browne's granddaughter—stood over us, Peewee and Storm circling us playfully. Rosie, who'd been reclining against the rocks, sat up, her hand at her chest as if to still her heart. "Jesus, you scared the shit out of me!" she snapped. "We were just reading about-about *things*, and then you pop up out of nowhere."

"Ooh, is it a *love* story?" the little girl asked excitedly.

"Sort of," I said, wishing she would leave so I could read on.

"Can I listen?"

Absently flipping through a few of the previous pages, I saw words like "selkie" and "drowning." I sniffed. "Uh, I don't think so."

"All the other visitors left on the first ferry," the little girl said. "Why didn't ye?"

Because my boyfriend transformed into a seal to go save his brother, who is also currently a seal. No big deal.

"Stuff to do, kid," Rosie supplied. Not the friendliest answer, but better than mine.

"What kind of stuff? Like reading?"

"We have to get going," Rosie said, climbing to her feet, brushing off her brand new Aran sweater, and holding her hand out to help me up. "Almost time for the next ferry."

"No," I said, panic filling me at the thought of leaving this place. This last place I'd seen Rory. "I need to talk to Seamus. There might be a way...a way for me to..."

"Cora," Rosie said through gritted teeth, "let's ditch the kid, then we can talk."

"I can hear you, you know," the little girl said in wonderment.

Rosie rolled her eyes, and I let her haul me to my feet before obediently following her toward the road that lined the back of the beach.

"But ye weren't leaving until *I* got here," the little girl pouted, traipsing behind us. "Ye can tell me what ye're doing. I'm great with secrets."

"Don't you have friends your own age?" Rosie muttered.

"Yes," the girl said, "do you?"

Even in my current state, a snicker escaped me as we climbed over the short wall at the back of the beach.

"Get lost," Rosie snapped, either to the girl or the dogs—or both—it wasn't quite clear. I brushed sand off my jeans as we headed down the road. It was a useless attempt. Sand seemed to coat my very skin.

"It's another forty minutes 'til the next boat, at least!" the little girl said, dancing in front of us. "Let me listen to your story! Or I could read for ye. I'm great at reading!" Peewee licked my hand, as if to add to her persuading.

"Believe it or not, we made it to college," Rosie said, "so I think we've got the reading part covered." I grabbed Rory's backpack from Rosie and slipped the diary inside. The bag smelled so strongly of saltwater, I couldn't believe I hadn't noticed it before. He'd brought the coat all the way from Galway. That meant he'd been planning it all along—at least as a contingency. My heart twinged. How had I not noticed?

"Come to the pub," the little girl said, changing tactics. "I know the bartender. I can get ye free drinks."

One of Rosie's eyebrows shot up.

I rolled my eyes. "Yeah, a ten-year-old's gonna buy you beer, Roz."

"I'm eleven!"

"Thanks, but we're just going to go wait by the boat." As the little girl stopped and let us pass her by, seemingly running out of convincing strategies, Rosie took the backpack from me and slung it over her shoulder, and I pulled the Aran sweater tighter around me.

"I saw him, you know. Your friend."

I stopped. Rosie was tense beside me.

"What?" she asked, half-turning toward the girl.

"The selkie boy."

I couldn't see her face, but her voice rang with triumph. She knew she'd just played a trump card.

Rosie was the first to regain use of her legs and walk back toward the girl as I turned around to stare. "What are you talking about?"

"I saw him walk out to the rocks. He started taking his clothes off, so I closed my eyes, because *ew*. And when I finally looked again, he was a seal."

"You're insane," Rosie said, shooting me a terrified look.

"I know a selkie when I see one," the girl said petulantly.

"What do you know about selkies?" I asked, finally finding my voice.

She grinned. "What do you want to know?"

"I'm gonna need that beer," Rosie muttered, pulling a hand down her face.

"Follow me." The girl smiled triumphantly. "I'm Róisín, by the way. Pleasure to meet ye. Are ye interested in renting bikes, by any chance? I get a com-commission."

There were a few pubs on the island, and we passed one as we followed Róisín, chattering all the way, but she didn't stop until we reached a light-green two-story building with spindly trees in front of it. There wasn't even a sign proclaiming it to be a place of business, but Róisín pushed right through the door like she lived there.

It was dark and musty inside, but nobody else seemed to notice. Róisín walked straight to the bar, climbed onto one of the high stools there, rapped on the shiny wood twice, and ordered,

"Three MiWadis, John, please."

"Róisín," the barman said, nodding. They pronounced her name like "*ro*-sheen."

"My what?" Rosie asked, scrunching up her nose.

"Mi*Wadi*," Róisín said. "Ye not have MiWadi in America?" She looked genuinely surprised.

Rosie and I looked at each other and shrugged. "Could we maybe go sit back there?" I asked, nodding toward one of the darker corners of the pub. There were a few people sprinkled about the place—an older gentleman alone, and a family of three slurping soup—and I didn't like the idea of being overheard.

Róisín nodded and handed a pint glass of a light-orange drink to Rosie and I. Then she grabbed her own and slid off the chair before leading us to a wobbly table near the back of the bar. The walls were covered with framed photos and posters and clipped newspaper articles, and my eyes roved them as I sat down.

"So what are ye doing here? And with a selkie?" the little girl asked, her eyes big as she sipped her drink. I tasted my own—it tasted like watered down orange juice.

Rosie sighed deeply, apparently resigned to this conversation. "Well, we *were* catching the ferry out of here. But you threw a little wrench in that plan. I'm Rosie, and this is Cora."

"Your name's Rosie?" Róisín asked excitedly. "Mine's the Irish for 'little rose.'"

"How delightful," Rosie said in a tone that indicated exactly the opposite.

"Róisín," I said, stumbling over the pronunciation, "how did you find out about selkies?"

"'Cuz I am one," she said easily. "I've never seen another one. Not on land, anyway. I know they're around 'ere, but they don't like to come on land. So it was quite exciting for me, really."

Rosie and I stared at her. After a long moment, I felt Rosie's eyes on me, and I met her gaze.

"So this place is like a hotbed of selkies?" she said under her breath.

I shrugged. This was a child, after all. She could just be repeating something she'd heard in books. But she had come up with some awfully accurate information. I stared at her as she sipped from her pint glass. She was small for her age, skinny as a rail, giving her the appearance of being made up of all limbs. Dark-haired and dark-eyed, she certainly looked like the only other selkies I knew to compare her to, but she didn't act like them at all. And she was so tiny. Not the kind of build one would expect of an expert swimmer.

"Of course, maybe there have been others to come visit 'ere, an' I just didn't know," Róisín said. "Cuz I'm not allowed to tell anyone about it. But I figured if ye knew about your friend already, it was okay. And you were reading all about it in tha' book."

Rosie snapped her fingers, her face lighting up. "You heard us!" she said triumphantly. "You heard Cora reading from the book!"

Relief washed over me. That was it! She'd heard me talk about selkies in Mrs. O'Leary's diary. Of course. I smiled as Rosie shook her head happily. "Duh."

However, that didn't explain how she'd known about Rory…

Róisín's dark eyes narrowed at us. "Ye aren't the first to discover selkies, y'know." She rolled her eyes.

"Pshh," Rosie said. "You're just a kid."

"And I already known more'n you!" Róisín snapped. I was about to get in the middle of the bickering children when the actual child said something that made me pause. "Bet you didn' know last night was a selkie storm!"

"What?" Rosie asked with a laugh. "What does that even mean?"

"Selkies can whip the sea into a frenzy." Her little face was scrunched up into a glower—there was no other word for it. "They say the sea controls the sky, and once the selkies are angry, the storms'll come for ye on land." Her brown eyes flashed with something not unlike pride, and Rosie scoffed.

I glanced around, but the barman and the family had disappeared. Only the older gentleman remained, and as I looked at him, he turned to look at us. He didn't look happy.

"So, what, are you trying to tell us selkies are wizards, then?" Rosie asked.

"Shh," I murmured. It was too early to be interrupted. Because we were finally getting somewhere. I just didn't know where. Something was niggling at my memory. Storms. Something Colm had said. About the night of the Great Storm in Oyster Beach, when he was out on the boat with Seamus, Kieran, and James. The night James had died. He'd said the storm hadn't begun until *after* they started hunting seals.

"The more we killed, the worse the storm got," he'd said. *"Mother Nature was punishing us."*

"Why were the selkies angry yesterday?" I asked Róisín.

She frowned. "*Dadó* sorta went after 'im, or so says me mam. Lost 'is temper about somethin'."

A chill came over me. Outside Seamus's house. Kieran had gone after the seals at the haul-out, throwing rocks at them in a fit. A fit sparked by finding us with Seamus. We'd assumed that he was scared we would find out about James, dying on their boat all those years ago in Oyster Beach. That we'd find out the hand he'd played in that tragic event.

But what if that wasn't it at all?

What if he knew what Mrs. O'Leary was, what we'd found out about her, and he was petrified we would find out his tiny, spunky granddaughter of his was a selkie, too?

"Okay, then," Rosie said, rather too loudly, "let's say you're a selkie—"

"I am," Róisín said, crossing her arms.

"Yeah? So go turn into one—a seal." It was a challenge delivered with the gravity of a double-dog dare. "Go. We'll wait."

"I'd have to have my seal coat, ya blockhead!"

The door to the pub blew open then, admitting a pungent, salty breeze.

"Howya, John?" the newcomer said as Rosie opened her mouth to lay into the kid again. But Róisín's attention had shifted at the sound of the voice.

"*Dadó!*" she shouted, her eyes going wide. At least she had the grace to look caught out. Kieran turned, pushing the sleeves of his sweater up his arms. There was a great hole near the left armpit, and I felt a twinge in my chest for the weathered old man in front of me.

Who knew what Kieran Browne had been through, the fear he lived with for the secrets he was hiding? I felt…sort of sorry for him.

It evaporated as quickly as his friendly smile slid into shock.

"*Céard in ainm Dé?*"

"*Dadó,*" Róisín said quickly, jumping to her feet. Her MiWadi swirled in the pint glass. "These are my friends. Rosie and Cora."

Kieran was beside us in a flash, belying his old, crooked frame. "*Cén fáth a bhfuil tú ag déanamh cairde le turasóirí?*"

Rosie shot me a look. I gulped.

"We were just talkin', *Dadó,*" Róisín said earnestly.

"*Faoi ceard? An féidir liom ceist a cuir?*"

I had no idea what he was saying, but the look on his face was enough to spur me into action. It was angry, sure, but there was more to it, I could see now. Below the anger, there was fear. Maybe that's what rocketed me to my feet, or maybe it was just the sad fact of this eleven-year-old lying to her grandpa. For us. Whatever the reason, I was on my feet.

"We were just going," I said, shooting a look at Rosie. She scrambled to her feet, too, and slung Rory's backpack over her shoulder. "We were just chatting, honestly. She's a sweet girl."

If anything, Kieran's gaze grew even more fiery. What on earth had I said wrong?

On the other side of the table, Róisín deflated but obviously knew better than to protest, so we turned to go. Kieran's lips were pressed into a tight line, and his gaze flew back to his granddaughter. Still, below that fire, I saw it again. Fear.

Feeling one last spurt of confidence, I turned back and looked

Kieran in the face.

"We… We're not going to tell anyone." My voice wavered, and I gulped, but I met his gaze. "About…anything." My gaze flickered to Róisín. "We would never do that."

He looked at me without breaking eye contact for long enough to make me feel uncomfortable. But it felt like a test, and so even when the door of the pub opened, letting a little more light into the dim room and setting the dust motes to flying, I held his gaze.

"John. Kieran," one of the new arrivals murmured as he pushed past us.

Kieran cleared his throat and his eyes broke away from mine as he mumbled something in Irish to the couple who'd settled at a table near us. He looked at Rosie, then at Róisín, and then back at me.

"I swear," I added for good measure.

Kieran cleared his throat once again, a deep, gravelly sound. "Don't swear, girl," he said in English. "The Lord won't smile kindly on that."

He was still facing his granddaughter as Rosie and I headed for the door.

"Girls," the barman called. "Ye staying at the hostel?"

"Not tonight," Rosie said. "We're going back to Galway."

The barman laughed humorlessly and nodded out the window. "There's the ferry. Last one of the evening."

In unison we turned toward the window. It was cloudy with age, but we could still see enough to get the gist. Far out in the middle of the bay, the familiar white double-decker boat chugged over wave after wave toward the horizon and the thin slip of mainland visible from here.

Rosie's eyes were huge as she turned to face me with exaggerated slowness.

"Sorry," I murmured.

She shook her head. "I hope you realize this is *exactly* how horror movies begin."

Chun Imeacht nó Fanacht
TO GO OR STAY

I SMELL LIKE AN OLD TOWEL."

"Trust me, I know."

Rosie glowered at me. We were back in the same room in the hostel, much to the delight of Evan, who was working the front desk. Tonight, though, all the other beds in the room were empty. Apparently all the other prisoners of the island couldn't wait to get off it.

All the better for Rosie to yell at me.

"We need to go back to Galway, Cora! What Rory did was really heroic and everything, but what are we supposed to do? Just sit here? Why do I feel like you don't want to leave here at all?"

Because I didn't.

"I just need to talk to Seamus again," I said instead.

"Fine. And then bright and early, we're on that goddamn ferry."

I didn't answer but climbed the ladder and slipped

between the sheets of the top bunk. The bunk where Rory and I had slept last night.

"Okay," Rosie said, taking a deep breath, oblivious to my emotional choice of bed. "We need to get our story straight. What are we going to tell Rory's roommates? Niamh and Niall—they're going to wonder why Rory's disappeared but we're still around."

The sheets were cool, and I imagined I could smell Rory on them, but the truth kept burrowing away at my hope—it was just detergent; they had been changed earlier in the day. Just cold sheets and the smell of detergent. I pulled the blanket up over my legs and hugged myself.

"Well?" Rosie said.

I shrugged unhelpfully. This was new territory for me, as well. Forget fantastical beings and international adventures, I wasn't even experienced at sneaking around *at home*. I was about as good at lying as I was at swimming.

"Well," Rosie said, taking over the situation, "I think we should just tell Niamh and Niall he went to visit his brother in Dublin, grab our stuff, then get the first bus to the airport."

"Leave now?" I asked.

She stared at me with her mouth open. "Are you listening to me at all?"

"You're the one who told me not to be mad at him!"

"Look," Rosie said earnestly, "I don't think you should be mad at the guy. He's struggling with this just like any person…or-or selkie…would. But that doesn't mean you should stay! Just wait here while he…he …" She waved vaguely toward the windows.

I sighed angrily through my nostrils.

"Look, I know you're, like, in love with Rory or whatever," Rosie went on, "and I don't blame him for everything that's happening, and I feel sorry for him, I really do, but this is some batshit crackers stuff, and I don't think we should stick around to see it out."

"Rosie—"

"Cora, I don't want to hurt you right now, because I know you're in a low place at the moment, but I have to say it. What if he doesn't come back? Ever? How long are you going to sit around here, waiting? The rest of the summer? The rest of the year? Maybe you should just apply for citizenship now!"

A vision of Mrs. O'Leary on her little porch came so clearly to me, I was sure for one moment that I was back in Oyster Beach. Back before any of this had started to unfold. When she would wax poetic on Seamus, and I would obediently listen to her imaginary stories, still believing they were just that—imaginary.

"Well?" Rosie prodded, the toe of her shoe tapping the linoleum impatiently.

I wasn't leaving. But Rosie was a fierce competitor. I had to think logically.

"Forget that I 'like love him,' as you so eloquently put it, and think about this from any other standpoint. If we leave right now, in a week, maybe two, when his roommates or his family can't get ahold of him and report it to the cops, who do you think will be the *first* people they contact? And then what? We tell the cops the truth? Yeah, that'll go down great. Can't wait to share a padded cell with you for the rest of our lives."

"Not only do I make a *fantastic* roommate, no matter the circumstances, you're forgetting that that scenario will not be any different if we hang around here!" She threw her arms up, her eyes wild. "How long do you think we can live in this hostel without people becoming suspicious?"

"I don't know, but I'm willing to find out!"

"Cora!" she groaned.

"Rosie, we can't just *leave*. If…if something…happens to Rory, we're going to have to tell his parents the truth."

"Oh, no! No!" Rosie gesticulated wildly. "We are *not* going to be responsible for telling their parents this! Besides, how would we even know if something happened to either of them? It's not like we've got a seagull updating us like the freaking Little Mermaid! We'd be waiting around here forever!"

Forever. Mrs. O'Leary, sitting on her porch for decades, watching the waves, her eyes roving, roaming, hoping. *Dying*. Slowly dying. Left all alone by Seamus.

It always came back to Seamus.

Sighing, I pulled my knees to my chest. "Look, I'm just as freaked out as you, okay? I think the only option we have at this point is to go talk to Seamus. He's the one who created this entire mess, so maybe he can help. At the very least, we should go tell him where Rory is."

Rosie shook her head indignantly. "You're seriously concerned about this guy being kept updated on the situation? Don't you remember that he *killed* a man, Cora? And he's got a best friend who's just as murderous! Do you want us to be the next two people to disappear on this stupid trip?"

I didn't think Kieran was a threat anymore. But I didn't tell Rosie that. Instead, I just shook my head, trying to knock all the confusing thoughts sideways so that maybe they'd fall into some semblance of order. "I know. But…but think of the position he was in! His friends were there hunting seals, while his own kids were out there in seal form. Not that I'm defending him—maybe he really had it out for the guy. I don't know! I just… I can't leave yet, Roz. I'm sorry."

Rosie pressed her lips into a grim white line. "There's a note in the backpack for you. He handed it to me with his keys and his phone. I wasn't going to tell you because it's probably telling you to go find some magic beans and join him in the ocean, and you'd probably freaking do it, but who am I to stop you?" With that, she threw the backpack on the floor, grabbed the hostel-provided towel, and stomped out of the room, slamming the door behind her.

You little—!

Climbing clumsily off the bed, I missed the second to last rung and landed on the floor on my butt. Scrambling to my feet, I stubbed a toe but finally managed to unzip the backpack. His cell phone was at the bottom—with several new notifications, but no missed calls, so I ignored it, assuming there would be a million missed calls if his parents had gotten Aidan's letter already. Letting it drop back to the bottom of the bag, I kept rummaging and finally found a wrinkled piece of notebook paper with jagged edges. There was a seashell in there, too, along with his keys and the diary. With shaking fingers, I picked up the seashell, by far the oddest item in there, and unfolded the paper.

Cora,
Call me sometime?
Hardy har. Get it? You can use the seashell to listen to the ocean? Okay that was a terrible joke. I'm sorry. I'm nervous. All I really wanted to say was:
Fan liom?
I love you, Galway Girl.
Love,
Rory

Closing my eyes, I thought of the last time he'd said that—two nights ago in the pub, when he'd sung my song. My song. *The ghosts that follow Cora, make her run a little faster, but she'll always find her way right back to me.* He had ghosts of his own, too, but he would always find his way back to me. I had to believe it.

And then I thought of the first time he'd said "I love you." It was last summer in Oyster Beach, and I'd called him out on it. *"Mrs. O'Leary doesn't even think humans are capable of real love,"* I'd told him. *"Well when I say, I love you, Cora Manchester, it means I'm head over heels for you as much as my schoolboy mind can understand."* That's what he'd said. I'd felt the same way. And it was even more true now.

Tears pricked at my eyes, but along with them came a renewed resolve to help Rory through this. Rosie would only be able to get me off this island kicking and screaming. When she got out of the shower, we'd go to Seamus. Until then, there was only one place to go for information on how to find a selkie. I dug the diary out of the bag and flipped quickly toward the back, looking for the era in which Seamus O'Leary had found his sons.

My heart fell. The back of the book was empty. The entries stopped in 1974.

Sighing, I sat down. Oh, well. Maybe there was something useful in the other entries. The book's spine snapped as I opened it and began to read.

Anchúinse
MONSTER

18 November, 1960

Dear diary,

Seamus and James just got back, and James came by to say hello. I do not like James but I try. He smiles too much at me but then says things that aren't nice. Today he told me my dress was too "loud," but he said it with a smile. Seamus just shook his head and went to the cabinet for the whiskey, but I did not know what to say. Can mean things be nice if you add a smile? I am happy always when James leaves.

Seamus says my English is yet very good, but I feel guilty for not writing to you every day. Seamus asked to see my diary to see how my writing is, but I don't want to let him see it anymore. I don't want him to see the things people say about me and him. What if he begins to believe it himself?

Martha says it happens, things falling apart for a woman and her husband. But I am a selkie. That means we are different, yes?

Still, I think I will always pretend everything's perfect so that Seamus will think it is, too.

But I hope he doesn't think I'm keeping secrets from him in here. I do not gamble or drink and I could never love another. What secret could I keep from Seamus?

Lia

24 November, 1960

Dear diary,

I'm thankful for Seamus and our yellow house and Oyster Beach and Mamaí and Phillip and Martha and the sea and this adventure I never want to end!

We had a feast at Doyle's Corner and now I sit beside Seamus on the scratchy couch as he plays the tin whistle.

Happy Thanksgiving, little book!

Yours,

Lia

5 December, 1960

Dear diary,

I must confess I've had my most difficult day since coming here. Before I left, Mamaí made it very clear that I approach my new life as a forever. That I should think not of the sea or yearn for it. And I never understand why she said that. I didn't think I would ever yearn to return once I was here. But for the first time, I've wished myself back. I wished myself back, all the way to tears.

Martha came over this morning. But not for a visit. Seamus was out, and

124

thank goodness he was, for Martha came straight into the house without knocking. I never seen anyone do a thing like that. She marched right in to the kitchen, where I was having breakfast, and began to shout.

"You're an animal!" she screamed. "You freak of nature! You're-you're a monster! You're the secret! You!"

I didn't know what she meant at first and simply dropped my spoon.

But she kept yelling. "You're the secret Phillip has been keeping from me! He thinks you're a…a selkie!"

And then I became afraid. I knew Seamus had probably told Phillip, his best man, in the early days before our wedding, for who could keep a secret like that? But I was terrified of anyone else knowing. Phillip is a quiet, even-tempered man. But Martha has fits and times of high spirits. And she was having one now in my kitchen.

I tried to tell her it was not true, but that made her more angry. She said she knew I was a freak since the moment she'd met me and that I had Seamus under some sort of spell. I tried to defend myself, but she was quite wild with emotion. She seized the whole set of wooden spoons on the counter, a wedding present to us from herself and Phillip, and threw them at me.

Before I could say anything more, she grabbed two knives.

"Release him!" she was yelling. "Release him from your spell, or I'll do it myself! You can't hold a spell over him if you're dead!"

Phillip came upon us then. He was out breath, like he was running. He caught Martha by the arms and took the knives away. She collapsed into his arms, crying, and he just looked at me, scared and shocked, and then led her out of the house.

I was shaking. I shook like when I'm so cold I can't control it. And I was cold. Except it wasn't my skin that was cold. It was deep inside me. Like my bones were in the dead of winter without a sweater.

When Seamus came home, I told him everything. He is furious. And still I can't stop shaking. He threatened to storm over to the Hall house and teach Martha a lesson. I begged him not to. For my mind is in such a jumbles I don't want to be alone. A spell. I didn't know what it was. But I looked it up in the dictionary Seamus taught me to use. Magic. Enchantment. Draíochta. That's what Martha meant. She meant this is not true human love. And what if she's right? How am I to know the difference when all love I know is selkie love?

I don't know what will happen now, but I think I have lost my only friend.

I must confess I never thought I'd want to disappear like this. I wish to just slip beneath the waves and let the saltwater wash away my tears.

Lia

12 December, 1960

Phillip is in distress. They fought and Martha left Oyster Beach. She hasn't been back. I can not believe she would let such a thing break her marriage, but I know I do not understand human love properly. I have that conclusion after trying to understand Phillip and Martha. I'm trying, for Seamus's sake, but I don't. Seamus tells me Phillip and Martha were having problems and that Phillip kept this from Martha was only the last fight.

But I worry. I worry if it can happen to Martha and Phillip, it can happen to us.

Do you know, little book, Seamus told me why he was crying that first day I ever saw him, on the jetty. Seven tears, Mamaí always said, it's a sign of such torment in the soul of a landsman that it calls to the ocean. And to us. And that's why I felt it in my heart, the pull to the shore. And since that day I saw him there in the sand, silent tears streaming down his face, I wondered what brought such a handsome, strong man to tears. And he told me today.

I asked him. For the first time. Because I was afraid that whatever it was would come back, and he would cry those tears again, and it might be something that drives him away from me. Like one of the secrets husbands have that Martha taught me about.

But it isn't anything like that.

Seamus told me his mother died. He'd been gone from Ireland two years, and his mother asked him again and again to come home. But he was having fun in America. He thought that is all that mattered. And then she died. Suddenly. And he could never see her again. That is what brought the seven tears that took me to him.

I asked him why he ever left Ireland to come here. He said whim. That many young men of Ireland were going to England and America, and he had heard great things in letters that boys sent back. He said there was nothing in his town for him, he thought then. He said then. Then is not now. I wonder if he thinks different now.

That conversation did not bring the comfort I was hoping for. Instead I worry that one day he will leave Oyster Beach like Martha did. And not come back. But how can I worry that when I still have my dreams? Those awful dreams I used to have only when Seamus was away at sea. But they're different now, little book.

Instead of me waking up one day, back in the waves, these dreams are much clearer. I sit up in bed, Seamus asleep beside me, swing my legs onto the cold floor, and walk through the yellow house to the bookshelf in the front room. There, my seal coat lies. I take it and walk outside. Across the porch, down the steps, and over the boardwalk. I walk barefoot across the sand, wrap my coat around me, and sink to my knees in the frothing waves. Instead of choking the breath from me, the ocean now accepts me, its child come home.

I checked, you know. Just to see. I went to the bookshelf in the front room. Of course my coat was not there. Seamus hid it more than half a whole year ago. I told him to. But I do wonder where it is sometimes. I wonder if he moves it. That would be smart. Then as much as I search, it would always elude me.

It's no harm, wondering. But I do wonder an awful lot. I wonder if these dreams mean I really want to go back. I don't think I do. I love Seamus. But the sea comes to me while I sleep, pulling me, pulling like the moon pulls the tide.

Lia

Bun an Bhuidéil
THE BOTTOM OF THE BOTTLE

POOR MR. HALL. POOR, POOR MR. HALL. LAST summer I'd thought ill of him for not helping Lia, being there for her. But it was no surprise he'd distanced himself from her after a secret that wasn't even his had destroyed his marriage. And there I'd been, a flippant teenager, prancing about the beach demanding he fix everything. Poor Phillip Hall.

It was all I could think as we trudged down the road toward Seamus's house, past the sleeping seals, the blinking goat, and the tiny fairy house. But when he opened the door, his bloodshot eyes flickering between me and Rosie in confusion, all I could think was: *He's been crying.*

"Mr. O'Leary," I said in surprise.

"What are ye doing here?" he asked hoarsely, apparently finding his voice somewhere in the depths of his soul. "I thought ye left."

"We…we missed the ferry," Rosie said, glancing at me. She was obviously just as uncomfortable with his tears as I was.

I wasn't expecting ye," he said, wiping his sleeve across his nose and averting his eyes behind us. "Wasn't expecting anyone."

The statement stabbed at my heart a bit as I wondered if he ever expected anyone. Did he live alone and isolated, as Mrs. O'Leary had in those final years? "We just … We wanted to talk."

He gulped and seemed to think for a minute. Then he stepped back, turned, and stumbled to the living room, leaving the door wide open.

Rosie shrugged and stepped in before me, so I followed and gently shut the door, the seals vanishing from my sight behind the bright red paint. In the living room, Mr. O'Leary was already sitting, and on the table beside him was a large glass bottle filled with an amber liquid and a black label I couldn't read. Beside it, a tin whistle. And a thick glass tumbler. Empty.

"What'd ye come for?" he asked, his eyes on the floor. "Ya should've left on the boat. Spring tide's over, you know. The tide's gettin' shorter now."

"He's drunk," Rosie whispered. For a moment I worried he'd heard her, but then his desperation began to annoy me as I remembered why we'd come. The circumstances we were in. All because of this man.

"We want to know what you said to Rory."

Something flashed in Mr. O'Leary's eyes, but his bleary gaze remained on the woven rug between us.

"Tha's between me and my son," he said, all the s's slurring savagely.

The anger was rising in me. Not because I didn't want to be left out. But because he had left Mrs. O'Leary and Rory and Aidan in another country to figure this out by themselves, and now that it had caught up to him—the one who had all the answers—he was acting like the injured party. Too angry to sit still, I stood. "You made this something between all of us when you left your wife and sons to rot in another country."

Outside, the goat in the yard bleated, but it only seemed to turn Mr. O'Leary's indignation into sadness. His eyebrows tipped up in the middle, and for a minute, I was sure he was going to burst into sobs.

Instead, his nostrils flared, and he whispered, "Keep reading, girl."

"What?"

"The diary. You've obviously not finished. Have you even started?"

"Yes." I glanced nervously at Rosie. "What's in there that you want me to see?"

"The only thing I want right now is for the two of ye to leave an old man alone with his memories. His regrets." The last two words were whispered so quietly, I almost didn't hear them.

Rosie nodded toward the door with a little shrug. "If he isn't going to talk…"

She was right. He obviously wasn't the type of drunk to be loose with his words. It would make more sense to come back tomorrow, when he was sober and his sense had returned. I nodded, and we both stood. But before I followed her into the hall, I turned and told the old man, "Rory left, but I think you know that. He followed Aidan. Your *sons*. It would be great if you cared."

"It's not the first time," he murmured. "Probably won't be the last."

My chest constricted. I certainly hoped it would be the last time Rory transformed and went back to the sea. But I hadn't really considered anything past the *now*. "You're going to have to face them," I said, swallowing down my fear. "Both of them. Whether they come back tomorrow, the next day, or a month from now."

I turned to go, but he quietly said, "It won't be tomorrow," and reached for the tumbler and the bottle, which I could now clearly see was whiskey.

I looked back at him, a pitiable sight as his glazed eyes stared unseeingly at the bottle in his hands. "How do you know?"

He gave a humorless laugh. "Spring tide, girl. The selkie moves with spring tide. I thought you knew everything there was to know about them."

My heart fell. Selkies could only change at spring tide. I *did* know that. But I'd forgotten. The next spring tide wouldn't be for...

"Two weeks," Seamus said softly, before taking a hearty swig of whiskey, straight from the bottle.

"Wonder what's got him in such a state," Rosie grumbled as we walked back to the hostel.

I raised an eyebrow at her. "Maybe it has something to do with his only remaining son turning into a seal."

"Maybe," she conceded. "But it's kind of his fault, isn't it?"

"I guess. He did give Aidan his sealskin."

"No, I mean all of it. Think about it. If he hadn't, like, fallen in love with her and everything, none of this would have happened."

I scoffed. "You can't blame this on *love*. But you're right that he started it all. Had he and Lia both handled this a little better, and a little sooner, things could have gone so much differently for all of them. They could've been a happy little family."

Rosie shrugged. "But then your boyfriend would be, like, eighty."

I gulped. Her math was a little off—it would be more like fifty—but the point was clear enough to make me nauseous.

"Two weeks," Rosie groaned. "But our flight home—"

"I know." I looked carefully away from her. "I guess we'll need to change our tickets."

Rosie scoffed. "No. Flipping. Way."

Well, that reaction was calmer than I'd been expecting. I thought I could bring her around from there. "Rosie—"

"Howya?" somebody interrupted.

Rosie and I looked up abruptly. Evan was walking toward us, his hands in his jeans pockets and a big smile on his face.

"Hey!" Rosie said as easily as if we were back in St. Louis. I envied her comfort with the world. I just gave a quick wave. Throwing me a glance, she hissed, "This conversation is *not* over."

"Thought ye'd be long gone by now." Evan gave a little half smile, and while I had to admit he was cute enough, Rosie having a crush was the last thing we needed right now. Her crushes were long, hard, and emotional. And my emotions were all wrapped up at the moment.

Of course, maybe if she had a reason to stay a little longer…

"We missed the last ferry," Rosie explained, just as Storm and Peewee came trotting up to us. Bending to scratch Storm behind the ears, I babbled in baby talk at Peewee, who nudged against me, almost sending me to the pavement.

"Who do these two belong to?" I asked, looking up.

Both Evan and Rosie were looking down at me, Evan clearly amused and Rosie humiliated.

"She's not good with people," she told Evan, giving me a pointed look. "Evan was *saying*, Cora, that he's headed to The Oak."

"The pub," Evan clarified.

"Oh, no thanks. We're gonna—"

"*You're* gonna," Rosie corrected.

"Right, I'm gonna—"

"Go read a diary written by a woman long passed." Rosie sighed. "And maybe take a long, hot shower, with plenty of soap? It will do *both* of us some good."

I gave her a tight smile. It was more or less accurate. Even if it made Evan throw us each a slightly uncomfortable look.

"A book, like?" he asked. And the way he pronounced "book" to rhyme with "spook" tickled me so, I smiled.

"Go have fun, Rosie. I'll see you guys later."

Before they could walk away, though, I had a thought. "Hey, Evan? Before you go, could I ask—do you know anything about selkies?"

He scrunched his face up. "Is that a Scottish book you're reading?"

I glanced at Rosie, who was glaring at me. "Sort of."

"Can't say I know much about 'em, but it might be worth asking somebody like Seamus. It's an old Celtic fairy tale, I think. They're like swans or something that can turn into people, right?"

Okay, maybe that theory about this island being a hotbed of selkies wasn't quite accurate. Clearly not *everyone* here was a selkie.

I forced a smile. "Something like that."

Réiteach
A RESOLUTION

21 December, 1960

My tears wrinkle your paper, leabhar beag, but still I can't stop them. I went to the market today. In the summer the market is full of people and families and couples who don't live here but come just for the sun and the beach. But in the winter the market is dreary and the smell of dead ocean life is biting and it is nearly empty always. So I was surprised when I saw Elizabeth Nelson and Laura Nolan.

They stopped me to say hello. They never do that. At least, their hellos are always for Seamus. But they were smiling brightly even though I was alone. May the heavens forgive me, but I thought maybe because Martha was gone now, they were eager for a new friend. I was even a bit excited.

The first thing Elizabeth said was, 'Look what the tide dragged in.'

They laughed so loud then that the men behind the nearest stall looked over with their eyebrows high. I wanted to laugh, too, but theirs was the kind of laugh that does not invite one to join in.

"Allowed to wander around on your own now, are you?" Elizabeth said to me, and I didn't quite understand. I was alone often with Seamus gone to the boat. But maybe I didn't go into town just as much as others. I liked to be near the sea or in our little house.

"Oh, Elizabeth, who's the one on the leash really?" Laura said then. "She follows him around so. He's quite stuck, I should think."

"Of course you'd think that," Elizabeth said with a giggle, and her eyebrows danced.

They laughed together, again a laugh I wasn't invited to.

I asked after the children, because Elizabeth has a baby, but Laura interrupted me.

"Tell us, did you drive Martha out yourself?"

The shock made me fall quiet, and I dare to say I looked as dumb as a rock. I finally told them that of course I was devastated when Martha left Oyster Beach, and I had never wanted her to go.

And then Elizabeth said, "Mmm, I'm sure that's true." But she said it in the most curious way, little book. As if she meant the opposite.

"Yes, you cozied right up to Phillip, didn't you?" Laura hissed it like a snake. She even looked around to make sure nobody was listening, and I was glad the market was quiet, for I didn't want more to see my embarrassment. "Martha said you were the wedge that finally drove them apart."

"Do you have your sights set on anyone else's husband?" Elizabeth asked, already turning away from me. "Do have the decency to warn us, won't you?"

I didn't know what to say. Because they are right. My secret is the secret that drove Martha away. But I didn't mean for it to happen that way! All I ever wanted was Seamus. To be with Seamus.

As they walked away from me, Laura gave me one last look and nearly spat at me. "Why don't you leave Seamus for a real woman and go back to where you came from?"

Oh, why do they hate me so? I didn't want Martha to leave, I am honest! She was the only friend I had. Seamus will be home soon. I went to the market to get things to make him a nice dinner, but I can not bring myself to go to the kitchen. My legs shake, and I feel as though the world is turning sideways. I just want to lie and cry. But my tears will upset Seamus, and after Laura's words, I am determined to be the best wife of Seamus that I can. So I must dry up before he comes home.

No more tears now, little book. We have a job to do.

25 December, 1960

Do you think the sea feels pain, dear book?

26 December, 1960

Dear diary,

Oh, how my head throbs. But I have so much to tell you and no time to waste, for I might forget. I never knew there were so many days of celebration on land! One is over, when already the next is here. Yesterday was ~~chris~~ Christmas, and I must confess I did not feel nearly as cheery as half the people on the street. Seamus was quite down, moping about the house in one of his silent streaks. But I didn't pay him mind because Harold spent many days last week in the kitchen with me, helping me to learn all the parts that go together for a feast, and yesterday I had to put them all together. I was at the stove from as soon as we got home from church until the evening, when Phillip came for dinner.

I was a bit annoyed that Seamus had invited Phillip to join us, for I can only imagine what Elizabeth and Laura are telling their friends now. But I know Phillip is lonely, and as soon as I thought that I wished he'd stayed home, I was all regret. Even more when I took the ham from the oven.

It was a great big ham Seamus bought at the market. Harold wrote a list for me, the things I needed to make all the foods he taught me, and Seamus bought them on Christmas Eve. He brought home the biggest ham, and I thought that was strange, for there was a sadness in his eyes when he went to sleep that evening. It was those eyes of his that I was thinking of as I pulled the ham, charred black, out of the oven, smoke pouring out after it. The smoke stung my eyes, little book, but that's not why I cried.

Seamus and Phillip came running to the kitchen when they heard. Maybe it was my crying and maybe it was the clattering as I tried to get the potatoes out of the oven, too. They were not nearly so black as the ham, but burnt enough to discourage eating.

I couldn't even look at Seamus. Here was my first time cooking a great big meal for us, trying to make him happy on a day meant for cheer, and I'd only gone and ruined it all. I was a heap on the floor in the middle of the kitchen, smoke still pouring out of the oven, when Seamus began to laugh.

I stared at him then, no longer afraid of his eyes, and Phillip joined in. Before I knew it, Seamus had taken the brandy bottle he keeps in the cabinet over the stove, poured three glasses, and offered me one. I'd never had spirits with Seamus before. I've always thought that is for men. But I was so sad while Seamus and Phillip so jolly, I wanted only to join them.

The brandy was so sweet it made my mouth and stomach warm at the first drink. While I had another glass, Seamus scraped the top brown layer off the pan of potatoes, and Phillip grabbed the uncooked carrots, and then they sat right there *next to me on the floor and together we had our Christmas dinner.*

It was the best Christmas dinner in the world. Sure it was my first Christmas dinner, but even Seamus said it was the best, and he tells me often of how glorious his Christmas days were back in Ireland with his mam and deaide. If he says ours was best, it must be true.

It was especially perfect when the sherry bottle was empty and the whole room glowed with a warmth I felt in my very bones. It was like a special magic had seeped into me and I could do anything I wished. We walked on the beach, and despite the wind, I felt warm and liquid. I told Seamus that—that I could feel it, the magic, inside, and he says that's the sherry.

But I don't think so. I think that's just Christmas. If only my head didn't smart so much today.

Love love love,

Lia

1 January, 1961

Dear diary,

It doesn't feel like a new year, but I suppose it would be unbearable if it did. People mark the passage of time so that they don't feel as though they're floating in a stagnant pool and are instead moving forward, Seamus says, but I can't think why you wouldn't rather float ~~then~~ than be carried along by a never ending tide you can't control. That's all time is, really. And just like I didn't know how the waves could hurt this new body of mine, I never thought time had the power to hurt. But, oh how I was wrong! It hurts to think how much time has passed since I was with Mamai. These land bodies are so fragile. So much hurts them.

Seamus has apologized. I wasn't thinking of it since, but he said he was somber on Christmas day because he was thinking too much of his parents and Christmas days past, and especially his father at home alone in Ireland. He said he was sorry for being sad, but his eyes still held a sadness that made me think he couldn't mean it. I know he doesn't write to his father often anymore, and his father's letters have become scarce, too. Seamus said this is the natural way of things, a growing apart, but I don't like to think that's true. Just in case, I went down to the jetty twice that morning to see Mamaí.

That evening we spent at Doyle's Corner, me and Seamus and Phillip, the odd little trio we've become. And even Harold was out of the kitchen and drinking brown lager that made his cheeks as red as the holly still hung all over the pub. He asked Phillip about Martha once, and Seamus says he wouldn't have done that if he wasn't drunk as a skunk, but Phillip merely shook his head and went to the bar for another pint. I haven't thought much of Martha since I saw Elizabeth and Laura in the market, and I can't say I miss the thought.

I didn't have drink, for I dread the thought of the headache I had after Christmas. So I sat and watched the others be jolly, and that in truth, little book, makes me just as jolly as drink. Just before midnight, Harold gave us all a little scrap of paper from the barman's notepad to write on it our New Year's resolution. As I thought, all that entered my mind were the white caps of the waves outside and the feeling of the water hugging me through my seal coat. I was quite flustered, ashamed of those thoughts, and not knowing what to write, but then Seamus put his hand on mine and showed me his piece of paper. It said:

To have a child with my love

He was smiling so broadly, my own face caught it, and then he hugged me tight, and Harold must have seen the paper because he laughed out loud, his big stomach jiggling, and then wrapped us up in a big hug and danced us across the room. I forgot to write my own resolution then.

But when we got home in the early hours, and Seamus fell immediately into bed, the lager catching up to him, I took the slip of paper from his pocket, tiptoed down to the jetty, and slipped it into the water. I want it so bad, this baby, because maybe then Seamus won't yearn for Ireland so. And maybe I'll be able to see past the sea. But first I need this one last gift from the waves.

Mmm, it's colder than ever today, but I feel warmer, little book. Seamus sleeps still, though the sun is high in the sky, and I think I shall not wake him and instead sit on the porch and think. I'll practice thinking of things other than the sea.

Like whatever I shall name our baby. I've always liked Áine.

Love,

Lia

Ag Insint Bréaga
LYING

THIS TIME, WE WERE AWAKE BRIGHT AND EARLY and ready for the ferry. Well, I was. I had to drag Rosie's hungover self out of bed, but it wasn't as difficult as I thought it'd be. Especially considering I'd explained to her in no uncertain terms that we were just going to Galway to collect our suitcases—and then coming straight back.

I'd had the nightmare again—the one where I'm in the jetty and I see a dead body. First it's Mrs. O'Leary's, then my sister Gretel's, and then Rory's. The images had jolted me awake, and I felt shaky with adrenaline as we got ready.

After grabbing Rory's backpack—I was too worried to leave it in the hostel—we were on the ferry into Rossaveal with ten whole minutes to spare, and though Rosie lost her return ticket and had to pay again, she was in too high a mood from the night before to care.

"You're in an awfully good mood," I observed as she

sat down, one hand pressed to her forehead, but a small smile on her face nonetheless.

"A hangover's not so bad when it was worth it, I guess." She looked at me through half-lowered lids.

"Did you kiss him?"

"Oh yeah," she said. "Irish boys taste like Guinness."

"Could that be because he was drinking Guinness?"

"Are you trying to tell me *all* Irish boys don't taste like that?"

I rolled my eyes. "I wouldn't know."

"I wish I could form my own theory, but the last time I kissed an Irish guy, I'd had a few too many to drink. Guess I'll have to try another to find out."

I gave a little groan. "Rosie, do you *really* have time for dating right now? We're on…well, vacation, I guess—"

"You call this vacation?"

"Okay, a weird mission trip that turned into some sort of vigil, but that doesn't leave room for boys, either."

Rosie laughed and dug a pair of sunglasses out of her purse. "Trust me, Cora. I am in no danger of losing my heart in a hopeless place. That's your territory."

"Hey! Last summer wasn't hope—"

"Shall we discuss one Rory O'Brien?" She perched the sunglasses on her forehead and turned to look me in the eye. "A magical creature who was just reintroduced to his estranged father after the disappearance of his magical mother, and who is now living underwater and searching for his brother who ran away *to the sea?*"

"Well—"

"Don't worry, Cora. This little island could not handle one more lovestruck American girl. This one"—she pointed at me—"is complicating things enough."

I swallowed. She had me there. "I would like to change the subject now."

Rosie smiled and flipped the sunglasses down over her eyes. "That's fine. I should stop talking before I hurl."

By the grace of God, Rosie didn't puke on the boat—that, apparently, was *also* my territory—and we both fell asleep on the connecting bus, waking up to the chatter of the other passengers just as it pulled through the tiny medieval streets of Galway.

The town felt surprisingly familiar, and I felt a strange feeling of relief as we walked to Rory's apartment.

"We need to decide what we're going to tell them," Rosie said, glancing around us. Shop Street wasn't all that crowded, so we could talk freely. There were several buskers on the street, dutifully adding their unique touch to the colorful storefronts, but that only masked our words more.

"I've been thinking about it," I said. "What you said before—he's gone to visit family. That works."

"Okay." Rosie dug Rory's keys out of her bag and then looked at me for a long moment. I pretended to be interested in the splotches of gum on the pedestrian street. "You suck at lying, Cora."

"I know."

She sighed. "Just follow my lead."

Rex was the only one in the sitting room, and he barely gave us a passing glance, but I could hear Niamh chatting away on the phone in her room. Rosie ushered me straight to Rory's room, glancing over her shoulder as if afraid someone would sneak up on us. God, lying professionally was nerve-racking.

Inside his room, we gathered our stuff quietly. Rosie was taking forever, and I found myself drifting over to his dresser. Among a sea of low-value euro coins stood a can of his aftershave, making the whole corner of the room smell like him. There was a photo of him and Aidan tucked into the corner of the mirror, and I had to look away before tears could form. Turning quickly, I came to face the bank of windows looking down upon Shop Street. That was no better. The two of us lying in his bed, watching the seagulls fly past these windows— the memories were everywhere.

I knew immediately that that was a price of love. Rory and I had only a fraction of the memories that must have followed Mrs. O'Leary after Seamus left. Or the memories that had been following my mother around for as long as I'd been alive.

My mother. My heart twinged. I needed to call them soon. Avoiding it would not make anything better. And it certainly wouldn't make the lawsuit go away. Things were going to be different when I got home, whether I liked it or not.

"Knock, knock." The words were followed by an actual knock.

Niamh was standing in the doorway to the room. "Hey," she said when Rosie and I turned. Rosie glanced quickly at me, and I understood—follow her lead. "Where have ye been? Went out with the lads last night, but we couldn't get a hold of Rory."

"Oh, we went out to the Aran Islands," Rosie said cheerfully. "There was a big storm, and we ended up having to stay the night."

"What a drag," Niamh said, leaning against the doorframe and peeking into the room. "Where is he now? Did he decide to stay out there forever? Americans sure love that place."

She giggled, but the word *forever* bounced around my skull, and I had to concentrate to listen to Rosie's reply.

She gave a quick laugh. "Hardly. No, he actually had to go to his brother's in Dublin. Something with his nephew. A baseball game or something."

"Baseball?" Niamh repeated.

"Um." Rosie gulped, then recomposed herself and gave a little titter. "Sorry, I wasn't really listening. Maybe it was soccer? Do you know, Cora?"

"Yeah, soccer," I squeaked.

Fortunately, Niamh bought it. Because she had no reason to distrust us. "So are ye up for going out tonight?" she asked.

Rosie shot me a hopeful look, but there was no way I could keep up this ruse for an entire day and drunken night. She read my look correctly and pursed her lips. "Unfortunately, we have reservations tonight for a hotel down in…Cork."

I was fairly sure that was the only other place in Ireland Rosie could name.

Niamh wrinkled her nose. "Never been. But have fun, I guess?"

Fun was *not* on the agenda, but I just smiled and waved as Niamh backed out of the room.

"Will ye be back through Galway before you leave?" she asked, but her attention was already on her phone.

"Maybe," Rosie said.

Niamh's phone rang then, and she gave us a quick smile. "Good. Then I'll see ye then."

We both gave a sigh of relief when she turned and answered the call.

"Baseball?" I hissed at her once the door to Niamh's room closed.

Rosie shrugged. "Sorry. I don't have as much experience in *Irish* lying."

But I had a feeling that before we were done here, we'd both be well-versed in the art of lying in Ireland.

While in town we found an internet café and changed our flights. Rosie fought it, but I finally got her to book the return for four days after the next new moon. The next spring tide. My heart beat quickly even as I clicked "book." What if he didn't show up? What if he got lost out there or something happened or…

Even worse, what if he *chose* not to come back? There was no way I could possibly imagine what it was like for him out there, in this form, and who knew what sort of thoughts and experiences he had? What if he loved it?

The fear was still hot within me as Rosie bought two tickets from a ferry company that was *not* Aran Ferry, considering our lifetime ban. Pushing management on the issue for a second time didn't seem like a good idea. And as we found seats on the ferry, Niamh's voice reverberated in my skull: *Forever. Forever. Forever.*

Forever is a long time.

"You okay?" Rosie asked, jolting me back to the present.

Not trusting my mouth, I nodded, because despite the day's practice, I was still not a good liar. So I hid my face, and my watery eyes, behind Mrs. O'Leary's diary.

151

Ceannach Mór
A BIG PURCHASE

21 January, 1961

Dear diary,

I know I haven't written in so long, but I did not have heart for it.

Seamus and I had our first fight. There is a new plan on the boardwalk, and with that arrived our troubles. A company bought the old Steiner cabin down the boardwalk from us, the big red one that's been empty for some time, and though I don't see how that can be a hotel, Seamus was very excited about it. He said it would bring much tourists to the area and make the town prosper. Including us. After all, what do tourists want when they come? The same a selkie does. Fish!

But his happiness was short. A man in a suit showed up on the porch and when I answered the door, he asked to speak to the man of the house. I thought it strange that he should wear a suit on the boardwalk, where sand rides the wind and coats everything in its path. I also thought it lucky Seamus was home, but when he sent the man away, his face was dark. We watched the man walk to the Starks' house next door and knock, and then Seamus told me that the man wanted to buy our house and so he'd told him to go to Mr. Acone, who owns it.

It wasn't a day later that Mr. Acone called Seamus, and though I heard not the conversation, at the end, Seamus slammed the phone down. Mr. Acone does not want to sell to the hotel, for they will knock down all the houses and build cabins for summer visitors. Mr. Acone wants to sell to Seamus instead. But Seamus calls him a rat. For he wants the money the hotel would pay him, and we don't have it.

Seamus talked of moving out of our little yellow house, away from the boardwalk, somewhere that prices are lower. He spoke of living in an apartment in town.

Oh, but you can't see the sea from town! The walk to the jetty would take ages. He even said we could live in a town inland, where there would be no tourist money. I can't help it, leabhar beag, I cried. How could he speak of leaving our little yellow house? How could he talk of leaving the shore?

How could he ask me to leave the sea? Again?

I begged him not to, for us just to buy our house, and I am sure my voice was too loud, and I can't explain why. I can only say that it hurt. Like so much that happens to this body, it hurt inside me.

Seamus was angry and told me something I did not understand, to get a hold of myself. He said we could not afford it and that if we ever had a child we would need even more money. If, he said. If. He doesn't know it's not an if for me, little Áine.

He says it was our first real fight. And then he smiled little and kissed me after he said it, but I didn't smile back. I don't smile still. And I am mad at myself that I can't smile. What right have I to stay angry with him when he has forgiven me since? I don't know, little book, but I do know this body doesn't always feel what my head tells it to.

Love,

Lia

24 January, 1961

Dear diary,

Seamus bought the little yellow house. He went to the bank to sign his life away he said. I didn't go with him. When he got home he was quiet. He still has not talked to me.

I do feel so lonely when Seamus will not speak.

Lia

4 February, 1961

Dear diary,

Many neighbors are leaving. I am surprised by how many on the boardwalk have sold to the men in suits. Seamus isn't. He says, "What did you expect?" I think he bought the little yellow house because I was sad, little book, and I too thought it would make me happy to not leave.

Telling Seamus that it did not work would break him. I feel what can only be guilt.

Yesterday, he has been to see about a job. He says the fishing aren't good in years past. And do you know why he says?

"The damn seals," he snapped at me. "They follow the boats eating right out of the net like we're serving them a feast. And their sharp teeth tear the nets, which are very expensive to repair."

His tone makes me mad. As if the sea exists only for the people to use. Why should we not eat what we have since the beginnings? Just because the landsman finds he has a taste for grouper!

But I do not wish to vent, little book. I shouldn't complain of my husband. The reason I tell you this is because Seamus looks for a job away from the sea. We stayed here and still he turns away from it. He went up the boardwalk quite far north, where there are big houses that the very rich people stay in when they come to see the sea in the summer. There is a job open for keeping the grounds of one of the big houses, and Seamus has been to speak to the man, a Mr. Gerald Ritz. I do hope he gets the work, for then our fights might stop. How quickly our first fight turned into our second and third.

Sometimes he says things like how easy it would have been to find work if we'd left the house. And maybe it would have been better to leave the boardwalk. For other reasons, too.

For it's still there, constantly, the pull at my heart. Asleep or awake now. Not confined to my dreams. It's like the blood in my veins is always rushing in the direction of the sea, and the rest of me has to follow or I'll be split in two.

Some days I wish I could split in two and leave one Cordelia here and let the other find her coat and slip into the waves.

14 February, 1961

Dear diary,

I am told St. Valentine's Day is meant to be a day about love, but we didn't quite live up to it, I think. And that just makes me ~~dubbly~~ doubly nervous that I won't ever know what true human love is. All day, Seamus was in a grand mood altogether, kissing me at random, when I sat reading about faeries on the couch or stood on the boardwalk watching the waves, little surprise kisses … until shortly before dinner.

I've been practicing cooking with Harold very steadily these weeks, and I've become so good that I cooked Seamus a whole dinner, with scallops and potatoes and all kinds of things Harold told me is perfect for Valentine's Day. But I made the mistake of asking Seamus if Phillip was coming.

Little book, a storm moved across Seamus's face, as clear as the clouds that come in over the sea and hover above the boardwalk. I was so surprised, I didn't know what to do. He said of course Phillip was not coming over and asked why would I think that? Well, I thought that, of course, because we have Phillip for every holiday since Martha's leaving—so he doesn't feel lonely. But I didn't tell Seamus that. We sat and ate in silence.

After dinner, Seamus said we were going to Doyle's Corner, but I didn't want to go. I don't like leaving far from the little yellow house, to places I can't see the sea. I feel unsettled when the waves aren't there, moving in the corner of my eye, a gentle rhythm that never ceases, like the beating of the world's giant heart.

I think it angers him, honest. Me staying near to the shore. I know I don't like to go into town quite so much as I used to, not since I thought I might have to leave it for good when Seamus talked of moving. But how can he not understand? He knows what I am. Who I am. How I am.

So he went without me. And though my eyes grow heavy, I won't sleep til he's home.

Maithiúnas
FORGIVENESS

MY PHONE FELT FOREIGN IN MY HAND. I hadn't talked with my parents since the day before Aidan disappeared, and it made me feel like a bad daughter. Especially since I was the only one they had. And not by choice. I dialed, the room blissfully quiet after Rosie had gone to get us some dinner.

Mom answered on the first ring.

"Cora!" she exclaimed happily. "We were beginning to think you were never coming home."

She said it happily enough, but its relevance to everything going on with the O'Brien boys made me cringe. "Just enjoying myself," I said softly.

"I bet! I know the drinking age, young lady." Mom laughed.

Her amusement annoyed me. If only it was the drinking age I was here to explore. "How's everything with the lawsuit?" I regretted it immediately, knowing I'd said it only to knock her down a peg or two.

She paused, and a gentle rush of air came through the phone. "It's okay," she said, her voice holding considerably less mirth than before. "Your father's preparing, and everyone at the company is busy getting ready for that. It'll be a few months before anything comes of it."

A few months. So I would be home for that. *Home.*

It was the first time I really considered this—the *after*. The future. What would happen after all this? How would I go back to a normal life? And what would that even look like anymore? With all this, and then my dad's lawsuit on top of it, was I really able to go home—to the way things were before? And what about me and Rory?

I gulped down my nerves. "That's good," I ground out. "Um, I was actually calling to let you know I wanted to stay another week…or so."

Mom sighed. "You must really like that boy."

"Um, I do."

"Of course." She cleared her throat. "It's summer. Enjoy it while you can." I heard Princess bark in the background, and a bit of homesickness pierced me. How nice it would feel to sit in the living room with Princess in my lap, no waves within earshot. "Have you told Beth Herzinger?"

My manager at the flower shop. I hadn't even considered her. It wasn't that I expected a serious future in flower arrangement, but a letter of recommendation would be handy at some point. It would be unwise to screw it up. "Um, not yet."

"Do you want me to speak with her?" Mom asked knowingly.

I closed my eyes. My mother becoming involved in every

problematic area of my life was exactly what had caused such a rift between us last summer. But what could I do? Was I really going to run home with Rory stuck in the ocean for the next two weeks? Maybe utilizing my mom's help every now and again wasn't the worst thing in the world. In fact, I reasoned, if Rory had asked for help all those years ago, when he'd first learned what he'd learned, maybe we wouldn't be here, in this hopeless place, right now.

"Cora?"

"Yes, please," I murmured.

Everybody needed help sometimes. It was a fact of life. And mothers were often poised to give some of the best of it. Especially mine.

I sighed. "Mom, can I ask you something personal?"

She hesitated but finally came up with the words, "Of course."

"When Dad really, *really* annoys you, or makes you mad, or does something that hurts you, how do you forgive him?"

There was a long silence on the line, and the only indication that the call was still connected was the sound of Princess growling at something—probably a faraway barking dog.

Finally, Mom asked, "Is this about that boy? Rory?"

My own hesitation was too long. I knew it as soon as I murmured, "Kind of."

Mom sighed. "What did he do, Cora?"

"No, Mom, I'm not talking about any one thing. I'm just saying…being in a relationship is hard. How do you forgive the other person when he…" What? Keeps a pretty major secret from you? Leaves you behind to go on a rescue mission for someone he loves?

Makes a big decision about *his* life without you? God, I sounded like such a baby.

"So you're in a relationship now?" Mom asked.

I groaned.

"Okay, okay. I'm sorry. I...I don't know what to tell you. It's not a twelve-step program, Cora, it's just...it's a state of mind. You choose to be with that person every day, and you don't let things that don't matter get in the way. And, most importantly, you talk about it. Everything."

Not so easy to do when the other person in the relationship is currently residing in the sea, but whatever.

"But...sometimes things do happen." Mom's voice was halting, and I was ready to cut her off—after all, I was being ridiculous. Maybe I'd been hurt by some things Rory had done, but I hadn't exactly been the best person this past year. We'd both made mistakes. When he got back, we'd talk about everything, and my mind would be at ease as soon as we were together again. But Mom kept talking. "And you...you have to learn not to assign blame. Never assign blame, Cora. It's a slippery slope that will only end in..."

For one moment, I was incredibly confused. I heard a waver in my mother's voice, and the heavy weight of tears pushing to the surface. Grief clumping in her throat.

Grief.

Blame.

Gretel.

Pressing my fingers over my eyelids, I squeezed them shut. "Mom, I didn't—"

"I read somewhere that divorce is up to eight times more likely among grieving couples than others. And we had our days. Weeks, even. The thoughts would get caught on a loop. Who wasn't watching? Who gave her permission? Who saw her last? Whose fault was it?"

We'd never danced this close to the topic of Gretel, at least not since last summer. Something was hardening in my throat, making it hard to breathe.

"But we learned to lay aside blame, shoulder each other's grief, and most importantly—forgive. We forgave each other and ourselves, and we decided every day to be alive and awake and together."

Immediately, visions of the diary came to my mind. In those early days, Seamus and Lia had done that. But then something had happened that had broken them apart, just like fate had torn my parents apart. But my parents had found their way back together. Seamus and Lia hadn't…

Even though I already knew the ending to this story, the recent entries about their bickering made me reluctant to go back to the diary. To keep reading at all.

"And then we had you," Mom said, "and we had something else to wake up for every day."

"Thank you," I whispered. For forgiving each other. For living every day—for me. But I couldn't say any of that. My throat was incapable of producing any more sound.

"I…I have to go now, sweetie," she said, clearing her throat. "Joan's here. Needs directions for, um, she's waxing the floor today. She—she says hello."

I doubted that, but didn't say anything. Deep conversation was still a relatively new terrain for us. "Okay, tell her I said hello," I played along. "I haven't forgotten the Belleek china for her. Give Princess a hug from me."

Mom sniffed. "I'll give her a firm pat."

"Okay, tell *Dad* to give her a hug from me."

"I will. And Cora?"

"Mm-hm?"

"I love being your mom."

Sometimes "I love being your mom" is all you need to hear.

"Come in!" Rosie called from her bunk.

Evan stuck his head in. "Heya," he said, his eyebrows raised. "There's someone here to see you."

Rosie and I exchanged a look. There were only about three people we knew on this island. None of whom were particularly thrilled with our presence at the moment. Except maybe Róisín.

"Seamus," Evan said, answering our confused looks.

Rosie raised her eyebrows. "Let's hope he came with an apology," she grumbled. I hopped out of bed and slid into my shoes. Apology or not, if he was willing to talk, I was willing to listen.

A flat cap on his head, he was sitting in one of the plush red chairs across the lobby from the check-in desk, where Evan seated himself, not-so-covertly stealing glances at us as Seamus stood.

"Hello," I said awkwardly. His eyes were still a bit redder than normal, but he didn't appear to be…indisposed anymore.

Seamus nodded at us, grabbing the hat off his head and slowly turning it in his hands. "I…came to apologize. I was in a state last night, and I shouldn't have taken it out on a pair of children."

Beside me, Rosie bristled at the word choice, but I wasn't going to pick apart his apology. At least he was trying.

"I came to invite ye to come talk again sometime. And I promise to be civil this time."

Rosie scoffed.

"And I also wanted to invite ye to a class I'm teaching down at the school," he went on, oblivious to, or not caring about, Rosie's attitude. "Students learning Irish come here every summer to practice the language, and I lead the beginner's class if you're interested. I know ye have some time on your hands." He grinned sheepishly.

"A bit," Rosie said through gritted teeth.

It was meant as a peace offering, and though I didn't relish the idea of more school, especially during the summer, what else were we going to do?

"We'll be there," I said.

"*You* might," Rosie grumbled.

Mr. O'Leary smiled. "My boys coulda done worse in the way of friends than the pair of ye."

Thinking about all the ways I'd messed up over the past year, I wasn't so sure this was an accurate assessment of the situation. But that didn't mean I wouldn't try harder when Rory returned.

If he returned.

Chun Spiorad Uisce
a Cheansaigh
TO APPEASE A WATER SPIRIT

25 March, 1961

Oh, it's been so long since I wrote, little book, for my English is fine enough now that Seamus forgets to make me practice. And, too, things have been inching upward and I have feared writing down my feelings will only rock our fragile happiness. Seamus and I haven't fought in weeks, and though they've begun work on the resort, cabins springing up all around us, there's a jolliness in Seamus that I'm afraid to break.

He's started working for Mr. Ritz, and he even has his own shed on the property to store all the things he'll need to keep the lawn trimmed and the flowers blooming. He likes the work, but I don't think that's the reason for his newfound happiness. I think maybe it has to do with his new friends.

The boatman he works for with James has bought a new vessel and recruited a few new immigrants to man it. Seamus says he hires immigrants because they'll work for little, and that's how he came to work for the man just after he left Ireland. I think that's a bit sad, newly lonely men from another country working in a new place, working hard—for the sea is hard on landsmen—and having little money to show for it. But the new boys are too jolly to feel sorry for!

There's Colm and Kieran, from the rural west of Seamus's Ireland, and Alan from a place called Stornoway in Scotland. Alan is a very thin, nervous man who can't see without his thick glasses, and I think he won't last very long on the boat, but I do not say that. He's too kind to douse with truths. Colm and Kieran, though, are too rowdy by half! They will no doubt make the best of fishermen. They both speak Irish, and Seamus delights in how easily I speak with them, and I delight in how the words feel on my tongue! I'd begun to believe they might wither from disuse!

It's wonderful to watch Seamus with them all. (And I won't pretend I don't enjoy an increasing absence of James.) They love to drink on the beach and though Colm and Kieran get quite drunker than Seamus is wont, the songs they sing are so entertaining, I can't fault them.

Indeed, I enjoy them like a breath of air after a long swim beneath the waves.

Love,

Lia

3 April, 1961

Dear diary,

Alan did the most fascinating thing the other night. They'd been drinking, and Alan waded into the waves up to his waist, lifted his bottle, and called out, "Shoney, I give thee this cup of...lager, hoping thou will be good and send us plenty of…*fish in the coming year!*"

I'm used to not understanding the things people here do, but this time, the others looked just as confused as me. Though they laughed loudly, for that's what they do when they've been drinking.

"What in God's name are you harping on about, Al?" Colm shouted out along with his laugh, which sounds much like the barking of a seal.

Alan threw his bottle as far into the sea as he could before trudging back through the waves and slumping onto the sand. He can't drink quite as much as the others, but he could still speak and said, "Shoney."

"Who?" Seamus asked, laughing uproariously with Kieran. I just stood quietly by because I was only happy to have been invited along for once.

Alan repeated, "Shoney. The water spirit."

He kept talking, but the others became disinterested when two ladies walked by. But Alan didn't notice and kept right on talking, and I was unable to move, fascinated by his words.

He said Seonaidh is a myth from the islands he comes from. That the people in the old times would bring supplies like malt to the church to brew an ale, and then one man would wade into the sea at night with a cup of the ale and offer it to Shoney and recite a prayer asking for enough seaweed to fertilize their ground for a good harvest. Then they would all return to the church before repairing to the fields to celebrate with the rest of the ale. This, Alan said, was thought to ensure a wonderful harvest.

I was about to ask Alan if he truly believed it, when the others rejoined us.

Kieran caught the end of the tale and scoffed. "How'd you ever make it over the Atlantic with that head of yours weighing you down?" he asked Alan.

The others laughed as they do, and they even went out into the water and yelled things at this Shoney, but I think it cruel to tease Alan for believing something.

Colm and Kieran are jesters, I know, and Seamus often jests when he's with them. But I watched as he lifted his empty bottle to Shoney, and I think, in his eyes, beside the mirth, there was a trace of something else. Hesitation, maybe. Or fear?

Seol
SEND

R ORY'S PHONE RANG, PULLING ME OUT OF THE diary. I immediately looked across the room to Rosie, who was supposed to be napping but instead was looking back with wide eyes. We hadn't discussed how to proceed when this happened. Looking back down at the phone vibrating helplessly across the table beside my bunk, I read the display: *Mum.*

It was afternoon now, which meant it was morning back in the U.S. Either they were just checking in, or they'd gotten Aidan's letter. Sucking on my lips, I watched the phone still as it fell silent. If they called again, they were worried. If they didn't, it was just a friendly call to say hello.

A second later, there was a chime—a new voicemail notification.

Immediately after, it began to ring again.

They'd gotten the letter.

"What do we do?" I hissed at Rosie.

She shrugged. "Not answer it, that's for sure."

"They're probably freaking out, Rosie! Think about how our parents would react."

"Maybe yours," Rosie mumbled.

"Regardless, I know *them*, and they're worried sick, I know it." And now I was starting to feel sick, too.

"And are you going to be the one to explain this all to them?" Rosie asked incredulously. "What would you even explain? The true story or the one she's been fed by her seal sons?"

"Roz," I groaned. "This is serious."

"I know! That's why you don't. Answer. The phone. Just send the email Rory wrote."

Staring out the window at the gray morning, I realized Rosie was absolutely right. I couldn't explain any of this with words. We would have to rely on Rory's. I opened the email app on Rory's phone and pulled up the draft he'd written to his parents. It said:

Hey, Mum and Dad,

Aidan and I are both fine. I want you to know that first. I'm sorry if you've tried to call, I've been dealing with Aidan. He's going through a bit of an early-life crisis. He took off a few days ago, and I've gone after him. He told me he wrote you guys about it, but I know the mail can take quite a while, so I wanted you to know now.

He tracked down our birth mother. She's living in Germany. I know it seems ridiculous for me to say at the moment, but please don't worry. He's an adult now, and this is something he needs to do for his own peace of mind. He's being smart and safe about it, but I think he was afraid to call you both for fear of hurting your feelings.

Please don't worry. I'm off to find him. My phone won't work while I'm abroad, but I will call you when I return in two weeks. Please please please don't worry.

I love you both.

Love,

Rory

Two weeks. He had every intention of returning in two weeks. For some reason, that didn't calm my beating heart. Rory didn't know what it would be like either, returning to that form. There was still no guarantee.

But I had other people to worry about right now.

Taking a deep breath, I thought of Mrs. O'Brien and how kind she'd been to me in Oyster Beach. The memory of the resort's front office, the hallway covered in pictures of all the O'Brien kids, reared up in my mind.

"It means 'little seal,'" she'd told me that day I'd gone there looking for Rory. Picture after picture of Rory with his brothers and sisters and Aidan, in the waves, on the beach. Those pictures had been taunting me then, and I hadn't even known it.

This whole mess would hit Mr. and Mrs. O'Brien the hardest, and they didn't even know about it yet.

After one last deep breath, I hit send.

Mum called three more times. Then Declan. They'd obviously called in reinforcements. Then *Dad.* Even *Home.* Then Declan again.

Rosie pulled a pillow over her head early in the barrage, but when the phone finally quieted, I grabbed it and scrolled through the messages.

A text from Declan: *CALL NOW.*

A text from Mum: *Rory please call me now.*

And an email from Declan that said simply: *Ror, call me NOW!*

I glanced at Rosie, who would no doubt advise me to unhand the device and keep my trap shut, but she had finally dozed off under the pillow. And my heart was banging around so violently, I was afraid the people in the next room could hear it.

Finally, I opened the email from Declan, and typed:

Declan,

It's Cora. Rory left his phone with me as it won't work abroad. He's not worried, but I know your parents must be. Please tell them not to worry.

- Cora

It would be little relief to the family, but I couldn't sit here ignoring their pleas. Sighing deeply, I turned off the phone's ringer and reopened the diary. The diary of the woman Rory might have called "Mum" had circumstances been different.

Na Rudaí Cronaíonn Tú
THE THINGS YOU MISS

20 April, 1961

Dear diary,

I'm so sorry it's been so long since I wrote, but we are so busy! I scarce fall asleep laughing before I'm awake to the sound of Colm and Kieran banging on the door, begging me to scramble eggs for them in the way Harold taught me.

Our days are filled to the brim with noisy men and dragging them to church—where I know all the words now—and constantly cooking and cleaning. They're rarely on the same fishing assignments, so when my Seamus is gone, I have Colm and Kieran. And when they're gone, I have Seamus and sometimes Phillip.

My favorite part of all is the music. Seamus has hardly put down the penny whistle since the boys came from Ireland. Colm brought along a fiddle in his bag—though hardly any clothes would fit alongside it! And Kieran sings like nothing I've heard before and plays the table in the living room like a drum. And all together? Oh, leabhar beag! It's the ceol of the sea, I swear to you.

I confess our days are so full, I sometimes forget even to go to the jetty, so happy am I to hear the song of the sea in my own home.

Love,

Lia

18 May, 1961

It's one whole year today. I didn't realize. Seamus is the one who reminded me. One year since I left for good. And though I still feel it in my bones, the me of the sea, it's harder and harder to recognize when I look in the mirror.

Love,

Lia

10 June, 1961

Dear diary,

I have to admit I quite forgot about you, little book. It was actually Colm who reminded me. We often sit on the porch while Seamus and Kieran kick a football in the sand. Seamus likes football, but he said he never had anyone to play with until Kieran came. They spend a lot of time in the flat patch of sandy dirt on the other side of the boardwalk, but Colm doesn't play. He says God didn't give him the calfs for it.

But I don't mind. Colm tells wonderful stories—even stories about unimportant things. He can make anything sound interesting. He says I can, too. "You have the gift of gab, Lia O'Leary," he's told me more than once. He and Kieran came from an island very close to Seamus's hometown. He says many young men have fled the area in search of work, and America is just one of the many places they end up.

Oh! And Colm tells such stories about their trips. I didn't know fishing was so dangerous, and I do worry after Seamus, but I take relief knowing that Seamus wasn't there for any of Colm's stories.

Of course, talking to Colm reminded me of the list Seamus made of things I needed to tell you, leabhar beag. Nearly a year ago he made that list, and it's been sitting here tucked between your back pages. I think I'll return to it for practice—to practice my gift of gab. Here's what it says to write about:

How we met

About our wedding day

Your new friend Martha

What you hear in Father George's sermons

Your favorite foods

Your favorite flowers

How the beach looks to you

Your favorite stories

How much you love me

Oh he was so funny, my Seamus, wasn't he? We had a difficult winter, but his eyes shine with summer now, and I am so thankful for it.

And I can't wait to write down my favorite stories! From the books Seamus has, what Alan told me about Shoney, maybe even what I see on the television.

Love,

Lia

4 July, 1961

Dear diary,

The shore is quiet tonight, so a storm is coming. Even from beneath the waves one would be able to tell. The way the surface undulates with a soft, soothing rhythm that is too exact, too precise to portend anything but a forthcoming opposite. Today was another holiday in America. It's one that Colm, Kieran, and Seamus don't feel deeply connected to, either, so I didn't feel so left out. Still, after dinner, things went wrong.

Seamus had to work all day preparing the Ritz house for the Fourth of July party they are throwing. He came home tired and crabby, but Colm, Kieran, and Phillip turned up and insisted we all go down to the beach for the fireworks show Oyster Beach puts on each year.

I don't like the fireworks for the terrifying noises they make, even beneath the sea, they pound and they crack like nothing in the world beneath those waves. But I wasn't speaking of that. I was telling you about Seamus.

Yes, I pretended the noises weren't scaring me, I pretended to be having fun because the lads were in great form, and nothing brings Seamus down like myself being down. And it worked, for a while. It wasn't until the finale, when I leaned over to tell Seamus it was beautiful, wasn't it, that I noticed the way he'd stopped drinking from his bottle. He held it by his side, his fingers grasped tightly around the neck, and I could see the gleaming in his eyes that should have been tears, but that he would never release around the others.

Once the fireworks ended and everyone on the beach broke out into applause, I quietly asked him what was the matter, but he only said, "Nothing," in the way he does when whatever it is feels too big for him to tell me. I know this because he will usually tell me after he's had time to think it into words. But tonight he didn't. Tonight, I went inside to go to bed while he sat on the porch with Colm and Kieran, after they'd gone to the shop for more bottles.

I could hear them through the little window in our bedroom. Not that I was listening, exactly. I often fall asleep to the comforting sound of their voices mixing and dueting with the sound of the sea, a lullaby more potent than any I could sing myself, their words dissolving into a melody that makes little sense but carries me into that place of dreams where sense doesn't follow.

But this night, Seamus's words came to my ears fully formed, wobbly from his drunkenness, but as clear as if he'd whispered them right beside me: "I hate it."

"Hate what?" Colm asked with a laugh. "The Fourth?"

"Eh, it's a little annoying, isn't it?" Kieran agreed.

Seamus didn't say anything, and I tried to breathe as quietly as this body would allow. I thought Seamus was happy. I thought he was content. What did he hate?

"What are you talking about?" Colm asked, the amusement gone from his voice. Seamus must have painted a stark picture to leak the ever-present laughter from Colm's voice.

"I just ..." Seamus huffed one of his sighs that I know so well, like the weight of the sea is flowing over him and he doesn't know if he'll sink or swim. It's a sigh I've heard from him often, but never has he ascribed words to it before.

I waited with bated breath. His friends seemed to, as well.

"Do ye ever miss it, lads?"

He said it so quietly, I almost didn't hear. But it finally soared through our window on the wind and rolled around in my empty chest. Miss it. Miss it. *How could I not? Even now, with it pressing against the shore, reaching for me, constantly grabbing, clutching at me.*

"You're drunk, mate," Colm said with a laugh.

"No, I mean it," Seamus insisted.

"Well, you are drunk," Kieran said, his voice still serious, "but I believe you. You carry it around on your face for half the world to see."

"What are you even talking about?" Colm asked. "Miss what? Home?"

There was a pause, and Seamus must have nodded, for after a while, Kieran said, "Sometimes, I do, sure. But not enough to make me frown like you are."

Another sigh. "Sometimes, I'll just be standing here—anywhere—in the market, in the house, at the Ritzes'—and the thought'll go through my head as if it weren't even my own mind that put it there."

"What thought?" Colm asked.

"I hate it here."

My heart twisted in my chest. He hated it here.

But no anger came. No anger could come, because I knew that I'd had the very thought more than once. Not for missing Ireland, but for missing another place, much closer yet much farther away.

One of the boys scoffed. "What do you miss about it?"

"The rain, the way the shop smells, people knowing my name, the people who have known my people for generations past. The colorful houses, the sound of a hundred accents like ours talking all around us. The comfort in it. The familiar."

"You're a right eejit to be missing the rain, y'know!"

"Seamus"—it was Kieran—"you've got a beautiful wife who loves the shite out of you, you've got a house that'll be worth a small fortune if you do ever give it up, and you've got steady work. That's more than half Ireland can say at the moment. So why are you talking like a fool?"

"What's the point of being here if my mind is constantly in Ireland?"

What's the point of being here if my mind is constantly there?

What's the point?

Little book, what's the point?

I love Seamus. I do. But my heart reaches for the sea, and his heart reaches across the sea, and why have we deemed love more important than that? Why have we deemed this intangible, inexplicable concept more important than the hard earth of the island where Seamus was born, or the clear, cold water of my home?

Colm told Seamus that there was nothing in Ireland that wouldn't be there waiting in five, ten, fifteen years. And I tiptoed across the room and closed the window. Softly. So he won't know that I've heard.

Rud Éigin na Farraige
SOMETHING OF THE SEA

E VAN ESCORTED US TO THE SCHOOLHOUSE FOR the first Irish lesson. Seamus looked ecstatic when we came in, and it warmed my heart a bit that our presence on the island didn't bring *only* desperation and despair.

There was a group of about thirteen Irish kids from the mainland. Learning Irish was part of the curriculum for their secondary school—or high school—and everybody took a test on it at the end. So a lot of the mainland kids would come to the Aran Islands, or any part of Ireland where Irish was still the main language spoken, in order to hone their skills. Even though they'd been studying it for years, their Irish seemed about as good as my Spanish. That is to so say, not good at all.

And the lesson wasn't like school at all. We all sat around in a circle, and Seamus just talked to us, mostly about the culture to start out with. He taught us all about

Irish dancing and traditional Irish instruments, and even brought in a drum called a bodhrán. Evan stayed to help him, and hearing the two of them speak Irish to each other was fascinating—and confusing as hell.

When it was time to leave, Seamus held us back and asked what we thought.

"It sounds like gibberish," Rosie said.

Seamus laughed. "That's understandable. Cora?"

"It sounds like…like you're speaking English but using words I don't know. Like the sounds are familiar but the words aren't."

He smiled. "Maybe it won't be so unfamiliar after a while."

"I hope so." Though it was unlikely. I'd had about as much success learning other languages as I had with math and science. School wasn't my thing, obviously. "I meant to ask you…" Fumbling in my pocket, I withdrew the receipt I'd stuffed there this morning. "What does this mean?" Knowing I wouldn't be able to pronounce it, I'd written *Is fearr Gaeilge briste, ná Béarla clíste* on the back of the paper. I'd been wondering about it since that night before Rory left.

Seamus squinted as he read, the wrinkles in his forehead even more pronounced than usual, and then his face slowly cleared and fell into a wistful smile. "*Is fearr Gaeilge briste, ná Béarla clíste,*" he repeated aloud. "That's in her diary, isn't it?"

I nodded as Evan looked over my shoulder to have a look. "She wrote that you used to say it and laugh," I said.

Seamus heaved a great sigh. "It means 'broken Irish is better than clever English.' It was a way of colonizing the Irish, you know, making us speak English. Our language was slowly killed by the Brits. Those of us who never let go, or even those who came back to it, we're proud. It might be hard for you to understand. But it's important to us. So much of our culture was decimated by invasion over centuries and…well, the language is a daily practice in regaining some of that culture." He gave a little embarrassed shrug before quickly saying, "Forgive an old man's ramblings. Enough lectures for today. I know it's not something ye'd understand, or want to, for that matter."

It was hard for me to understand—I mean truly understand—but it was difficult not to feel the import of what he was saying, the emotion in his words.

"It's also how we met," he murmured, before I could formulate a response.

"Who?" Rosie asked.

Seamus looked at her for a moment before focusing back on me. "Lia and I." I saw Evan throw us a sidelong glance but ignored him. "It's what she came out…" Seamus broke off, throwing a wary glance Evan's way. "It was her native tongue." He cleared his throat. "When I met her, I was with friends, but I was the only of them who spoke Irish. It's how we got to know one another."

He'd told as much before, but I wasn't about to interrupt when Seamus seemed to be trusting us—such a sharp contrast from the last time we'd sought answers from him.

"It was a bit of luck, I suppose," he mused. But I wasn't so sure. Was it simply luck that an Irish man met a selkie halfway across the world, then came back to Ireland and settled down on an island that just happened to be home to *more* selkies—that is, if a child was to be believed. And I was pretty intent on finding out just how trustworthy little Róisín was.

"I have to get going," Evan said then, clearly uncomfortable with the gloomy turn this conversation had taken. "I'll be back next time, Seamus, if you'll have me."

"Of course, lad, same time same place."

"I'll head out with you," Rosie said, following Evan toward the door.

But as I made to go, too, Mr. O'Leary called out, "Oh, and, Cora?"

I paused in the doorway and turned. Rosie and Evan didn't wait for me, already pushing out the front door of the school.

"I am sorry about the other evening. I shouldn't have treated ye that way." He gave a sheepish smile. "Or answered the door at all."

"It's okay," I mumbled, embarrassed by his apologies. "You were having a rough night."

"I was. Do you know what I was thinking on?"

Now alone, I exchanged a nervous glance with the empty hall, but nodded anyway.

"They don't feel like my sons."

I gulped. "Sorry?"

"Ronan and Fionn. They don't feel like my sons. And it's my own fault."

The silence of the little school was suffocating, and I cursed Rosie for leaving me, mostly to avoid thinking about the words he was saying.

"I tried so hard for so long to get them back…my boys…but they were never really mine. When they arrived here in Ireland, they were like…strangers."

My heart was hammering in my chest, and I was so uncomfortable

I seriously considered walking straight out of the building. I was sure he'd understand, and as far as the rude meter went, he did owe me one. "They're just grown up," I said quietly. "They're still your boys."

He shook his head. "Time is the greatest interloper of all."

The baby picture of Rory came to me then, and I understood how different he was now. It was impossible not to change in the intervening years. But I also knew Mrs. O'Leary had stayed on her little porch for decades and my mother had grieved for a lost daughter for years, and I wanted to say that time didn't have to be an interloper if you didn't let it. If you loved strongly enough.

But philosophical arguments aren't easy to have with a person you don't understand. And despite how I'd come to know Seamus to some degree since we'd gotten here, I still didn't understand him. Instead of telling him I thought he was wrong, I said, "Well, you can know them now."

He gave me only a sad smile. "It's near impossible, child, to know something of the sea."

Bláth Beag
A LITTLE FLOWER

21 July, 1961

There's a furious glow about all the world today, leabhar beag, and I should tear out all your pages and start anew for that is exactly what has happened! We're starting anew. I've been to the doctor and he has confirmed!

I'm expecting a child! Áine has come at last! Dr. Griffin says she'll be here in Aibreán, and I can't imagine how I'll wait that long. Seamus is away on the boat, and so I won't be able to tell him for two whole days. I don't know what I'll do til then. I feel I must tell someone or I'll burst. Maybe I'll tell the girl in the shop and then swear her to secrecy. Or maybe I'll content myself with telling you, little book!

Love, love, love,

Lia

23 July, 1961

Dear diary,

Seamus is delighted! After I told him, we sat on the porch and he held me for hours, and he's scarce let go of me since. I sit now, his arm around my shoulders, writing away as he reads, and it feels like when we were first married. Like there is nothing else in the whole world but me and him, and now our Áine.

I think we will finally know, for sure, that ours is a true love comparable to that of any human couple.

The doctor says I'll be quite uncomfortable in the coming months, but I am ready. I think it will be worth it. And I'll bear it in silence, because Seamus says it was quite a risk to go to Dr. Griffin. I've never been to the doctor before, but Seamus sees Dr. Griffin often, so I didn't at first understand Seamus's trepidation. When I asked why, he said, "You're different, love."

Of course he's right. The doctor's job is to inspect one very closely, and since the day I stepped foot on Oyster Beach, people have been telling me how very odd and different I am. Luckily, Dr. Griffin didn't seem to notice.

Then Seamus said, "Will the baby …"

And I didn't know what he meant. But his eyebrows were low over his eyes, which shone with a fear and hope that made sense when I remembered that word: different.

Will the baby be different?

"No, dear," I said and cupped his face with my hand.

It was a lie of course. I'm different and so my baby must be, right? I don't know. It is nothing Mamaí ever discussed with me. But for Seamus's sake, I hope not.

It has brought many of those thoughts back. All those things Martha used to tell me about, the things others in town say about me.

I am different. And it seems that I'm eternally destined to be so.

But I won't let that bring me down now. Nothing can bring me down! Dr. Griffin says everything happening in my body is also happening to Áine, and so I will stay happy for her. And when Seamus holds me so, it's very difficult not to be.

Love,

Lia

17 August, 1961

I've had the most horrid day, little book. Seamus is on the boat, and so I went to the post office to check his post box for bills, and the things he likes to read when he gets home. Laura was there, as usual, and her leering brother Frank. But as I approached the corner with the post boxes, a strange smell hit my nostrils. It was like a fish out of water.

I pretended not to notice, as that is most polite, just in case it was one of the several people around me. But as soon as I put the tiny key in the lock and opened our box, the smell increased tenfold. I had to press my handkerchief to my nostrils to keep from gagging, and it was quickly apparent why.

People whispered and somebody laughed, but I didn't dare turn around, just stared at the great big dead fish stuffed in our post box. And it stared unblinkingly back at me. The whispers grew louder, and somebody nearby said, "What a strange thing to keep in a post box."

When I turned around, Frank was trying to control his laughter, and Laura stood behind the counter with her arms crossed over her chest and her mouth curved up in a satisfied sneer. It shouldn't have bothered me, a simple fish, but I knew enough to know that such a thing would humiliate a normal girl, and knowing that it was intended do so served to accomplish the task. Tears sprang to my eyes, but I wouldn't cry in front of her.

Thankfully, somebody spoke behind me. "Come on, Lia."

It was Colm. He put a hand on my arm and led me out of the post office. I couldn't stop the tears, and he just whispered, "Shhh," and walked me home.

I'm not near enough to showing yet, and today I wish I had been, for maybe then Laura would accept the truth. That I am Seamus's wife, and Áine's mother, and I'm here to stay. I am, amn't I?

Colm sat with me until dinner, when he went to Doyle's Corner and returned with dinner and Kieran. We're out on the porch now, and though I wish Seamus was here, these two lads are the next best thing at keeping the tears away.

I've asked Colm not to tell Seamus of this. I don't want to worry him. Not when he's in such great spirits with the baby coming. But I shall have to endeavor to hide my own despair.

I'm sorry to only write with bad news, little book, but I needed to speak to you and I just haven't had the energy in ever so long. I've been so sick. Even before the fish. Dr. Griffin warned me of this that first day, but it is quite different to hear someone say something than to experience it oneself. I spend many mornings sitting on the cold tile of the bathroom, the closer to the toilet bowl the better, but the sight only makes Seamus chuckle.

"She's a fierce one, isn't she?" he says of Áine. I hope so. She'll need it to handle being "different" in this town. For her sake, I try not to complain.

Love,

Lia

20 September, 1961

Dear diary,

Seamus came home from the Ritzes' today with the most sweet surprise. A bouquet of tiny blue Do Not Forget Me flowers! He remembers! I often go back through your pages to the day I wrote about our wedding, so I can relive it with every detail, and I didn't think it meant so much to Seamus. But today he handed me the bouquet and said, "So you do not forget me, Mrs. O'Leary. Or the day you became mine."

Every time I think he's so very far away, his mind all the way in Ireland, he does something to show that he is right here, listening, in Oyster Beach, with me.

That is on the list. The list of things I should write about—my favorite flowers. I've just decided my favorite flower shall be the Do Not Forget Me. They're so tiny and perfect, and I wish to keep them forever, though I know they won't last forever. Instead, I'll keep Seamus forever, my own Do Not Forget Me. And Áine. Our little flower.

Seamus has suggested a birth at home, with one of the midwives from down the coast. "Just in case," he said. I know he means in case Dr. Griffin should notice anything…different about me. Or Áine.

I suppose he's right, but I do so wish I could escape all the gazes constantly seeing me as different.

Love,

Lia

Na Seacht Séipéil
THE SEVEN CHURCHES

I T WAS ONE MORNING WHEN WE RAN INTO RÓISÍN with Seamus in town that I got the idea to isolate and interrogate the little girl—nicely, of course. I needed to know whether the stuff she'd said before was just the ramblings of a kid or…

Rosie and I had just gone out for a walk when we saw Róisín talking Seamus's ear off as they crossed the square toward the bike shop. She had to take two steps for every one of his, as he hadn't moderated his stride to accommodate the little girl. It made me think of what he'd said yesterday—about the boys not feeling like his sons. It struck me as unbearably sad, seeing Róisín scurry to keep up with him, who was clearly uncomfortable. Maybe he would have been more comfortable with children had he been given a chance to raise his own.

"Cora! And the other Róisín!" the little girl yelled when she noticed us across the street. Rosie rolled her eyes, but I nudged her to make her stop walking. We'd so far managed to avoid any more interaction with Kieran Browne, but I wanted to talk with Róisín some more, and taking this opportunity before she reached the shop seemed the best option. I seemed to have appeased Kieran somehow that day in the pub, but I still wasn't eager to revisit our tenuous acquaintanceship.

Seamus lifted a hand to wave but kept walking. "Need to open the shop," he called, nodding down the street.

I nodded and walked over to the friendly kid instead. "Róisín, we're going for a walk. Wanna come with?"

Her face lit up and she turned around to yell at her coworker, "*Táim ag imeacht le na Yanks a Shéamus*! But I'll send people to the shop! Don't forget my commission!"

"Why does everyone call us Yanks?" Rosie muttered.

"I can give ye a tour!" Róisín squealed, twirling back around to us. "I'm gonna give bike tours when I'm old enough. Will ye let me practice on you? We can start at Dun Aengus, I know all about it!"

My chest gave a twinge. The last time I'd been to Dun Aengus, it had involved baring my soul to Rory in a painful apology. I didn't quite feel like reliving that yet.

Luckily, Rosie snapped, "I'm not making that hike."

"Okay," Róisín said, unperturbed, "how 'bout the seven churches? Have ye been there?" I shook my head. "Follow me!"

She immediately launched into what sounded like a practiced tour speech. When she said, "On your left we have lots of fields," Rosie shot me a look that said I was going to pay for this inconvenience. She'd been hesitant to agree to a walk in the first place.

It wasn't until we'd been walking for some time that I was able to get a word in edgewise. "Hey, Róisín," I said, trying to keep my tone light. "How do you like being a selkie?"

Rosie suppressed a laugh. I knew what she was thinking. *Smooth, Cora. Real smooth.* Luckily, this was apparently normal fodder for conversation with eleven-year-olds.

"Oh, it's all right," Róisín said with a shrug. "It'd be better if I had my seal coat, but for now I'm just supposed to be a kid."

"You don't know where it is?" I asked.

"Oh, Mam and *Deaide* say I can have it when I'm older. They promised. But I'm not old enough for the responsibility yet. Not like your friend."

Not like Rory. Someone who'd gladly give up the responsibility of it all. I wondered at the easy way Róisín talked about this, if there was truth in the promise her parents made her of giving her the sealskin when she was older. It was such a stark contrast to the way Mr. and Mrs. O'Leary had handled the same situation.

"How long have you known about it?" I asked.

Róisín shrugged again. "Forever, really. We don't have secrets in our family."

Every family has secrets, I thought. But aloud, I said, "And is your mom a selkie? Or maybe your granddad?" Maybe that's why Kieran had been so irate about Seamus speaking with us. It wasn't just his granddaughter—he was a selkie, too.

"No," Róisín said easily, squashing that theory. And, really, I realized, wouldn't he have been more open with Lia if that were the case? The diary seemed to indicate he was no closer to Mrs. O'Leary than any of Seamus's other friends. "I'm the only one in my family," Róisín explained, her little face full of gravity. "That's why we have to be careful. Mam and *Deaide* don't really know how it all works."

Of course I didn't know how it worked either, but I'd always assumed it was a genetic issue. What if that wasn't the case? What if anybody could become—

"Are you seriously believing everything she says?" Rosie hissed at me, grabbing my arm to pull me back. Proclaiming that we were almost there, Róisín darted on ahead down a skinny road bordered by short stone walls and overgrown hedges.

"She knows a lot," I said defensively. "More than anybody else we've encountered so far. Even more than Mr. O'Leary."

"Really, Cora? Does she? Or has she just read a lot of books?"

"At this point, who knows?" I snapped, pulling my arm out of her grip and jogging to catch up with Róisín.

"This is the seven churches!" she proclaimed happily.

A break in the wall opened into a grassy area enclosed by those same stone walls that were all over the island. And that gave way to a tiny town of ruins. Small buildings, crumbling and desolate, lay before us, their roofs open to the sky. It was beautiful.

"There's only two churches," Róisín said, popping through the short doorway of the bigger crumbling stone structure in front of me, "despite its name." I ducked through the doorway and joined her in a tiny temple, the stone walls giving way to vast blue sky above us. "This one's from, like, the 700s," Róisín explained. "But Da says nobody *really* knows."

Through one of the windows in the church wall, I could see just the foundations of other buildings, their walls long fallen, all the stone splotched with white. "The rest were houses where, like, the monks woulda lived," Róisín explained, moving through the church to point at different small stone structures. "That was a well. And that was a well…"

But I wasn't really paying attention. Behind the churches was a cemetery, an expanse of scraggly grass littered with headstones, some shiny and new-looking, others so worn their inscriptions were illegible. Most of the graves were enclosed in little stone rectangles overgrown with the bright green blades of grass I'd come to associate with Ireland, and here and there were shabby relics of large, stone Celtic crosses, perfect likeness of the ones people wore on necklaces back home.

"Over here's the seven Romans," Róisín said, deftly winding her way along the edge of the graveyard to a back corner, where a row of rough-hewn slabs stood upright, their engravings worn. "That one says VI Romani and that one's Tomas AP, for Thomas the Apostle. Deaide says this is one of the oldest pilgrimage sites in Ireland." She climbed up onto a collapsing stone wall at the edge of the ruins and turned toward the sea. I climbed up after her, Rosie on my heels.

All three of us instinctively looked down at the waves. The cemetery gave way to a slope of rocky fields and spindly trees, leaning toward us, always leaning, leaning away from the sea—away from the wind.

"God, you can never get very far from the ocean here, can you?" Rosie grumbled. "Not even in death."

"Why would ya want'uh?" Róisín asked, genuinely perplexed.

As we trailed behind her to the next stop on her tour—something she called "Dun Eochaill"—I realized how comfortable I'd become here. It wasn't difficult, what with the islanders being so welcoming and used to outsiders gawking at their way of life. But it still surprised me to realize that I *was* comfortable here. Me, a girl raised in landlocked Missouri, almost as far from the ocean as you could get, a girl who hadn't learned to swim until she was eighteen, felt at home on this little island.

"I come up here when I need to think," Róisín said, grabbing me from my reverie. The thought of this kid needing some serious thinking time put a tiny smile on my face. "This is the lighthouse," she explained. "The old one." She'd led us to the top of a hill, the top of the island, really, and a lighthouse was visible above a high stone wall. We followed her through a doorway into a grassy courtyard around the lighthouse. She called it old, but compared to everything else on this island, it looked rather kept up. "It was no use, really. This is the highest point on the island, but you can't see everything from here. The dummies!" Her giggles were contagious, and I found myself laughing as she kept trudging on past the lighthouse and led us through another break in the wall. Field after field of stone walls in concentric circles drew out in front of us, the center being a circular fort.

"Hiya!" Róisín chirped, grabbing my attention. Storm and Peewee had come running out of the fort through the wall in front of us and were circling Róisín's legs, their tails wagging. Peewee ventured to sniff my outstretched hand but then returned to Róisín.

"Dogs love selkies, you know," she said proudly.

Rosie snorted, but my smile wasn't derisive. I couldn't help remembering how Princess had adored Mrs. O'Leary last summer. Of course going to Mrs. O'Leary's house was one of the most exciting things to happen in her daily doggy life. But maybe there was something else to it…

"Lots of things do," Róisín went on "They say selkies have an almost magical lure. Maybe that's why ye like me." She gave a big smile, but my chest felt cold.

Mrs. O'Leary had wondered about this in her diary. And every time I'd read about it, it had made my head spin. Was there really a chance that's what was between me and Rory?

"Mam jokes that I'll be glad of it when I'm older and wanting boys to like me," Róisín said, pulling a face. But the face wasn't quite so convincing and I did wonder if the idea wasn't so unwelcome to her after all. "What do you think? Does your friend have it?"

Rosie looked over at me, and I looked away, sure my cheeks were blazing. I didn't need her to confirm the doubts I already had. If selkies really had some sort of magical lure, like Mrs. O'Leary suggested in her diary, what did that mean for me and Rory? Was I only attracted to him because of some inexplicable lure of legend? Did that make what we had not…*real?*

The memory of him holding me came so strongly to mind, I felt warm, much too warm, despite the wind whipping around us. Was that magic?

"I think he does," Rosie said stiffly. I could still feel her eyes on me, but I wasn't about to give in.

The line between what was real and what wasn't was so blurred, I wasn't sure there was a point in trying to discern it anymore. I cleared my throat. "Tell me more about selkies, Róisín."

Of course I didn't know what the little girl did or didn't know. She could've been reciting things she'd read in children's books. But what if she wasn't?

Rosie gave me an incredulous look, but I kept my eyes on Róisín. "What else do selkies like?"

She grinned widely and rolled her eyes. "Swimming!"

I mBrionglóidí
IN DREAMS

17 March, 1962

I've never felt more alive, nor closer to death, more full, nor more alone, more devastated, nor any happier. I've been torn open and put back together, and though I can scarce keep my eyes open, to let this day pass without writing it down would be unforgivable.

Seamus has just fallen asleep beside me, and Scarlet, the midwife, has the baby downstairs.

It isn't Áine, little book. It's a boy.

I wanted to name him at once, for it doesn't sit well with me for a baby to live in the world without a name, not a day longer, but Seamus hushed me and said we had plenty of time. He said it isn't even imperative until the baby is baptized.

18 March, 1962

I'm so delighted I can hardly write, leabhar beag.

Today when I woke, Seamus was holding the baby, more perfect and tiny than I remember even from yesterday. He has lots of dark hair, and his skin is velvety soft, as if there's a layer of down all over him. Before even good morning, I said, "Seamus O'Leary Junior."

Seamus laughed heartily but shook his head. "I wouldn't weigh down a boy with a 'junior' now," he said. "Let him look forward, not backward."

We sat quietly as I kept thinking, and Seamus must have noticed my concentration, for he said again, "We have plenty of time, love. Don't dwell on the name. The right one will come."

But I don't like it. A boy needs a name.

18 March, 1962

Seamus is reading aloud from a big book of Irish baby names he found in the bookstore where Phillip works. He says the baby must have a good, sturdy, Irish name, in case he goes to Ireland one day.

Stephen. James. Michael. Connor. Brendan. None feel right.

In fact, I can't get rid of the feeling that nothing has felt right since the baby came. As if something has shifted in the world, and we're all off-kilter now, but I'm the only one who's noticed.

18 March, 1962

Ronan. Ronan! It means "little seal." Seamus suggested it himself. Ronan Stephen O'Leary. Stephen, after Seamus's father.

14 March, 1962

Oh, no one told me how much work a baby requires. I haven't slept at a normal hour since before. But it is so worth it, when I hold Ronan's tiny fists in my palm. And I've never seen Seamus so happy. It's as if the world fades away when he holds his son.

I'm happy, too. But tired. And I'm having dreams again. The ones where I wake up in the sea. Only now, I'm desperate and flail wildly through the water, trying to get back to Ronan. But when I reach the shore, I can't shed my coat. I'm stuck. Separate from him forever.

I think it's the fatigue, leabhar beag. I'm so tired that when I do finally sleep, it is troubled.

14 May, 1962

I did something tonight Seamus wouldn't approve of. So I haven't told him.

We spoke today of the baptism. Father George has been asking and asking Seamus to have Ronan baptized, but Seamus says we're in no rush. Father George says were a baby to die before baptism, it would not go to heaven. I've spent many Sundays at church, and so I know much of heaven and of hell and what the bible says of each. So, today, Seamus finally set a date. June 15.

I'll tell you that I always trust Seamus, and so I didn't think on it any more. Seamus told me all the town would be there, and we would celebrate little Ronan and his entrance into the church. Then something occurred to me and I asked him, since I wasn't baptized, would I not go to heaven while Ronan did?

Seamus turned quite red then. He said it was all very much nonsense, but I could tell he didn't mean it, little book. I asked him if I could be baptized, and he became very annoyed. He said it wasn't possible, for Father George thought I already was. Seamus lied to him in order for us to be married in the church.

I got very angry at him and said I didn't want to baptize Ronan. That he wasn't going to be going somewhere I couldn't go, too.

Seamus got very still then and asked me, "You would have your son condemned to hell simply because you are?"

I was so mad, little book. I know that Seamus understands who I am, what I am, but he's never said anything to make me think he sees me as different. Odd. Strange. But it's true. He thinks I'm going to hell. I'm so inhuman that I can't possibly be going anywhere but damnation. If that's what he thinks, it can't possibly be true love that we have.

Laura and Martha were right all along. This isn't real love.

That's worse than fifty Elizabeth Nelsons mocking my accent and a hundred fish in my post box.

"I didn't mean it," he said quickly, reaching for me, but I scooped Ronan from his chair and went upstairs.

He came to the bedroom door once and asked me to open up, but I told him I couldn't speak to him at that moment. My shaking voice lent truth to that.

Colm and Kieran showed up a few hours later, and I watched Seamus go with them down the boardwalk. Then I did something I can never tell Seamus about.

I put on a sweater, swaddled Ronan in his warmest blanket, took a towel from the bathroom, and went to the boardwalk. Ronan fussed in the cold wind at first, but the more I hummed against his ear, the calmer he became. So that by the time we reached the jetty, he was quiet and napping softly.

I made sure no one was near, then unwrapped Ronan, and his big eyes popped open as he shivered and his face screwed up to cry. For one moment, I thought I was just as terrible a woman as Laura Nolan thinks I am. I even began to cry. But then something stirred in my veins, like a wave running toward shore, and I lowered Ronan into the water—just one leg at a time.

The water lapped over my fingers, and I felt a warmth inside that I haven't felt in nearly two years. ~~I haven't been in the sea since~~

But that isn't important. What's important is that Ronan's little face relaxed, and he sighed as though I'd wrapped him in the biggest down comforter in the world. And before I could marvel at his comfort in the water, his skin grew warm beneath my fingers. Through the green of the water, I could just make out the brown tinge moving like a blush across his leg.

Reaching one thumb down, I touched it. Smooth and sleek under the water. As smooth as glass.

It was happening. I was right.

The excitement made me frantic. I pulled Ronan out of the water and wrapped him in the towel before he could react. Then I wrapped the blanket around him, kissed his sweet, now salty forehead, and hurried home.

And now I know. My baby is a selkie.

I can't tell Seamus any of this, for I don't know what he would do. I know he has always cared for me, but…

If he thinks I'm damned and going to hell, if he thinks I'm an animal, why does he stay with me? Could Martha be right? That I have some sort of spell over him? I've heard whispers of it, little book, in the sea. But I've never given them a thought. And when I saw Seamus, I didn't care how it happened. I just wanted him.

But now that his real thoughts are there, in my own mind, I can't unthink them. I can't unknow them. And so I wonder, if Seamus thinks I'm going to hell, what will he think when he finds out Ronan is just as inhuman as I?

I'm afraid to go to sleep now, though Ronan sleeps peacefully for once. What if I have the dreams again? And what if dreams are windows to our deepest desires?

23 May, 1962

I went back once more, leabhar beag. Just to see. Seamus was at Doyle's Corner with Colm, Kieran, and Phillip, and I wanted to make sure. What if that night was a dream?

But it wasn't. I let the velvety coat form all the way to Ronan's chubby neck this time before hauling him out of the water. It disintegrated in the air, and I wrapped Ronan up in his blanket, so scratchy and unnatural compared to his coat before it, and hurried him home.

Seamus wasn't home when I fell asleep during one of Ronan's naps, but that rest didn't last long. I had the dream again, but this time, when I found myself beneath the waves of the ocean, I was happy. There is no mistaking the joy that coursed through my veins. I'm afraid feeling the water at the jetty that day was a mistake.

I woke up with my forehead damp from sweat, and it wasn't until Seamus mumbled, "What's going on?" that I realized Ronan was wailing. I hurried to his crib and brought him downstairs. Now he's asleep again, but I can't go back upstairs, up to Seamus, knowing what I know and dreaming what I dream.

He never brought it up again. What he said about the baptism. Nor have I. Instead, we carefully tread around it in our little life, and June 15 marches closer, and I would be lying if I said it didn't frighten me. The pomp, the beliefs, the legends. I fear this baptism will take my son somewhere he'll never return from. A place I can't go.

While existing as a monster to his own father.

I consider the possibility of never telling Seamus about my trips down to the jetty, but how will I keep Ronan out of the water his whole life? Colm and Kieran already talk of teaching him to swim, and Seamus listens with such a brilliant smile on his face.

No, Seamus will find out. Unless…

Why should Ronan keep hidden his whole life? He doesn't belong here, waiting for a death that will take him to heaven, hiding who he is, living a half life, a half truth. He's like me. He isn't like Seamus.

The possibilities that fly through my mind now are too great to contemplate. Not with Seamus asleep upstairs.

4 June, 1962

Dear, dear diary,

This night I dreamt my dream, but this time, when I found myself in the water, Ronan swam beside me, making bubbles with his tiny nose. And I can't tell Seamus, and I can't tell Mamaí, and so I tell you.

I looked in Seamus's drawers tonight, in the dark. Quietly, so I wouldn't wake him. I'm ashamed that I did it, but it was as if another being controlled my arms. There was nothing there but his clothes.

As I sit in the kitchen now writing, I have to, again and again, bring my mind back to you, little book, and stop thinking of nooks and crannies. I've searched the kitchen and the living room and the dining room, but I must stop. I don't want to know.

I don't want to go back.

I hear Ronan crying now. I must go to him.

Saol an Oileáin
ISLAND LIFE

IT WAS SURPRISING, THE EASE WITH WHICH WE settled into a routine. Even Rosie, who grumbled about missing a vacation to the beach with her father, agreed that not many people got to experience life on a remote Irish island—it just wasn't necessarily an experience she would have chosen for herself. But I noticed with each passing day that she complained a little less and explored a little more.

Evan's presence certainly helped there. Along with the constant stream of tourists we shared a room with—when we didn't have it all to ourselves. And then there was Evan's cadre of charming friends from around the island. They invited us to "bonfire night," which was apparently a popular holiday celebrating the summer solstice on the islands. Not that I paid them much attention. It was strange, the way the feeling of the Claddagh ring on my finger became comfortable, as familiar as the waves outside the windows of the hostel, and my crushes on other boys faded away to regular thoughts of just one. I began to think maybe that's exactly what love was. Unfortunately, for now, I had to content myself with sitting on the beach, reading, and exploring the island with Rosie—and sometimes Róisín.

And we still went to Seamus's Irish lessons. He even told me one day that I had a real affinity for it, the Irish language, and told me about a cool Irish language and culture program at a school called GMIT in Galway. I wasn't sure I was *that* good at Irish, but I did enjoy making Evan speak to me in Irish in the evenings when he and Rosie would drag me to the pub. Sometimes Róisín was there, and I'd make her tell me everything she'd heard about selkies. After a while I realized Rosie was right—Róisín was just reciting things she'd heard in stories—but I was so desperate to pretend otherwise that I didn't care. Eventually, though, Róisín's parents would drag her home, the sun still out on this tiny island so far north. Sometimes the light would linger until Rosie and I had trudged back to the hostel. "I want to live where there is no sunset!" Rosie cried more than once as we walked home from the pub in light befitting an afternoon.

And every night before bed, I checked Rory's phone, alight with more missed calls and texts. And a response from Declan O'Brien. He only begged me to make Rory call him. Oh, how I wished I could. Instead, I'd slip the phone back into his backpack and try to sleep, only to wake up in the midst of my nightmare once again.

But the days were better. When we weren't at the pub, swapping stories, or walking the gravelly roads, or climbing to the old lighthouse, or chasing Storm and Peewee, I was reading.

Baile
HOME

13 June, 1962

I thought a child would make everything right, everything perfect. Instead it's made everything different. Wrong somehow. The bigger Ronan gets, the more I worry he will spend his life ridiculed and feeling different. Other. Wrong. Outside everything. Far away from home.

That, at least, is a feeling Seamus can relate to, can't he?
This isn't where he belongs. Ronan. Seamus.
Me.

14 June, 1962

I did it.
I don't know what I've done.

14 June, 1962

I tried to go back to the jetty, but Seamus sent me home again. The lifeboats are out now. They won't find him.

They won't ever find him. And the way Seamus cries, I want to be sad. I want to feel what he feels. For us to be together again. But I'm not. I'm not sad. I'm not crying. I feel nothing but a rightness in my heart. And that, I'm afraid, means Seamus and I will never be happy together again.

15 June, 1962

Still Seamus is at the jetty. Officer Harville and many from the police have questioned me thoroughly, but no one will tell me what they're doing. Seamus told them the baby fell into the water while I was on the jetty with him. And I think, maybe, he wishes that was the truth.

15 June, 1962

But I'm not sorry! That's what scares me most, leabhar beag. I'm not one spot sorry. Kieran and Phillip were out searching with Seamus in their vessel, but I know they won't find him. I think Seamus knows that too. But he must pretend. And in his heart, I'm sure he hopes otherwise.

Colm came to sit with me while they were out. He tried to comfort me, and I confess I pretended to need the comforting. For what would they say if I didn't? A steady stream of women from the church have been by to drop food and different dishes, for they say I'll be too devastated to cook. They whisper around me. I do not know why. Father George has been several times to pray with me. And I pretend to pray.

But inside, I know my baby is with my mamaí, and the world is as it should be.

16 June, 1962

Finally I have a moment. I told Father George I needed to rest, and he said he would keep vigil downstairs and answer the door while I lay down. I must tell you everything, leabhar beag, before my heart bursts. Two whole days I've not told a soul.

I think it was when Seamus put Ronan in his baptism gown to make sure it fit that the wave inside me broke. When Seamus went out on the boat that day, I took Ronan from his cradle and went down the boardwalk to the jetty. I met only one or two people, and I am as a ghost to them. On the jetty, I sat with my toes in the water, Ronan in my arms, and I tried to think, think so hard, but the ocean made my mind as bleary as sherry does.

And then I saw her. Mamaí.

And there was no more thinking to be done.

I slipped Ronan's blanket away and lowered him into the water. He awoke and gurgled happily up at me. The coat took only moments to form, and then I lowered him further. The waves were calm, as though the sea knew what I needed in that moment. What we needed.

Mamaí came closer, and I let go.

My heart skipped two full beats before Ronan breached the waves, as part of the sea as I ever was. He barked once, twice, then turned and swam toward Mamaí.

I watched the water for hours, tears streaming down my face.

It is with shame that I admit I didn't think of Seamus, not once. Not until he said, "Where's Ronan?"

I turned, and he stood there, in the bright glow of a young afternoon, blinking into the light. He's so handsome, my Seamus. But his face slowly gave way to fear as he took in the sight of my empty arms. He went tearing off toward the house.

Colm came then and asked me what was wrong, where the baby was, but I just shook my head. He led me back to the house, and I let him. Seamus was frantic and shouted at me, "Where's Ronan?"

So I told him. Right there in front of Colm.

Seamus went running out of the house and I followed as fast as I could. He looked up and down the jetty. He looked to the waves.

Ronan and Mamaí bobbed with the ebb tide.

Seamus let out a strangled cry.

"No," he said. "That's not … That's … Lia, tell me where Ronan is!"

I saw the desperation in him. And I knew what he would do next.

I yelled across the waves, "Go! Get out of here!" Mamaí and Ronan simply looked at me, hunkering below the waves, their eyes just cresting the surface. It was the look of a selkie scared. My heart lurched to have made them feel that way. But there was no other way.

"Go!" I yelled. "Please go!"

"Lia!" Seamus wailed, a sound so primal and broken I was sure it would break me, too.

I grabbed a stone wedged in the boards of the jetty and launched it toward my mother and my baby. It splashed into the water a few feet from them, and they turned and disappeared beneath the waves.

"Lia!" Seamus cried as he dove into the water. He surfaced just as Ronan surfaced, several yards out. His lament changed just before he dove under again. "Ronan!"

Shivering, I crossed my arms over my chest, and watched our son swim out of my sight. "He's going home," I said, as much a celebration with the sea as an explanation for Seamus. "Home."

"Ronan!" Seamus spluttered, struggling against the waves now.

If a man cried seven tears into the sea, a selkie woman would come to his rescue. But what if a selkie caused the tears to begin with?

He didn't come back to me. He waited for the waves to wash him up on the shore, then he ran straight toward town. Only moments later he returned with Officer Harville and two other policemen. Before long, they'd multiplied, and a paramedic took me to the back of an ambulance, where I stared sightlessly as he checked my pulse and a policeman asked me questions and everyone handled me as delicately as a piece of blown glass.

And all the while, it was so hard to hide my smile.

Deora
TEARS

Y SNIFFLES MUST HAVE ALERTED ROSIE, because she sat up from her bunk and looked at my wet face, the tears streaming down my face. "Cora?" she asked, alarmed, running to my bed. "What on earth—"

"You have to read this, Rosie," I gasped between sobs. "It's awful."

"What is?"

"The way she…she…she sent Rory away. Mrs. O'Leary. I can't believe she did that. It sounds…horrific."

Rosie produced a tissue from her luggage and then joined me again. "Here. You've got snot everywhere. Wipe it off and then read it to me."

And so I blew my nose and reread the passage aloud. Then, Rosie's arm tucked around me, I read on.

Tar éis
AFTER

17 June, 1962

An older woman from the church came by with breakfast today. Seamus was already gone, probably off searching in the boat, but Colm had begun his vigil on the porch. The old woman came bustling inside, all authority, and demanded I have a muffin as she set a big basket and the newspaper on the table. In that moment, my eyes met Colm's. He reached for it at the same time I did, but I got there first.

"Really!" the old woman huffed.

"She shouldn't be reading tha'!" Colm barked at the old woman.

"She's going to be expected back in the real world eventually," the woman said.

I stopped listening to them bicker as I unfolded the paper. There, on the front page, was a picture of the jetty, a police vessel in the water beyond it. Below the grainy photo, in giant letters, it said:

Missing infant presumed dead

Presumptions like that will make this easier.

18 June, 1962

Seamus can hardly look at me in the spare moments he does come home. Our love, or spell, or whatever it was, it's over. And so I spent an hour today looking for my coat. It's difficult to do with the house so full of well-wishers. But now, with Ronan out there, the pull is like another limb, slowly tugging me home. I want to let go, give in, let myself be pulled back, but I know that without my seal coat, I'll just bob in the waves, forever separate, forever other, never home, until I sink.

19 June, 1962

He spoke to me. For the first time since, he spoke to me. "Why?" That's all he said. At first.

How do you make someone understand? I didn't know. I opened my mouth to tell him what's in my heart, but I don't know words enough to make it clear to him.

So he yelled again, "Why?" and slammed his hand against the wall.

I didn't want him to hurt himself, so I said, "He's home. He's safer there." And that's true. But it's more than that. More than words.

"Can we bring him back?" he asked then.

And I lied. I lied without words, because I'm not a strong liar but I knew he would stop at no lengths if I did not lie. There was no other way. So I shook my head.

There were tears in Seamus's eyes, and for the first time since that day, it made me sad. I'd made Seamus sad. He looked broken. Like a ragdoll that's been ripped apart. I don't regret what I've done, but I do regret making Seamus a broken man. The heart of a landsman is so easily fractured.

I did try to explain then that dear Ronan was with my mamai and so much safer among the waves than he was here. There was so much more to make him happy there.

Seamus only shook his head and left. I don't know where he's gone, but the sun has set and he still hasn't come back.

3 July, 1962

It's funny, isn't it, how quickly the rest of the world goes back to before? When you can't fathom it. The meals and visitors have stopped, and while I thought it would be a blessing, I find myself lonely.

I've found out where Seamus goes. He spends nearly all his time in his shed on the Ritz estate. And he's been volunteering for double the shifts on the boat than normal. I see books he's left around, books with chapters on selkies. I know he's looking for a way, a way to get Ronan back. But I'm not worried. Those books don't hold answers like that.

Colm still visits from time to time, but I find Phillip and Kieran reluctant. Their loyalty is with Seamus, and I'm sure they think the worst of me. As well as the rest of the town. I don't have to know what they're saying to interpret the looks from men and women alike when I go to the shop.

They think I killed my son.

It would wound my heart if I didn't already know that they'd always thought ill of me.

I visit Ronan and Mamaí often. If I go to the jetty, I can be sure to see them within the day. I never run into anyone out there, and I wonder if that's because I'm there. I know they avoid my gaze in town, and perhaps they do the same on the beach. Sometimes I wonder if I'd rather they know the truth. A murderer? An incompetent mother? Or a selkie torn between land and sea? What is the worse fate? No matter what they think, I couldn't bear not to visit Ronan. Until I find my seal coat and we're reunited, the jetty is all I have.

I can see men setting up for the Fourth of July party down the beach. I won't go this year.

21 July, 1962

It has been one month since Seamus spoke to me. Not using my voice is not hard for me, like it might be for others. But I know in landsman terms, the silence is meant as a punishment. And so I feel the intended hurt. He spends all his time away from the house, and when he's home, his beautiful emerald eyes stay far from mine.

Colm brought me a bouquet of flowers yesterday—daisies—which was very kind of him, but I confess I have no need for flowers. If he could tell me where my coat is, that would be a true gift. With Seamus gone off, I've had ample time to search this house. I can't imagine where it might be.

And I do wonder. Is the hate and anger Seamus is feeling, is it enough to make him return it, if I were to ask him...

It makes me ill to think he may hate me that much, wish me away, but the pull, the yearning to go back, makes my stomach tumble and my head spin. Does that mean I am destined to feel sick the rest of my life?

Creid
BELIEVE

I NEED TO GO TALK TO SEAMUS," I SAID, TAKING A deep, shuddering breath. My grief felt so visceral, as if someone had just taken Rory away from me, just like in the diary. And, in a way, they had. Except all this time I'd been blaming Seamus O'Leary. And now, for the first time, I could clearly see her part in this. The woman who'd brought me into this mysterious world, and had shown me such kindness last summer—I'd been so loathe to place any blame on her. How could I not have seen the role she'd played?

For once, I felt *sorry* for Seamus O'Leary.

"I'm coming," Rosie insisted as I scrambled into my shoes.

It was late evening, but the Irish summer sun had a solid hour of play left in it. For once, I wished it wasn't quite so cheery. A good rain would have done my soul justice.

The haul-out was empty of seals, but Seamus's goat bleated at us when we climbed to the stoop and knocked.

Seamus answered the door at once, and a kind smile crinkled the skin around his eyes. "What an unexpected surprise," he said, opening the door wide. "I imagine you're just looking for a cuppa and some biscuits? I'm afraid I can only offer one of the two, but I'm sure it's cozier here than that hostel you're in."

"We were just reading the diary," I said, stepping inside. "And…and we read the part where she sends Rory…away."

Seamus's smile faded. "Oh," he said simply, turning his back and disappearing into the kitchen, which appeared to be the only room in his house with the light on. It struck me as intolerably lonely.

Shaking myself out of my melancholy, I went after him and gestured for Rosie to follow. The electric kettle was on, and Seamus was fiddling with mugs in a cabinet. Tears pricked at my eyes, but I couldn't find the words. *Sorry* seemed to want to pour forth, but I wasn't quite sure my emotions were correct yet. After all, the man had still left Mrs. O'Leary to rot in Oyster Beach as he started anew in Ireland.

"Did you believe her?" Rosie asked. When I looked at her in surprise, her own eyes were misted over.

There was a clink as Seamus set the mugs on the counter and turned to face us. His face was inscrutable. "Believe what?"

"When…when he disappeared," Rosie said, looking to me for help.

"Did you think…" I gulped, remembering the rumors that had swirled around Oyster Beach, even all those years later. "That she'd…"

"Drowned him?" Seamus asked. He let out a long breath and

shook his head. "It's certainly what the neighbors thought. Not a day went by that I wasn't asked why I didn't have her locked up. Murdering her own child, they said. It was clear as day."

When Mr. Hall had told me of the town's whispers and rumors about Lia O'Leary, I'd been outraged. I couldn't believe it. But now, for the first time, hearing it from Seamus's own lips, I thought that maybe, just maybe, it would have been what I'd believed had I been a neighbor in Oyster Beach all those years ago. "Why didn't you believe it?"

"I told you before, I loved her," Seamus said simply. "Always have."

Then why did you leave her?

The kettle *clicked*, and Seamus poured boiling water into each mug before bringing them to the table and sitting at the far end.

"To be truthful, I'm not sure what I believed back then," he went on. "It was around that time that she began to look for what she called her seal coat. I kept it hidden, because I was scared. And maybe it was then that I knew it was all true, deep down, subconsciously. If not only because I couldn't believe her a murderer. I never did. I mourned Ronan and believed he'd left this world by nobody's fault. Certainly not my precious Lia's."

"So you tried again. You had another child," I prompted him.

"Fionn was born in 1964." A phantom smile was on his face, and I wondered whether he told this story often. Whether he'd told anyone else at all. Or perhaps it only felt practiced because he told it to himself, reliving his memories, as he lived alone in this house. "A perfect, tiny human being. I thought we would begin again. Things would be different. Better." He shook his head, and a strand of his neatly kept white hair fell into his eyes. "It was only a few days this time. And I was there."

A cold wrapped around my heart, despite the fact that I *knew* this story. At least the bare bones of it. But there was a difference between allusions, whispers, and the truth laid bare, the unfathomable made clear with familiar words. But I wanted to know. I had to know.

"I found her out on the jetty with the baby one evening, and of course I was frightened. Frightened that the rumors were true. That she was disturbed and was going to kill our other son. I think that's the only moment in which I believed the rumors. She was frantic and kept telling me he wanted to join Ronan. I thought she meant in heaven, and I begged her then to hand him over. To let me take Fionn back to the house. She jumped into the water then, and I jumped in after her, but I was too late. She'd let go of the baby. He was swallowed by the waves."

The sound of the ocean outside Seamus's little house seemed to grow louder in the silence, teasing us, taunting us, saying, *Yes, that's right, I did that.*

"Of course I dove in, searching, but I recovered only his blanket. And then…" Seamus closed his eyes. "I saw it happen. It was as if the water was a catalyst in some grotesque science experiment. Where there was an infant one moment, the next there was the dark shape of an animal ducking underwater. And then nothing. Just me, floating there, holding a sodden blanket, as Mrs. O'Leary cried tears of joy. After then, well…"

"Then you believed," I whispered.

"Then I believed."

Chun Selkie a Gabhadh
TO CATCH A SELKIE

ROSIE SNIFFLED, AND WHEN I LOOKED OVER, tears were streaming down her face. "But they're here," she said. "Teenage boys, on land. At least, they were. How?"

Seamus smiled faintly. "You won't find that in the diary. Toward the end she became…well… She lost the ability to write, and after a while even reading escaped her. I think … I think she became a little less human as the years went by and she stopped trying at it."

The statement was chilling, and I wondered if that was happening to Rory right this second.

"So how did you find them?" I felt a little desperate, like maybe I could use the same technique to get Rory back now. But at the same time I knew that was unlikely.

"I searched for them," Seamus said simply.

"Searched for them," I repeated, disappointed by the mundane answer.

"For thirty years."

Thirty years. That was a long time to miss someone. Longer than Mr. O'Leary had been gone from Oyster Beach.

He took a sip of his tea, which, if it was anything like mine, wasn't warm anymore. But I didn't mind. I wasn't actually drinking mine.

"How did you find them?" I asked.

"It was a bit of luck in the end. For years, Mrs. O'Leary had told me we couldn't get them back. That it wasn't possible. But she'd become quite a hermit after Fionn was gone, and she let down her guard. She would sneak out on the jetty to look for them. Talk to them. D'you know, people thought she was covering up the murders by pretending to grieve. It's amazing what people will come up with when they don't want to believe the best of someone.

"The truth was, she wanted to be near them, even after they'd gone. And that's when I realized that maybe she was lying. I used to read everything on the topic that I could get my hands on, and I finally found a book that spoke to the selkie's human body returning, unaged, from the sea. That's when I knew they *could* return. That it was possible. I used to try to catch Lia down there on the pier, but seals are skittish at the best of times, and she would fly into such a fury when I tried to catch them …

"Besides, I hardly knew which was a seal and which was …" He sighed. "I gave up for a time, considered returning to Ireland. But I couldn't leave them there. Not knowing what I knew. I tried off and on for years, setting elaborate traps near the jetty, but I didn't want to raise suspicion. I'd told Phillip Hall in the early days, and Colm overheard what Lia said the night Rory disappeared. But I don't think he believed.

He never really knew, nor Kieran."

A cold creeped up my back. Kieran. He certainly knew about selkies. Could he really not have noticed who—or what—Mrs. O'Leary was back then? Or was it possible he knew more than Seamus was aware of?

"They were my best friends in those days," Seamus went on. "I had to be careful. It hurt my heart to do it like that, setting traps, like my boys were … animals. But what choice did I have? I didn't know what to expect if I succeeded. In the end, one of my less ingenious traps near the jetty worked.

"It was Ronan."

Seamus disappeared down the hall and returned with the same wooden box of keepsakes we'd seen before. He opened it and took out a picture newer than the last, a little boy in the bright colors of the 90s. He had dark, tousled hair, and Rory's grin. It looked, for all the world, like any of my childhood photos—not like the childhood photo of a boy born in 1962.

Seamus sniffed. "The night I found him, tangled up in my nets, just a baby, his tiny fists clutching his seal coat … I remember it like it was yesterday. Being simultaneously horrorstruck and elated. But Mrs. O'Leary stumbled upon me then, out at the jetty. As I untangled Ronan and brought him back to land, she fought me."

Head hanging, Seamus sipped his tea again, which was surely ice-cold by this point. But he didn't seem to mind. "Luckily," he continued, "the O'Brien boys were playing nearby, like they often did at dusk, and that's when I hatched the plan." His eyes twinkled like he still believed his scheme to have been genius. "Leaving the baby there on the sand, I dragged Mrs. O'Leary back to the house and locked her there. I'm not proud of that, but I did what was for the best. I sat on the porch and watched over Ronan from afar. The O'Brien boys discovered him almost immediately, and the oldest took charge, picking up the baby and taking him home to his mother. Good boys, they were, the O'Brien children."

"And you told the townspeople the baby's mother was some poor young girl," I whispered, remembering what Mr. Hall had told me.

"Yes, when nobody could identify the strange infant found on the beach… Imagine the furor it caused. They called him 'The Beach Baby.' But I came forward and told the guards I knew the young woman who'd given birth to him. She was a troubled young local girl who couldn't take care of him, and I managed to convince them not to press charges for leaving the child exposed."

"Are you kidding me?" Rosie said.

"I knew the chief at the time," Seamus said easily. "Chief Harville. He was a friend of mine. And it wasn't a big town. Not like the big cities where no one knows one another. In Oyster Beach, everyone cared for each other. The chief thought he was doing nothing less for a poor girl in trouble."

"Any relation to the current Captain Harville?" I asked, my suspicions mounting. No wonder he'd been around at the end—just before Lia disappeared. He probably knew everything. Or some at least Seamus's version.

Seamus nodded once. "Like father, like son."

"But this hypothetical girl could've *killed* the baby!" Rosie interrupted. "And the cops didn't care?"

"Of course they cared," Seamus said, "But I covered all points. The public knew this girl could be in serious trouble with the police for child endangerment, but I spread the story that she needed to remain anonymous for another reason. Because she was a young, Catholic Irish immigrant. Her family would disown her for even becoming pregnant. Luckily for me, Americans don't know much about modern Ireland."

"They suspected he was your illegitimate child," I said. "That that's why you cared so much. They probably knew the baby was never in danger, that you'd facilitated the whole thing. Isn't that funny? They were right. But for the wrong reason."

Seamus looked at me long and hard, his eyes narrowed. "How did you hear those rumors?"

"Mr. Hall told me. Last summer."

Seamus shook his head. "The idea of my looking elsewhere for love is absurd. I've loved Lia O'Leary every day since I met her on that beach."

I just barely resisted rolling my eyes. *Sure, sure, that refrain again.* Then why hadn't he had more trouble walking away? I decided not to bring that up just yet. "But how did you keep Mrs. O'Leary from interfering?" I asked. "Telling everyone who the baby was?"

"At first, I locked her in the house. Which wasn't difficult to do. She'd been shunning any social calls for years. And after I told her what I'd done, she grieved fiercely. I thought she would get over it, knowing that the boy was safe. But she didn't. She was getting a reputation for being quite insane, and I was getting a reputation for being a cruel husband. So I made a deal with her.

"I'd hidden the boy's sealskin with hers, so I told her I'd never return either if she ever so much as approached the boy."

His words rang with such confidence, it made the hairs on my arms stand on end.

"That's not a deal, that's a threat," Rosie pointed out.

"It wasn't either, I'm afraid," Seamus said. "Because I never had any intention of giving them up no matter how well she behaved. Which she did. For a time."

"So she had to sit there," I said, "and watch her son grow up a stone's throw away?" The pity I'd felt for him after reading Mrs. O'Leary's diary entry was melting quickly away.

"What would you have had me do instead?" Seamus asked quietly. "I just had to make sure she didn't approach the boy. She was locking herself up in the house of her own accord."

"Probably to avoid seeing her beloved son!" I snapped.

"So how did she react when you brought Aidan back?" Rosie asked.

Seamus sighed. "She didn't. Because I never told her. I did the exact same thing with Fionn, but this time I didn't tell her. It was 1996, the year of the Great Storm. I was out in the boat with Colm and Kieran and James, God rest his soul."

My blood ran cold at the mention of the man who'd drowned at Seamus's hands. All those years, Oyster Beach believed Seamus had disappeared at sea, probably drowned, but it wasn't he who'd lost his life to the sea at all. Had people missed James Cassidy? Did they wonder where he'd gone?

"We were fishing—"

"We've heard this story," I interrupted, "from Colm Vesey."

A shadow passed over Seamus's face. "Oh, yes, Colm certainly does love this story."

"*Love?*" I cried. "He's horrified by it! He's been scarred for life! You…you *killed* a man!"

The words hung in the kitchen like some great shadow.

Seamus never met my eyes. But he finally spoke.

"In all my life, since the day they were born, I have done nothing but what I thought was best for my boys. I have only *ever* wanted what was best for them."

"Yet here we are, both of them back out there," I said, nodding toward a window. "So I guess after all your efforts, it happened anyway." *You failed them.* The accusation went unspoken, but I could tell by the look on his face that he'd understood it all the same.

Finally, he looked down at his tea and murmured, "I think it's time ye go."

Cinneadh Iontach Mór
A GREAT BIG DECISION

12 August, 1962

The rain thunders against the roof, but that's not the reason I won't sleep tonight. I can't stop watching Seamus, his chest rising and falling, a sure sign that he's alive.

He's alive.

The waves are terrible this August, and for those toiling above them, it's dangerous. Colm says Seamus was reckless, not careful like he usually is. Nobody saw what happened, but he hit his head and fell overboard. A weaker swimmer would have drowned.

Little book, I can't tell you what I felt when I answered the door and found Phillip on the porch, his face streaked with tears. They thought he was going to die, you see. Phillip didn't say that, but by the way he said, "Lia, you have to come to the hospital," and the fact that he was speaking to me at all…I knew.

Even after the month we've had, my heart flip-flopped in my chest as I imagined the reality of a world without Seamus. Kind, sweet, funny Seamus. When I thought he was going to die… Oh, I've never been so scared.

It felt as though I was below the waves and couldn't breathe. Like I was going to die myself. And all the ill thoughts I've had of him, all the trouble we've had, it evaporated like mist on the water. I wanted nothing more with my heart—not to go back to the sea, not to see Ronan and Mamaí—I wanted nothing more than to hold Seamus and see that he was all right.

He looked so broken in that hospital bed. Even more broken than before. I've never felt so wretched. I was there, crying in his room, eight hours before he woke up. When he did, he found me sitting beside him, and I reached out and took his hand, and he didn't pull away. When I gently squeezed his fingers, he squeezed back. He even looked me in the eye until Colm entered and interrupted.

He said, "For God's sake, we thought ya were done fer, lad!"

We all laughed then. But even the sight of him breathing and talking wasn't enough to still the shaking in my limbs. His head is injured, but the doctors said the real miracle was that he'd not drown. He held my hand as much as he could, and though we spoke little, with people and nurses and doctors coming in and out, I felt it in my heart. This mending of something broken between us.

We were there three days, but today he came home. I can't bring myself to do anything but watch him. Make sure he eats, help him up the steps, settle him on the porch to sit, tuck him in to nap, and now I watch him sleep. He's like a child I feel I must protect with every last piece of me. My arms still shake and my breath is shallow, and I can only watch him.

13 August, 1962

Everything is going to be all right. The storm has passed, and the beach is full of seashells. I walked and picked out a basket of them for Seamus. And when I got home, we spoke.

"Lia," he said, "I'll give you your coat. You can go. Or you can stay. But it's not up to me anymore. You once told me to hide it from you at all costs. But I won't do it anymore. You have to make a decision."

He offered to let me go back, little book.

He offered to let me go back, and I said no.

I said no.

No.

It echoes in my head like a church bell, too loud to truly appreciate. Tears sprang to Seamus's eyes at the same time that I tried to decide if I'd meant it. That tiny, easy word. No. No. No.

"Lia," he said, the tears brimming in his beautiful eyes, "if you stay, you have to promise me. You have to be fully present. You have to see someone, a therapist, about being happy. Somebody who can help us learn to love each other again. You have to promise me that-that what you did, that it won't … That you can be happy here. Just you and me. You have to promise me right now that I'm enough for you."

Images ran through my head so fast, I could barely make them out. Ronan, a tiny baby gurgling in my arms. Seamus, holding me in our bed. Ronan swimming away from me toward Mamaí. Martha screaming at me in our kitchen. Colm smiling kindly and Kieran addressing me in Irish. Seamus kissing me senseless in the early days after I came here. The days just after I made the decision. The decision in which I chose Seamus.

I chose Seamus. This beautiful man with the striking dark hair and glimmering emerald eyes. I chose him. I chose this. And we loved each other.

We love each other. I choose him.

The therapist will come next week. We will speak of Ronan as though he's passed, but I'll do it if it will make Seamus happy. We're going to be like we once were. Other people may still whisper words like "murderer" and "psycho" when I pass in the shop, but Seamus knows the truth. Seamus knows the truth and wants me anyway.

We're going to be like we once were. We're going to learn to love again.

Love,

Lia

12 October, 1962

Dear little book,

It has been so long since I wrote. Seamus noticed and encouraged me to write again. So I told him I would. Even though he was the one to give you to me, writing in here feels like a betrayal to him. You hold all my secrets, things Seamus can never know. And these months I've felt so close to Seamus. Closer even than we were at the start.

Dr. Holden comes every Monday, and we sit in the living room and talk. In the beginning, Seamus came, too. But he's often away on the boat, and those weeks Dr. Holden comes anyway, to talk to me alone. He says it's important that I'm happy both in my marriage and independent of it. I'm not sure what that means, exactly, or if it can be, when Seamus is the only thing I'm here for.

Dr. Holden thinks Ronan drowned, an accident, and I let him think that, as all the town does. That is the thing he thinks makes me unhappy, and I don't correct the notion. In truth, I find I'm not unhappy. Seamus is more loving and caring than he ever was, and though I visit Ronan at the jetty daily, I begin to think we are both in the places we are meant to be.

Seamus asked me again, just once, if we could bring him back. Ronan. I almost told him then, leabhar beag, because the image of the three of us, one happy family, was so strong in my mind. But then Martha charged into my vision wielding a knife. Ronan is safer and far happier with Mamaí than he could ever be here. He is selkie, and no wishing on Seamus's part could change that.

There was a time when Seamus grieved in private. I would find him alone in the bedroom, the tears streaming down his face, and my heart would hurt. He would wipe them away and pretend to be fine, but I knew the truth. There was one time I even considered taking him to the jetty to watch Ronan. But I knew it would be a risk. Who knows what he would do if he saw him right there in the water? That is, if he even believed me that it really is our Ronan.

It was easy to convince myself I was doing what was best for everyone. And eventually Seamus's tears dried up. Maybe he cries somewhere else now. Or maybe he realizes that Ronan is in a better place. Maybe he's determined to be happy with me.

We have dinner together every night that Seamus is on land, as the therapist instructed us. And the more time we spend together, the closer I feel to him. He's like the Seamus of old, funny and kind, playing the tin whistle in the evenings before bed.

Even Kieran and Phillip have begun to visit again with Colm. I think maybe Seamus asked them to, for sometimes I still find Phillip looks at me strangely, when no one else is paying attention. He looks at me like I'm a monster.

It is a relief to me when he leaves. I like our time alone better—just me and Seamus curled on the couch as he reads aloud from fairy tales. Like we used to.

It's not so hard to learn to love again.

Love,

Lia

Leithscéal
AN APOLOGY

AFTER ONLY A FEW MORE DIARY ENTRIES, I regretted pushing Seamus that far. Back then, he'd no doubt been tormented. And today, he was an old man whose sons had just reversed the rescue mission he'd performed nearly two decades ago—a mission thirty years in the making—and this time they'd gone back by choice.

And, knowing what was coming next in the story, I was reluctant to keep reading the diary. It didn't help that the next spring tide was bearing down on us. The logical side of my brain knew I had to make plans, contingency plans, in case Rory didn't make it back in time. Would I sit around waiting another two weeks? I knew Rosie wouldn't allow it. Not to mention my parents. But I was still too shaken up by the diary and our conversation with Mr. O'Leary to be able to make any real decisions.

All of which made for a few gloomy days for me. Much to Rosie's chagrin.

"If you don't snap out of it, I'm going to do something drastic!" Rosie groaned on the morning before our last lesson with Seamus. I'd been checking his phone incessantly, for no other reason than to make myself feel even worse about not being able to answer his parents' calls.

"Like what?" I challenged her.

"I don't know! Like, fall in love with a mythical creature! That would really get back at you, wouldn't it?"

I gave a halfhearted laugh. "I think I would feel better if I apologized," I said quietly. "To Seamus. We're digging around in the most painful parts of his life. That isn't … it's not right. I just need to apologize."

And I did. When all the other students had filed out of the classroom after our Irish lesson, even Rosie and Evan, Rosie tugging on his arm and giving him a pointed look before he left without me.

"I'm sorry," I said, as soon as the front door of the small school closed.

Seamus nodded, accepting the apology with the quiet embarrassment stereotypical of most of the Irish I'd encountered so far. "You've nothing to be sorry for."

"That's not true. We shouldn't be digging up all this stuff that's so painful for you. I'm sorry about what I said the other day."

Seamus nodded again, clearly uncomfortable. "Ye aren't doing me a disservice. I can't say it's not a relief to be talking about it with someone after all these years."

I looked him in the eye until he grew uncomfortable and looked down at the desk he was sitting on. "If that's true," I said carefully, "you won't mind answering one more question?"

Seamus didn't look up but gave a little shrug. I was sure he'd been expecting what I needed to ask.

"Did you kill James Cassidy?"

His eyes closed briefly, but when he opened them, he looked me right in the eye. "It was an accident. Did you know seal hunting was illegal for a great many years? But it was legalized in the 90s because the seal population was decimating the fishing industry. You can't imagine my terror. I'd grown a bit lax over the years, but that news made me renew my efforts. And when my own friends took it up... Please try to envision my fear when James, God rest his soul, went after the seal I knew to be my son. I attacked him, I don't deny it. I just had to stop him. But he lost his balance. And did my anger and fear in that moment, and a great many other things, the way he looked at Lia, talked to her... Did all those things cause me to dart faster, tackle him harder than I otherwise would have? I...I don't know."

The look on his face seemed to be imploring me to believe him, to understand. And the surprising part was, I did.

"It was an accident," Seamus repeated. "And the greatest regret of my life."

I nodded. And I actually believed him. Seamus O'Leary had the air of a man with nothing to hide, despite the great many things he'd been hiding for a great many years.

"I would have done anything for those boys, for her," he murmured.

"Except stay," I cut in.

Seamus grimaced. "She ... she just didn't return my love."

I thought of Mrs. O'Leary's constant longing to return to the sea and wondered if Seamus was right. Mr. Hall had told me that people in the town thought Seamus loved her more than she loved him. I'd thought it was just people's disinterest in truly understanding Lia and her kind, gentle nature. But maybe I was wrong. Maybe she hadn't loved him. After all, she was a selkie. Maybe it was all magic.

"Mr. Hall was mad at her. Or afraid of her, or something," I said. "Is that why he never told her where her seal coat was? He knew all those years."

Seamus shook his head. "That, too, was my fault. I asked him to keep that secret. I feared what she would do if she ever found her coat, and Ronan's. You can't destroy a selkie coat, d'you know? I tried. And that night of the Great Storm, I managed to convince Colm and Kieran to take Fionn's coat away with them. But Ronan's, it was still there…and I was running out of ideas for trying to get rid of it. So instead I chose the easy path. To give up and fear her. Fear what she would do if she found her coat and tried to take the boy with her. Because above anything else, I believed those boys deserved a real, normal life. A human life."

"Mr. Hall must have grown tired of keeping the secret," I mused.

"Yes, there is only so far and so long you can push an old man," Seamus murmured.

I wondered if that was a veiled threat, but it didn't stop me from asking, "Then what made you leave? You didn't leave right away. Colm said he and Kieran left immediately after the Great Storm. They were so frightened. And you finally had Aidan back, and in safe hands with the O'Briens. But you stayed. For a while, at least. Only to one day disappear in your boat? What made you leave her in the end? And like that?"

"Oh," Seamus sighed, letting his gaze settle on mine, heavy and full of regret. He took a deep breath and then said, "I'd long felt a deep desire to leave, but I harbored an inability to do so." It had the air of a lie, even when I knew what he was going to say next. Something I'd already heard: "D'you know, they say there's an allure around a selkie that affects a human's mind and emotions."

Those words made it sound like he hadn't had a *choice* in loving her. But the way he said it made me think he didn't really believe it, either.

"Are you saying you never truly loved her?"

Mr. O'Leary closed his eyes. "That's the opposite of what I've been telling you all along child. I loved Mrs. O'Leary with all my heart. Always have, and, I think, always will."

"Then why did you leave?" I demanded, unable to hold my anger in check. "If you loved her, why—"

"You haven't finished the diary," he said simply. It was a statement, not a question. "Finish the book, child."

Ag Lorg Freagraí
LOOKING FOR ANSWERS

S PRING TIDE WAS COMING UPON US WITH SUCH speed, I felt harried. Like there was so much I had to discover before time ran out. Before Rory came back. It felt as though if I could discover what had driven Mr. O'Leary away from Mrs. O'Leary, I could find out how to make sure what Rory and I had was real.

But the diary was long, and I didn't have the time. Bonfire night was two days away, and the morning after, I'd sit on the beach, or perhaps the haul-out, unable to peel my eyes from the waves. So, instead, I used a technique perfected by the average American high-school student. I wasn't a selkie, but I had my own skills. I could skim a book the night before a test and perform … well, not great. But there wouldn't be a test this time.

In an April 1963 entry, Lia wrote that she was pregnant again, and she was terrified to tell Seamus. I skimmed the passages where she tried her best to reassure him that everything would be okay this time, and I wondered if she was lying. There was no hint of subterfuge, she seemed to believe it herself. I skipped ahead a good chunk of pages, unable to stomach their misplaced trust in the future.

When I got to January 1964, I grew leery, for I knew the year Aidan was born, but not the date, and that's how I stumbled upon the description of a long and grueling birth on January 16. Lia's tone was so very different from the previous entries I'd read from the spring, expressing extreme sadness. And sure enough, in the next entry, I read only one sentence: *I've done it.*

I couldn't bear to read about her sending Fionn to the sea. Not after reading about the time with Ronan and then hearing Seamus's account of Fionn's—what would you call it? Not death. Not really. It was like hitting a pause button.

Squeezing my eyes shut, I flipped through more pages, this time a great deal. In November 1964, Lia described Seamus taking a weeks-long assignment on the boat, and she feared it was because he couldn't bear to look at her. But in August 1965, she admits that she barely misses Seamus when he's gone—him recently having been on a month-long voyage—because the pain of her longing for the sea is too great.

Flipping to 1966, I felt a great weight on my shoulders. Reading Mrs. O'Leary's words, hearing her voice, it was becoming too much. It felt as though I was living inside the mind of a dead woman, a friend long passed, and maybe it was the effort of trying to read her scraggly handwriting, but my head hurt and I felt weary.

In the early '70s entries, her handwriting began to deteriorate, and I remembered Seamus saying she became less human. Her entries were few and far between here, too, and I wondered if being out of practice had any effect.

Seamus continued to take longer assignments, and Lia continuously expressed her deep desire to return to the sea. But Seamus's staunch position never changed—that he could never let her go because she was his only link to the boys. His only hope of ever finding them again. In several entries, she said she assured him there was no possibility of retrieving the boys, but still he wouldn't relent, as if he knew that if she disappeared, so too would his only hope of seeing his sons again. And there were details of her days. Her waiting, her trips to the jetty, and again and again—as constant as the waves—her desire—no, her *need*—to go back.

There were a few bits and pieces about other people—Kieran getting married and having a son, Phillip buying the antique shop, Dr. Griffin telling Lia she was too frail to have any more children—but for the most part, it was boring. It was repetitive. It was mundane.

Is that what Seamus had wanted me to read when he told me to finish the diary? That they'd gotten stuck in this mundane world of married life, and once he got his sons back in Oyster Beach, he could take it no longer and left? It couldn't be. Wasn't that what married life was? Learning to love the mundane with someone who managed to make it just a little less mundane?

"You look like a wreck."

Setting the diary on my lap open to my current spot, I looked up. "I feel like a wreck."

Rosie closed the door to the room and did the cursory glance around to make sure no fellow tourists were lurking or listening. Today was sunnier than usual, so everyone had scattered outside fairly early on.

"Are you worried about him?" The bed bounced as Rosie sat next to me.

"Of course."

"He's gonna come back, Cora. He doesn't *want* that life. He's not like Aidan."

"But what if he *can't*? Or what if, now that he's down there, that's all he wants? Or what if something happened to him?"

"Whoa." Rosie pushed her palms out. "Calm down. You could drown in what-ifs…" Her face went scarlet, but she quickly recovered. "I'm sorry! That word choice, I'm so sorry, Cora."

I shook my head. "It's okay. I don't think I could feel worse at the moment, to be honest."

Rosie sighed deeply. "Maybe you should stop reading that thing," she said quietly, knowing I would protest.

But she was wrong. I was beginning to think the same thing. "I think you're right," I said.

She looked at me, surprised, before suggesting, "Let's go for a walk or something. Or we can collect seashells, I know you like to do that. Or—"

"I don't really feel like leaving," I said, snuggling deeper under the covers on what had come to feel like my bed these past weeks.

"Okay," Rosie said, chewing on her lip. "How 'bout a board game? They have some in the lobby. I can go grab us one."

She looked so hopeful, so eager to distract me, that I finally nodded, despite not being the least interested in a game—and I didn't think Rosie was, either.

"Awesome!" she said, leaping up. "I'll see if Evan wants to play too!"

When she'd bounded out of the room, I picked the diary up and ran my hand over the dried ink. Lia's words. They were too hard to read. I should put it away and let Rory read it someday—if he wanted to. But my curiosity was still there.

As well as that niggling doubt that what Rory and I had wasn't real.

I flipped through the remaining pages, and the steady *thrum* of the paper was interrupted by one page with an offbeat pause. Because the page wasn't flat. It was all wrinkled.

Opening the book to that entry—January 10, 1973—I saw that the page was warped. As if it had been sprinkled with water … like maybe a deluge of tears, now long dried. Curious, I decided to read the first line, just the first, to see what had made Lia cry. It read:

I am an animal.

Pheaca Fiú a Dhéanamh
A SIN WORTH COMMITTING

10 January, 1973

I am an animal.

Oh, *leabhar beag*, forgive me. I tremble to write even to you of what I've done. These weeks since, the winter sea has turned like a monster within me, and I've walked the world unseeing, starved of the one thing that can give me life.

I can't stay here. I've been desperate, dear book, and that's the only justification I can give for what I've done. Seamus is gone most nights, and I do not sleep. Never do I sleep, until the sun rises over the ocean and the limitations of this body overcome my mind. And when I sleep, I see the smoke.

In those desperate, dark hours, I've thought of many things. Many ideas I don't wish to reveal, for the shame is great. Mortal sins, Father George used to call them. But the one thing I finally acted upon—you have to know. It was the memory of Martha Hall, young, kind, suspicious Martha, being driven away from her *marriage by a secret.*

I knew that if I could have a secret as big as the one that drove Martha away from Phillip, just maybe it would be enough to make Seamus drive me away. Banish me from Oyster Beach. Throw me out with my coat so I'd never step foot on land again.

I was dying for it.

And on that day that Martha came to the house, upset, and told me she suspected poor Phillip was keeping something from her, she taught me what I needed now. She told me all the many things that husbands keep from wives. And why, I thought, could it not be the wife keeping them from the husband?

It would be enough, I knew it, to make Seamus throw me out with only my coat.

She yelled at me that day, saying I should be worried, for Seamus was always away on the boat. And so he was yesterday.

Colm has always been so nice to me. He was hesitant at first, and I almost went home, but then he said that he's always liked me. It embarrassed me, little book, and my cheeks must have blushed, for it isn't right. But Colm wasn't embarrassed. He says our marriage has been falling to pieces for a while now, it's plain to see, and Seamus knows it. That may be, but I hadn't even walked home before I regretted the entire thing.

It hurts my heart to think of what I've done, but I know also that it just might be enough to make Seamus stop loving me. And as awful as that truth is, I think it is the only way I shall ever go home.

16 January, 1973

Oh, I can scarce breathe in this little apartment! Colm comes to the door, yells through the windows, he wants to see me, and I won't, I can't. I don't want to. He wants us to be together again, and I want only to forget what I've done. I can't use this transgression to get what I want. It feels foul and wrong, like my soul knows it has done evil.

Seamus will be back tomorrow, and I can't, won't tell him. I never fathomed how it would feel, this secret in my soul, and it hurts more than any scar I've ever gotten on my body. How I wish that I had never met Martha Hall!

That every day Seamus has been gone I had sat, unsleeping, in my empty bed and waited for sunrise to tug me into sleep, for the unending torment of being on land is nothing to the feeling I carry with me now—that of my chest rending in two.

I can only live this lie and hope Seamus never finds out.

This is my penance.

21 March, 1973

I no longer feel as though I belong in this human body. Fate has betrayed me. I'm with child. I've been to the doctor, and am to give birth in October. Dr. Griffin looked sad, for he's told me before that after the boys...I'm too frail to have children.

But fate has played her cards.

Seamus is gone again, but he will be home tomorrow, and I know not what shall become of us, of me. I can't tell him, the words won't come, even when I try to practice in my mirror.

To undo it all, it is all I want.

8 April, 1973

I've never wanted more to slip beneath the waves and disappear, sealskin or no. My stomach grows rounder by the day, and today Seamus realized. Before I thought I could not form the words, but in the end, it is harder to form a lie.

He asked who, and I told him. Little book, he didn't even look surprised.

And when I tried to tell him why, he just shook his head and said, "And your plan's gone horribly wrong. Now you can't go back. I can't let you take one more child away like that and still face my god in the end."

How is it that you can try so hard for things to go one way and they end up the complete opposite? Fate is a fickle god.

And worse, still, is me.

I will never be able to right the wrongs I've done.

Áine
ÁINE

S HE HAD A CHILD WITH COLM. LIA O'LEARY HAD deserted Seamus long before he did her.

"Wait!" Rosie stood helplessly in the hall, *Monopoly* tucked under her arm. "Where are you going? I thought we—"

"I'm sorry, Roz!" I called out, turning to face her as I walked backward. "I have to talk to Seamus!" With the diary tucked under my arm, I saw her roll her eyes just before I turned around and darted out of the hostel.

I was just dashing by the bike shop, when Róisín yelled, "Hiya, Cora!" That caught my attention enough that I stumbled and looked at her—she was standing beside that Patrick guy, helping some visitors find bikes the proper size for them. And when my eyes drifted to the shop window behind them, I spotted Seamus through the window.

"Hey, are you rentin' a bike?" Róisín called after me.

"I get a commission if you get it—" The door shut on her pleas.

There were a few people in line to speak to Seamus behind the counter, and though my heart was pounding and my lungs working overtime, I knew I couldn't just barge right up there and embarrass him. Instead, I waited my turn, trying to calm my nerves.

By the time I got to the front of the line, the shop had emptied out, and when Seamus looked up at me, his eyes reacted instantly. The light in them dimmed.

"I can't believe she did that to you," I said, my voice still weak from my mad dash from the hostel.

Seamus glanced around the place then nodded toward a doorway that led into a back room. He went to the front door and called the man named Patrick inside so he could take a "break," then he nodded once more at the back door and walked through it, beckoning me to follow.

There was a small kitchenette back here, and Seamus gestured for me to take one of the chairs around the small, chipped table.

As I plopped down, the words came rushing out. "I'm so sorry. I always thought of Lia as the-the victim, and I … I didn't know. I just read about … I'm so sorry."

Seamus inclined his head and murmured, "Colm?"

I nodded.

Seamus went to the counter that lined one wall and flicked on an electric kettle there before removing two mugs from an old cabinet. *Jesus, does this country run on tea?* I thought, exasperated by his steady demeanor.

Finally, as the water in the kettle bubbled angrily, he said, "It was a difficult time."

A disbelieving scoff escaped my throat. "Talk about the understatement of the century. He was one of your best friends!"

Seamus carefully placed both mugs on the table and stared at me for a long moment. Then, after a long sip of tea, he acknowledged, "Human nature defies logic at the best of times."

His stoicism was about to make me blow a gasket. "What happened to the baby? Colm's baby?"

Seamus narrowed his eyes at me. "You didn't read far enough."

Embarrassed, I shook my head. "I ran straight over here."

He nodded at the diary in my hand. "August second," he said, holding his hand out. I placed the worn book in his palm. He flipped it open, turned a few pages, and read aloud:

"The second of August, 1973. Dear little book, no matter how I heap the blankets upon me, my bones are too cold to ever be warm again. I woke last night to blood. Too much blood. And too early. The baby wasn't expected for two more months. But sometimes nature doesn't follow rules given by a doctor.

"Seamus is the only reason I'm still alive. The baby was coming too fast. He tried to call Dr. Griffin, but nobody answered. And I had her, little Áine, right there in the bedroom. There was so much blood, and I could scarcely see for the tears and the room kept wavering before my eyes. And she was too small, leabhar beag. Much too small. She couldn't breathe.

"She died, my Áine.

"Little book, I'm in hospital now, the doctor calls it a miscarriage. He berated Seamus, reminding him that I'm far too feeble to have children. And Seamus took it, his mouth a thin, straight line.

"I asked him, just once, if he wanted to send me away now. All he said was,

'Why? You couldn't possibly do anything more to me.'

"It is an honest answer, and I knew I deserved it. But, oh, little book, I feel too empty to know quite what I should say or do. The tears won't stop, and I fear they never will. Not until I am a dry husk of skin. My Áine is gone. And it is all my fault. Help me, little book."

Silent, Seamus stared at the page for a moment, and then he whispered, *"Love, Lia."*

My breathing sounded too loud in this small room. I could hear my heart pounding over the sounds of the shop just on the other side of the wall. But they felt a million miles away.

"The baby died?" I whispered.

Seamus finally tore his gaze from her handwriting, clapped the book shut with one hand, and set it carefully on the table, as cool and collected as a schoolteacher who'd just finished a lesson on ancient history.

"No," he said.

I stared at him. When he offered no other explanation, I repeated, "No?"

"No," he said again, drawing a deep breath. "I tried calling the doctor, but there was no answer. As I watched the little thing struggling to breathe there in our living room, I panicked. I wrapped her up and ran down to the jetty."

He looked at his hands and swallowed. "It worked. She turned. She swam circles and then swam away into the dark."

The room felt cold all of a sudden. There were voices in the shop, but they felt a million miles away. "You, you put her in the ocean?" I asked breathlessly. For all those years after Ronan and Fionn disappeared, the people of Oyster Beach had suspected Mrs. O'Leary of purposely killing her boys. Living in the midst of that, maybe Seamus thought it would be an easy way to move on and forget the child his wife had had out of wedlock. Maybe he wasn't trying to change the baby at all …

"I panicked," he said quietly, and I saw that his eyes gleamed with something more than a simple retelling of history. "The poor thing was dying, and I couldn't get a hold of the doctor and I … panicked. And, I can't explain it but … she felt like mine. I know she wasn't. But she was Lia's, and so I loved that little girl, too. I was hoping for a miracle and … and I got it."

And I wanted to believe him. But I would never know what exactly had been going through Seamus O'Leary's mind as his wife prematurely gave birth to another man's child.

"Why did you stay?" I asked instead. "All those years, after she cheated on you. Here I thought she was the one wasting away due to the man who'd abandoned her, when really she'd abandoned you years before!" I felt more betrayed than ever, but I realized I'd just heaped a lot on his plate so I honed in on one question: "Why didn't you return her coat? Let her go?"

"She was my only link to that world." He sighed and ran a hand through his thinning hair. "I knew she was my only hope for getting my boys back. Without her … the hope would die. And sometimes the only thing you need in order to keep living is hope. More than breath, more than food, more than love… And as long as she was there, anchoring those boys, that magic I didn't understand, to that place, I had hope."

Letting my face drop into my hands, I inhaled deeply, utterly exhausted. "I guess there's not a lot of hope to be found when you make the mistake of falling in love with a selkie."

Seamus gave a little laugh but shook his head. "Oh, it wasn't a mistake."

I looked up at him. "How can you say that? After all of that, and everything that happened before, and everything that happened after, how can you say that?"

Seamus smiled and absently tapped the rim of his mug. "I loved her, and she loved me. And just because it couldn't last doesn't mean it didn't exist for the time that it did. We were … enchanted."

Those words made me uneasy. "You've said that before. And it was in the diary. And even that little girl Róisín told me about it." Tears creeped into my eyes as I finally put it into words. "Selkies have some sort of lure over humans."

Seamus blanched.

"So it's true?" I demanded, taking his shock for confirmation.

He gulped, stared down into his tea, and shook his head. "It was real. It was always real. The good, and the bad. The bad doesn't make the good any less real."

"But that … that allure."

"What's the difference between a 'magical lure' and attraction? Isn't one just the phrase people use when they don't know the science behind it? How do we know the science of attraction isn't the same a man feels for a selkie?"

I shrugged, uncomfortable. It felt as though he might know we weren't talking about him and Lia anymore. "So that's why you stayed?"

Seamus shook his head. "No, I've told you why I stayed all those years. And it finally worked. I finally got my boys back. But I was an old man by then. There was nothing left for me in Oyster Beach. Or in America."

"So why keep her there? Why not give her back the coat? Then you could both move on. Keeping her there, after you left… Telling Mr. Hall not to tell her where her coat is… It seems almost…"

"Cruel?" Seamus murmured.

I shrugged. "She was so desperate."

"I was afraid if she found the coat, she'd find a way to take the boys back with her. At least Ronan. Fionn was safe as long as she didn't know who or where he was. As you said, she was desperate. I didn't know what she'd do… In those later years, she was going quite…wild. As if the animal inside her was taking over the finer aspects of humanity, like reading and writing…I was…scared."

Nodding once, I swallowed down my comments about how on earth anyone could be scared of the kind old woman I'd met rocking on the porch of the little yellow house in Oyster Beach last summer.

"There's an old saying," Seamus said. "An Irish proverb. *Ní thagann ciall roimh aois.* Sense doesn't come before age. I've never known it to be truer. I know it wasn't right. But once I was here, everything else seemed far away…"

Nodding, I swallowed the urge to point out that maybe he'd been the tiniest bit bitter, too. I didn't want to use the word "revenge," but after everything Mrs. O'Leary had put him through, I wondered if Seamus had gotten any sort of satisfaction in seeing Mrs. O'Leary deprived of something she wanted dearly. But I didn't think I would get him to admit it, and what was the point, anyway?

"So she stayed there, until Mr. Hall took pity on her last summer," I murmured. "He was avoiding her, you know. But I guess when I started poking around, he realized how bad she'd gotten."

"I've long said Phillip is a better man than me," Seamus said softly, his eyes on the floor.

"You left him too, in the end," I pointed out. "Eventually." Which got me to thinking… My forehead scrunched up. "But you stayed … for a while, after the Great Storm. Treating Rory and Aidan as your neighbors. You taught Rory to play the tin whistle."

Seamus looked at his hands.

"Why? After James Cassidy died in the storm, weren't you scared? Kieran and Colm, they both left … You could've gotten into trouble for what happened to him. Why did you stay? Only to leave a few years later? What caused you to finally leave?"

After lobbing so many questions at him, I didn't expect him to answer them all. Or any of them. But I certainly didn't expect him to clear his throat and say, "I can't tell you that."

I didn't know if he meant he wouldn't tell me or couldn't because he didn't know himself. But I couldn't press him further, because Róisín came careening around the corner into the room.

"Someone just ordered *eight* bikes, Seamus!" she squealed, delighted. "Deaide needs help getting them sorted. And guess what? I get commission on *all* of them!"

Giving her an indulgent smile, Seamus took our mugs to the sink, which I'd recently learned was Irish for "please leave now."

An Selkie is Lú
THE LITTLEST SELKIE

I T FELT AS THOUGH I HAD ALL THE PIECES OF THE puzzle now, but I couldn't make them fit together to form a congruous image of the Rory and Aidan, the Seamus and Lia O'Leary I knew.

But Rosie wasn't interested in completing the puzzle. She dragged me to the pub late that night with Evan, and I only acquiesced because I couldn't face the thought of reading any more of that diary. As stupid as it sounded even to myself, I felt betrayed. Like Mrs. O'Leary had purposely convinced me she was an innocent old woman with nary a sin in her past. Likewise, Colm Vesey. I'd thought him blameless, a bystander somehow entangled in the plight of the selkie of Oyster Beach. Little did I know he'd thrown himself in there quite willingly.

The pub was crowded with tourists and locals alike, but I wasn't in the mood to mingle, especially not when I spied Seamus in a far corner with Kieran Browne. Rosie and Evan immediately pushed to the bar to order drinks, and I waited nearby, growing increasingly uncomfortable. The place felt too hot, and I felt too full of new information. Like I was going to explode if I couldn't talk to somebody about it. And worst of all, there was just over twenty-four hours left before I learned whether that person would be Rory.

Stop, I reprimanded myself. *Of course he'll be back. First thing, probably.*

Trailing behind Rosie and Evan to a table full of Evan's friends, I felt out of place and a bit drunk, like I couldn't focus on the room in front of me if I tried. There was too much in my head. After a few abandoned conversations started by the guy sitting next to me, I told Rosie I needed to go to the bathroom, and to my disappointment, she said she'd come with.

As I led our winding way through the crowded tables, I spied Róisín perched on the edge of a stool at the bar, in an apparent argument with a redheaded boy a few inches taller than her. It never failed to surprise me when we saw children in the pub. Especially a child screeching at another one in Irish. She stopped when she noticed us, however, and yelled, "Cora!"

We had to walk by her anyway, so I paused to say hi. Rosie bumped into my back and groaned. "Great," she muttered, already a few beers in. "The selkie."

The redhead boy snorted.

Róisín turned on him, her eyes narrowed. "Do ya have somethin' in your nose?" she snapped, as vitriolic as I'd ever seen her.

"Do you really think yer a selkie?" he said with a laugh. His freckled face was contorted in mean amusement, and I immediately disliked him. Even if he was just a kid.

"I don't think it," Róisín said proudly. "I know it."

"Yer outta yer mind!" the boy laughed.

"Jesus," Rosie muttered. "Didn't mean to start a kiddie fight."

"Cora!" Róisín demanded. "Tell him it's true! That I *am* a selkie!"

Hazarding a glance at the bartender, who was busy at the end of the bar, I decided we couldn't be heard over the music blasting through the pub. Besides, this kid couldn't have been much older than Róisín. There was no harm in confirming it—eventually he'd ask another adult, and they'd tell him it was just a story. "It's true," I said, staring him down.

He grinned wider and shrugged at us. "So they're mental, too."

"It's true!" Róisín yelled. "You can ask my *dadó*! He's not mental!"

"He's not your granddad!" the older boy said with a mean smile.

"Shut up!" Róisín said.

"He's not," the boy said in Irish, his eyes narrowed.

All of a sudden this didn't feel like a schoolkid fight anymore. Rosie was tugging on my arm in warning, and I wanted to escape, too, but Róisín's little face had crumpled, her brows low over her eyes. "What d'you mean?"

"He's just messing with you," I said, patting Róisín on the back.

"Am not!" the boy cried. "*Is leanbh uchtaithe í!* My brother told me. Go ask your granddad!"

Before I could blink, Róisín's tiny fist had launched through the air and landed on the boy's freckled nose.

The boy shrieked just as I yelled, "Róisín!" and the bartender came barreling over, having seen the whole thing.

"*Cad a cheapann tú atá tú ag déanamh?*" he yelled at her, rounding the bar as people turned to look and the little boy went running off to the back, probably to find a parent.

Tears were springing to Róisín's eyes as she slid off the stool, and I asked her if she was okay, but the bartender promptly took her by the arm and pushed her back toward the table where her grandfather sat with Seamus. I trailed after them, eager to defend her.

She tore her arm free of the bartender and ran to her grandfather who took her into his arms while the bartender spoke to him in Irish, and I could understand enough words from my lessons with Seamus to figure out that he was telling Kieran what had just happened, his arms gesturing about.

"She was upset," I put in when I could. "The kid was being a jerk. He said—"

Róisín interrupted, telling her grandfather something in Irish, blubbering through her tears. Whatever she said made Kieran turn a forbidding shade of red.

Seamus eyed me quietly, and when the bartender strode away, Kieran pushed back his chair loudly, Róisín in his arms. He spat out something at Seamus in Irish.

Seamus immediately shook his head. Later, I could only assume he wanted us to hear. To understand. To know. After all these years, he wanted to be free of the secrets. Maybe we'd forced them out of him in the beginning, but once they saw daylight, he must have liked the feeling. There's no other reason I can think of that he switched to English just then.

"Don't blame the sins of old men on the young," he replied, his eyes darting toward us.

"Are you talking about us?" I asked, stepping right into the trap.

Kieran's sharp gaze turned on me. "She didn't go spoutin' off about this stuff until you lot showed up here!" It wasn't exactly our fault Róisín suddenly felt comfortable talking about her selkie heritage now, and I thought maybe she would stick up for us. But she didn't. "What'd you go tellin' them for, anyway?" Kieran demanded, rounding on Seamus.

"He didn't," I said, feeling newly protective of Seamus. Whatever we'd learned about selkies from him had been nearly pulled out of him. He didn't deserve to be scolded like this now. "Róisín told us herself. And everything else, well, Mrs. O'Leary told us. And Colm Vesey."

Kieran's face froze, and then his eyebrows lowered as he looked from me to Seamus, whose eyes were now on the floor. I had the strange feeling Kieran was even more confused than I was at the moment, and the mastermind was currently studying his toes.

Kieran stared at him for a solid twenty seconds before shifting Róisín in his arms, looking back at me, and quietly asking, "Told ye what?"

I glanced at Rosie. What was going on here? "About…selkies," I murmured, glancing around the pub to make sure nobody was listening.

Well, I don't know about listening, but everyone was definitely watching. I guess brawls in Irish pubs weren't as common as the stereotypes would lead us to believe.

"And James Cassidy," Rosie piped up.

Kieran looked at Seamus one more time before apparently realizing his mouth was hanging open, and he snapped it shut. *"Tá sí níos fhearr as an amadán sin!"* he hissed at Seamus, already rounding the table. With three long strides, he was out the door, Róisín still in his arms.

As I turned to look at Rosie, whose own bewildered face must have mirrored my own, Evan stepped up behind her, one arm on her back. "What on earth have the pair of ye gotten mixed up in?" he asked quietly, as murmurs broke out around the pub.

"I have *no* idea," Rosie said. We both watched Seamus stand, set his flat cap on his head, and leave without another word.

"What did that kid say?" I asked Evan. "What did he say to Róisín?"

"I didn't hear him, but she told her granddad Colin told her she was adopted."

"What?"

"Well, it's true," Evan said quietly. "Everyone in town knows that."

"*She* obviously didn't!" I snapped.

"And when he was leaving," Evan went on, like a regular gossip, "Kieran told Seamus that she was 'better off here' than with 'that lout.'"

His use of air quotes would have been comical had my mind not been working at a thousand miles a minute. Or whatever unit of measurement Ireland used.

"She's adopted," I murmured.

"Cora, what are you thinking?" Rosie asked, probably recognizing my dawning look of apprehension.

"She's a selkie," I whispered to Rosie, then turning to Evan, I asked, "How old is she?"

Evan shrugged, his face scrunched up in confused. "I don't know. Nine? Ten?"

"I'm eleven!" she'd corrected Rosie nearly two weeks ago. I could hear it as clear as anything, and see her face too—her dark hair and dark eyes suddenly as wild and searching as another pair I'd met over a year ago.

"Where are you going?" Rosie shrieked as I darted out of the pub. I couldn't get any words through my throat, because my heart was now lodged there. The wind was buffeting the poor little building, but it seemed only to propel me onward as it swirled around my legs. I ran all the way to the main crossroads, my feet sliding on the gravel as I took the turn too fast.

The island was quiet and empty, only the cheery windows of houses hinting at the people hunkered down for the evening. I was no great runner, so I was heaving by the time I reached the patch of grass in front of Seamus's house.

Gravel spit up in front of me as I skidded to a halt. There was a figure moving—down at the seal colony. An upright figure.

My heart lurched, and my breath hitched. It couldn't be—

With a deep sigh, I closed my eyes. It wasn't spring tide yet. It couldn't be Rory. The goat beside Seamus's door bleated at me, and when I spared him a glance, I saw that the house was dark. Both windows were pitch black.

Down at the seal colony, the figure raised a hand and adjusted something on his head. A flat cap.

Without delay, I climbed over the short rock wall and started across the muddy field. I didn't waste any time. We'd already wasted enough. There was another rock wall I had to climb, and then the grass gave way to seaweed-strewn rocks.

And there he stood, facing the water, his hands clasped behind his back. If he heard me coming, he gave no indication. I jumped from slick rock to slick rock, my feet sliding on the slime and came to a standstill beside him, the rock big enough for two.

Finally, breath still heaving, I said, "She's Áine."

He didn't say anything, just stared out at the water.

"You didn't leave that night—the night of the Great Storm, when Kieran and Colm left—because you hadn't gotten them all back. You weren't just looking for your boys. You were looking for her, too. Because she felt like yours."

Limned in the soft light of the slim moon, his Adam's apple bobbed.

"You got her back somehow and brought her here."

It was becoming uncomfortable to keep staring at his profile, but he finally broke his gaze at the sea and looked at his feet.

"It didn't feel right to leave her there," he said, his voice quiet under the thundering of the waves. "Nobody but Lia knowing she was out there. Living as … an animal."

"Jesus Christ," I muttered.

For some reason, that put the ghost of a smile on Seamus's face. "Oh, he's long since abandoned me, child. Sometimes I think he's abandoned us all."

"How … How did you do it?"

His gaze returned to the ocean and it roved back and forth through the dark, so like Mrs. O'Leary's weary gaze on the sea, it sent a chill through me. Or maybe that was the soft spray of the ocean landing on my face.

"Well," he said, "all those years, I wasn't sure she was still … alive. But I tried. And I did find her. Out at the pier. More than eleven years ago. And I feared she'd still be sickly, but when I took her out of the water … it was like she hadn't been ill a day in her life. The healing power of the ocean, I suppose."

The healing power of the ocean.

Oh, Aidan. Was it possible his mad scheme could really work? Could the ocean cure him of the attack his own body was mounting against him? It wasn't as though a tiny infant born too soon was anything like an ill teenager, but the way Seamus said it—the heading power of the ocean—it was enough to give me hope.

"Anyway, I couldn't very well fool the O'Briens again, so I did the only other thing I could think of. I took the child with me. It was easy to disappear—me, an old man nobody would miss, and she, a child long presumed dead. But I had to do it immediately. I was able to sneak into the house for a few things, but…I couldn't get into the shed. On the Ritz estate. There was a party that evening, and I couldn't be seen hauling around a strange infant." He shook his head. "I couldn't wait around. I had this…this infant I couldn't explain. So I took us out in the boat, went far enough we wouldn't be recognized, and got us out of there. It wasn't difficult to have papers falsified, all it took was money, and then I got here and …"

"Does Colm know?"

His headshake was so slight, it could have been the force of the wind. But my heart fell all the same.

"Colm is 'that lout,'" I said, more to myself than anyone. It broke my heart, imagining Colm unaware of having a daughter.

"He thought the same as everyone else in Oyster Beach—that Lia had had a miscarriage. And if he suspected that poor soul was his child, he never said. We never discussed it. And when I got here … well, I had every intention of taking her to him, in the beginning." Seamus touched his flat cap, readjusted it. "But he wasn't well in the years after the Great Storm. He'd always been in danger of it, but by then, he was firmly a drunk. It was Kieran who I found first. He'd come straight back here to the island. He's the one who took me to Colm. He was living on the mainland. And it was true. He was in a bad way. A terrible way. He'd stopped working, was living on the dole, which gave him just enough to drink."

"So you didn't tell him? You left her with … Kieran?"

Seamus shook his head. "Kieran's son had married the year before, a lovely girl from the island, and they'd just learned she couldn't have children. They were devastated. It seemed to be divine intervention to me."

Divine intervention. Maybe. Maybe Áine—Róisín—really wouldn't have been better off with Colm. Maybe he wouldn't have been able to raise her properly. Maybe he wouldn't have *wanted* to. But he still deserved to know his daughter.

"You have to tell him," I whispered.

Seamus nodded. "It weighed heavily on my conscience for many years. When I decided to retire and move to the island, I admit … there was a small part of me that wanted to know her again. To see if she was anything like Lia. And she is…"

He sniffed, and that tiny noise shifted something in my heart that threatened to topple the careful façade of calm I'd managed to erect sometime after running out of the pub.

"I told Kieran we need to tell him. I've said it many times," Seamus said. "But…the longer you live a lie, the more difficult it is to remember the truth."

I closed my eyes. Rory had said something so similar not so long ago. To explain why he'd kept his secret so long.

"Besides," Seamus said with a shrug, "who am I to say what's best for the little girl?"

"You thought yourself best to decide that eleven years ago," I pointed out.

Seamus nodded once. "And I was wrong. But now it isn't just about us and our sins. Now it's about a vibrant little soul who never knew her mother didn't give birth to her."

"But she knew she was a selkie," I said.

Seamus nodded again. "They were told as tall tales to entertain the teller—her mother, Kieran, myself. Little did we know the child took them to heart." He wiped a hand across his face. "I don't think she knew just how right she was."

It was too much to comprehend. Too much to *feel*. I was horribly sorry for Colm, even though I didn't want to be. The man who'd been with his best friend's wife. But he deserved to know.

"Maybe now that she knows, she'll want to meet him. Colm."

Seamus didn't say anything for so long I began to think he wasn't going to. Goosebumps were popping up on my arms and legs, despite my jeans and sweater. Summer was a savage mistress on this little island.

As I contemplated whether to just walk away, leave him to his thoughts so that I could work through mine, he said, "I don't envy Patrick, Deirdre, and Kieran the conversation they're having with the child tonight. It's a hard truth for her to learn. And maybe harder for them to keep it. We'll leave them to it tonight. Things sometimes seem less cruel in the light."

He was right. There wasn't very well anything I could do tonight but go back to the hostel and contemplate what a tangled web one selkie had managed to weave. No wonder there were such legends written about them.

Turning to go, I froze as Seamus said, "I never meant to hurt anyone."

It was my turn to be silent.

"None of us did. Not even Colm, to be honest. But hearts are broken anyway. It's an unfortunate consequence of living."

Oíche Naomh Seán
ST. JOHN'S EVE

THE STORM DIED IN THE NIGHT SO THAT THE dawn of St. John's Eve was bright and the island picturesque.

"How are you feeling?" Rosie asked me over a lunch of cold sandwiches from the shop. "Twelve hours to go."

I shrugged. "I'm nervous he won't show. What if something … happened? Anything could have gone wrong."

I'd already told Rosie all about Róisín and everything Seamus had told me last night. She was as dumbstruck as I was. I kept looking around, expecting to see the girl running around the island like usual. But the only familiar faces to be found were Peewee and Storm.

"What could go wrong?" Rosie asked, taking a big bite of her sandwich.

"Anything!" I said.

But before I could expound on the *many* scenarios I'd

envisioned, she went on, "He'll be here. But first, you need to relax. And there's only one solution for nerves."

I raised my eyebrows at her. "Yoga? Meditation? Prozac?"

"Beer, Cora. Beer. We're gonna get drunk tonight."

It wasn't like a holiday in the U.S. There was no pomp or fanfare. Most of the tourists had no idea it was a holiday, and the only indication that the islanders were preparing for something was a rather larger number than usual buying beer at the shop.

As we walked by the bike shop, we saw that it was closed. Although it could have been due to the holiday, I had a feeling it wasn't. Several clumps of disappointed tourists milled around the front, trying to find a list of store hours—a useful feature a lot of Irish shops didn't seem to display.

I thought about poor Róisín, finding out about her adoptive parents in such a way, but as the day wore on, my thoughts turned back to the ocean again and again. When I saw the waves, there was only one person I could think of, and that made me feel as though I finally knew how Mrs. O'Leary felt. In those first years of her marriage, every time her eyes touched those waves, had her mind gone to her life before she met her Seamus? Her family, her life, her whole previous existence. And later, those same waves were an instant reminder of her boys. How would that have felt?

Still. As heavy as that burden could be, I couldn't imagine it justifying what she'd done to Seamus. And it had only made things worse. After that, those same waves remained an instant reminder of her little girl, and, eventually, once Seamus left, he, too, would have haunted her, another ghost of the sea. And she was *always* within sight of the sea.

The sky didn't begin to dim until quite late, making it truly feel like the longest day of the year. Rosie and I sat in front of the window in our hostel room, scrolling through the missed calls from Rory's family and watching the sun set, silent but for the chatter of the other tourists bunking with us. For once, Rosie seemed to understand I didn't want to talk right now.

It wasn't yet dark when Evan came to our door. He smiled broadly at Rosie, and then gave me a small, weak smile. Apparently my anguish was contagious. But he turned quickly away from the pitiful sight I must have made, back to Rosie.

We walked with him in the gathering dark to his own village's bonfire, me trailing behind the two of them as they chattered excitedly, Rosie's quick American accent loud in the soft island night. Each village on the island—if they could be called that; they seemed more like tiny clumps of houses to me—had its own fire. We could see two fires burning in the distance.

Evan's village was on the same stretch of road as Seamus's house, just past the seal colony and around a bend in the road. A great, flickering bonfire had been set upon the rocky shore that stretched from the rutted road all the way down to the sea. In front of us, the way was clogged with people moving toward the flames like moths to a light.

There were a few guitars playing to the night, and bottles of beer clinked together as neighbors said hello. And everywhere, children were running. Running, dodging, laughing.

"Look," Evan said, pointing out over the water.

Rosie and I followed his gaze and off in the distance, small dots of light danced in the darkening green of the mainland.

"That's the Connemara coast," Evan said. "They've got their bonfires goin', too."

Connemara. I imagined Colm in his tiny house, alone, with a bottle of something. Or would he have gone to the bonfire? It was too late, it was true, for me to step in and tell Róisín's parents what to do. But Colm, lout or not, still deserved to know.

Evan led us over to his friends, who offered us beer. I thought about it for a moment, but my stomach was queasy, and I realized then that the feeling was *nerves*. I was nervous. What if Rory didn't come back?

Rosie pulled me down to sit on a large rock beside her, and being stationary, with the sounds of island life around me, helped me to forget exactly why my stomach was tumbling. It was sort of nice to sit and listen to the boys play classic rock songs like "American Pie," their neighbors singing along. And the bonfire cast waves of heat upon me until it almost felt as hot as a summer at home. The nipping sea breeze was cast away by the flames, and a warmth suffused me that felt bone-deep. And all the while the fire grew taller, as people continued to throw wood upon it.

It was well past ten o'clock when night finally fell in earnest, cloaking everything outside the bonfire's light in a deep black. There were no streetlights and hardly any houses to create an ambient light. But the little island felt even more alive in the dark.

The songs turned to Irish tunes I didn't know, rolling and lively. A man with one of those drums showed up—a bodhrán, and suddenly a pair of children in jeans were dancing in the traditional style on what appeared to be a piece of plywood thrown over the rocks. Again and again, I looked around for Róisín, even though I didn't know where she lived or which village fire she might be at. But it didn't matter. The flames threw all the faces around me into stark relief, and I wasn't sure I'd recognize her even if she was here.

There was one face I did recognize, for I'd first seen it in a grainy picture almost a year ago, back in Oyster Beach. Seamus ambled into the firelight and stood behind the activity, his hands clasped behind his back. He never looked my way, but I was sure Rosie couldn't be missed with her loud joking with Evan.

Her voice only tapered off when Evan elbowed her, and I realized everyone around the fire had grown silent. The music had stopped, the young dancers were still, and a man was calling out. Singing, in a throaty, primal call that felt less like a song and more like a lament. Everyone instinctively grew quiet and bowed their heads over their pints.

Except the sea. On and on the sea roared, a disrespectful constant that bows to no other presence.

Toward the end of the ballad, a fiddle picked up, and then a tin whistle, and as my eyes wandered around the solemn group, I found it was Seamus, his shoulders heaving as he played the penny whistle. His eyes were closed, but I knew they glowed green behind his lids. As green as the sea.

Rosie nudged me. "They're all going to hit up another bonfire," she said, nodding at Evan and his friends. "Should we go?"

Tugging my phone out of my pocket, I looked at the time. Eleven.

"Still another hour to go," Rosie said. "Might as well live it up."

I sighed. She was right. It's not like I really knew how tides worked, and it was unlikely he was going to appear at the stroke of midnight like some seafaring Cinderella, but it wasn't like I was going to be able to sleep tonight either way. And how else was I going to waste another hour?

"Okay." I turned to follow her. Behind us, fires dotted the landscape as it sloped upward to the highest point of the island, where the lighthouse was. Looking back over my shoulder, I gazed at the sea, a pitch-black stretch of the unknown, an entity that didn't know nor care that it was St. John's Eve. And on the other side of the water, the dimming lights of the fires scattered across Connemara. It was at once so close and so far away.

And Seamus stood, a figure alight with the flames of the summer solstice cast dark against the mainland. His whistle was clutched in his hand now as he watched the children begin dancing again.

"Let's go!" Rosie said, tugging on my arm.

"One second." I hurried back and around the fire and stepped up next to him.

He didn't look at me, but a small smile moved across his face as he watched the dancers. He'd known I was there all along.

"That was lovely," I said.

Seamus's eyes flicked to me, then back to his neighbors. "I don't practice as one should, but it was near enough to the original."

"You taught Rory," I said.

He inclined his head, a tiny nod.

"Seamus?" I said softly.

"Mmm?"

"Will you go with me…to the U.S.…if he doesn't come back? To explain everything to Mr. and Mrs. O'Brien? They deserve to know."

In the dark, his eyes glowed with the reflection of the fire, two shining orbs intent on my face. I wanted him to tell me that it was a ridiculous notion, that of course Rory would be back. At the stroke of midnight, most like.

He didn't. And considering how his life with selkies had gone, it was foolish of me to hope otherwise.

Instead, he said, "Of course."

Sniffling, I nodded once. Then twice. "Thank you. I know this is hard for you. Everything that's happened. Everything she did to you… I'm sorry."

He looked at me a moment. "Do you understand why she did it?"

"Not really. I know she wanted to go back to the sea, but—"

"You didn't finish the diary, did you?"

I squirmed, afraid to tell him I didn't want to. I didn't want to hear any more about Mrs. O'Leary's mistakes. I wanted to remember her as she was last summer. At least as she was to me. "No," I finally admitted.

"Do an old man a favor and read the entry for 5 July, 1972."

The thought of opening the book again felt as heavy as my heart did at the moment, but Seamus didn't wait for my answer. He knew I would do it.

"You know, I don't regret a thing, child." The flames danced in his eyes, and I wasn't sure if it was that or real mirth that softened his weathered features. "Because I know something you can only learn with time. To have a broken heart is to have irrefutable proof that you've lived. Really lived."

Caillte
LOST

T HE ROAD SLOPED EVER UPWARD, TOWARD THE old lighthouse. The structure was limned in gold, due to our destination lying just behind it. I couldn't see the fire from here, but its effect on the lighthouse was almost magical.

"There are sixteen villages," Evan was saying, to Rosie's delight.

"So we could be bonfire-hopping all night!"

My legs felt shaky, and listening to another round of Irish men pouring their souls into a ballad would threaten my emotional stability at this point. So I said, "I'll meet you guys down there. I'm going to go walk up by the lighthouse."

Rosie looked at me sharply. She seemed to study my face as best she could in the dark, probably looking for tears or other signs of distress.

"I'm fine," I assured her, and even though it was

mostly false, I didn't feel bad lying to her. My despondency was the kind that wanted solitude at the moment. "I just want to walk a bit."

"Well, I guess it's okay," Rosie said. "I mean, what trouble could you get in on an island this small?"

When the path broke off toward the wall around the lighthouse, Rosie and Evan and his friends kept walking. It became incredibly dark inside the walls, so I pulled out my phone and turned on the flashlight app. Leaning back against the old stones of the wall, I let my head fall back. My eyes were immediately drowning in stars, stars brighter and more numerous than in any sky I'd seen before. With no light for competition—and the moon only a sliver—each star burned brighter than the bonfire we'd just left.

Rosie's chatter with Evan faded away, and the farther her familiar accent went, the wilder my heart beat. Until it felt like a bodhrán pounding in my chest. I'd been looking so long at the sea, I had never noticed the stars. And I'd been thinking so long on whether Rory would come back, I didn't think much on what he was going through right now.

What if he couldn't find Aidan? The ocean was a big place, in the biggest understatement of the century. It wasn't inconceivable that he couldn't find him. But then again, what if he did find him? Aidan had been so sure of what he wanted. And I couldn't exactly argue. It wasn't for me to decide how Aidan handled his illness. But Rory wouldn't be happy unless he had his brother beside him.

Either way, he would be changed, no doubt. You couldn't go through something like that and *not* be changed.

But hadn't I changed, too?

Meandering toward a broken section of the lighthouse wall, I noticed it was an old tower. Stepping over the tumbled-down part, I found myself in a tiny, dark room, the ceiling opening up to the stars above. I leaned against the wall and gazed around me.

And the darkness moved.

"Ahhhhhhhhh!"

An answering scream matched mine in pitch, but broke off quickly.

"Cora!" Róisín stepped into a soft patch of light cast on the rocky ground by the dim sky through the hole in the ceiling.

"Jesus! Róisín, you scared me half to death!" I put a hand to my chest as my heart resumed tapping at a wild pace.

"That's not my fault!" Róisín said. "You're in *my* lighthouse, you know."

"Oh, it's yours, is it? I didn't see a sign."

The snark was gone from her voice when she said, "I come here to think."

She had told me that. When she'd brought me and Rosie here on her practice tour. And it was obvious she had a lot to think about.

She went to the pile of tumbled stones I'd just climbed over and perched on it. When I joined her, I could see her face glistening with moisture.

"Are you okay?" I asked gently.

She heaved a sigh fit for a much older person. "Have you ever thought one thing your whole life and then found out it wasn't true at all?"

She was talking about her parents, of course, but I could relate on a tiny level. "Selkies," I said.

She looked at me, a question in her eyes.

"I never believed in any of that. Magic, all that stuff." I shrugged. "Until I found out about selkies last summer."

Róisín gulped. "It's kind of like that. Except I thought my parents gave my birth to me. And they didn't."

"I know," I murmured. "I'm sorry. That must be so hard to hear."

She was staring at the bonfire on the horizon, and I wondered if her parents were there. And Kieran. Or if this St. John's Eve was too hard for them, too.

"It's as if you think you're one thing all your life. And then one day you find out that's wrong. And suddenly you realize that every day you've ever woken up as you, that was wrong. So you were really lying to yourself and everyone else every day, weren't you? But you didn't know it, so it's not wrong, is it?"

"Róisín, no, that's not what this means," I said, putting a hand on her shoulder. "You're still you. That hasn't changed. Which is a good thing, because you're pretty cool." Okay, my attempts at comfort were sort of lame. But I was in way over my head here. Besides, I didn't know how much they'd told her. About Mrs. O'Leary, Colm. Rory. Even what me and Rosie were doing there. Had they told her she was born across the ocean forty years ago to a desperate selkie? That she'd spent decades in the ocean? I had to tread carefully.

"Me mam was a selkie," she murmured. "I'm still a selkie. That's the only part that was ever true."

"No, there were other parts, too. Like that Patrick and Deirdre love you. And Kieran. And all your neighbors here on the island."

She didn't respond, and I could tell she was a million miles away from me. Her eyes were no longer on the bonfire, but beyond it—on the inky-black expanse that was the sea.

Neither of us spoke until I pulled my phone out of my pocket. Eleven forty-five.

"Róisín, I need to go. But … you can come with me." I didn't know how much she knew, but I couldn't leave her here like this. "Remember my friend? The selkie you saw? He's due back now, and I'm going down to the beach to wait for him."

"My brother," she whispered.

I nodded. They had told her that at least.

When she turned to me, her eyes were bigger and rounder than a baby seal's. "Is he going to like me?" she asked, as quiet as a breath.

The smile on my face felt at odds with the frantic beating of my heart. I reached out and slipped her hand into mine. "He's going to love you." As we walked down the hill toward the beach where we'd last seen Rory, I told her all about her brothers, carefully avoiding any mention of the selkie who'd given birth to her.

She listened intently, but when we reached the sand, she stopped, her eyes on the water.

"Cora, do you know what my favorite part of swimming is?" she asked softly.

"What?"

"You can't cry underwater."

An Oíche
THE NIGHT

SOMETHING GRITTY GROUND AGAINST MY TEETH. Spitting, I sat up, jostling a heavy weight against me. The sand moved against my hands as I spit the grains from my mouth. How long had I been sleeping? It was still dark, but I felt groggy, and there were goose bumps up and down my arms.

Róisín sat up, rubbing her eyes, and suddenly I remembered where we were. My heart jumped in my chest as I made to stand up, but then I saw them—Rory's clothes.

Still sitting neatly folded a few feet from the rock we had curled up against last night. The tide had gone out, and Rory had not come back.

A chip broke away from this fragile thing in my chest

"What time is it?" Róisín asked.

"I, uh, don't know," I said, willing myself not to fall to tears in front of this girl who'd been through so much more than me these past days. "We both fell asleep."

As I moved to pull my phone from my pocket, a call reached us on the wind. For a split second, my heart soared—and then I located the speaker behind us, across the beach. He was accompanied by a group of flashlight beams frantically bobbing toward us. And several people were yelling. That must have been what woke me.

"Shit," I muttered, scrambling to my feet. "Your parents must be worried sick!"

"He's not here," Róisín said sadly, turning away from the search party to point at Rory's clothes.

"Róisín!" The flashlights came closer, Róisín's dad in front, his shoes slipping and sliding in the sand. Behind him, Deirdre. Behind her, Rosie. And up on the road, several more people, flashlights pointing in all directions. A real search party.

"What the hell?" Rosie yelped seconds before I was slammed into a hug.

"She's here!" Patrick shouted, and the other beams of light all flashed toward us before the group up on the road regrouped and stayed put, giving the family space.

"When you didn't show up at the bonfire..." Rosie pulled away and held me at arm's length. Her hair was a mess, and even as I looked at her, the wind whipped strands around her face, the picture of worry. "Don't *ever* do that again!"

"I'm sorry," I said, sniffling, whether from the cold or the disappointment, I wasn't sure.

"God, what were you thinking?" Beside us, I could hear Róisín getting much the same lecture. "Have you guys been out here all this time?" Rosie turned to look at the little indentation we'd left in the sand, and her eyes landed on Rory's clothes. "I'll take that as a yes."

"I ran into her up at the lighthouse. She was upset." I glanced over my shoulder at Róisín, but she was invisible beneath her father's coat and her parents' fussing arms. Guilt twisted my gut. "We went back by the hostel to get his clothes and then came out here. She wanted to come. She wants to meet him. And…I wasn't thinking."

Kieran only reached us then, a hand clutched to his side, his dark pants covered in sand to the knees. He glared at me before stepping to set a hand on his granddaughter's head.

"We fell asleep," I said lamely. "I'm so sorry."

Patrick glared at me while gathering Róisín into his arms and shuffling through the sand toward the road. Deirdre shook her head and followed, not meeting my gaze. Kieran stared after them, his shoulders bent forward with the weight of worry.

"I'm sorry," I said again. "I didn't… I wasn't thinking. She was just so upset and…I'm sorry."

"Cora," Rosie said gently, wrapping an arm around my shoulders, "let's go back. Let's get to bed. You're exhausted."

"No, can we—can we just sit out here a little longer?" When I turned to her, she was blurry, and I realized I was crying.

Rosie swiped her thumb beneath my eyes and nodded, her face creased with worry. She guided me to the nest in the sand indented from where we'd slept and sat. Before I joined her, I stepped toward Kieran, my legs still shaking.

"I'm so sorry, Kieran."

He seemed frozen—as if too many years of too much subterfuge had finally rendered him unable to function. But when he finally tore his gaze from the small dark smudge that was his family in the distance, he looked at me. I was sure I looked a fright, for the wind was still pulling my hair into a knot as tangled as my gut felt. But I held his gaze, and he didn't seem strong enough to chastise me, for his gaze bounced quickly to Rosie, and the rock we'd been sheltering against, and then the clothes.

"Did the boy come back?" he asked, his voice scratchy.

"No." I gulped. "Not yet."

Kieran nodded once, gave the sea one cursory glance over his shoulder, then turned toward the road, not sparing me another look. "It's a sad life you'll build waiting for a selkie, girl. Keep that in mind. *Go n-éirí leat.*"

Fós Fan Liom
WAIT FOR ME STILL

F*AN LIOM. FAN LIOM. FAN LIOM.*

The wind whispered it. The waves repeated it. The gulls shouted it.

I could only squeeze my eyes shut and promise, I am. I am. I am.

Every now and again time feels like a living, breathing thing, a conscious entity who knows how you dread its passing and thus decides to move more slowly, dragging its feet, flowing over your skin like a sticky reminder of what's decidedly not happening.

Seventy-two hours. It's a long time to wait. To sit in the sand. To watch the waves.

Mrs. O'Leary watched for decades, and you can't wait three days?

Yeah, but she certainly did her part to deserve that penance, I thought grimly.

On the third day, after the sun had begun its long

descent through the sky, sinking behind my back, a shadow fell over my rock.

"That was quick," I said, because Rosie had left only a few minutes before to find us something for dinner.

When she didn't answer, I turned.

Seamus looked down at me, the creases on either side of his eyes more pronounced than usual. My heart fell, and I turned away from him, back to the sea.

"Go home, child," he said.

Sniffing, I ignored him and pulled Rory's hoodie over my bare legs.

"You can't wait here forever, wasting away on this island—"

"Isn't that what you're doing?"

My barb was meant to silence him, but once it did, I wanted him to fight back. To argue. I looked at him. He was squinting at me like I was a foreign species he didn't quite understand.

"Maybe that's why I'm in a position to advise you. Go home."

I ran my sleeve under my nose, which had started running chronically sometime in the last three days. "I can't leave him," I murmured.

Seamus took in a great breath and let it out slowly. "I wish I could tell you not to worry, that he'll be here. But a life with a selkie is a life of waiting." He nodded at the horizon. "It isn't far to the mainland, girl. He could be there. Go back to Galway. I'll wait here. If he's going to come, he'll come."

I nodded. He was right. Rory had said so himself—the distance to Galway was small by sea. He would probably expect me to be there. And if he wasn't...

"Will you still come with me? If …"

Seamus nodded. "I can be in Oyster Beach by July."

I nodded and looked back out at the water. I gave myself one more moment, then slipped my arms into the sleeves of Rory's hoodie and stood. Turning my back on the water was easier than I thought it would be. But before I'd gone two steps, Seamus called out.

"Whatever happens, girl, promise me you won't waste your days sitting on a cold beach waiting for something you have no control over. Sometimes you have to leave what you love."

I turned halfway. "Like you did?" I asked the wind.

Seamus was silent, and when I finally looked at him, he was squinting at the sea, though the sun was behind us. His face was unreadable.

"I'm sorry. About all of this. If only you'd never met her…"

Something shifted in his gaze. "You still haven't finished the diary. July 5, 1972."

"I forgot," I lied. Because there is a great difference between forgetting something and consciously avoiding thinking about it.

"Try to remember," Seamus murmured. "Don't condemn the actions without knowing the heart."

"Can you ever really know the heart of a selkie?" I said.

A tiny smile tipped Seamus's face upward. "He's only half selkie, child. The other half is pure Irish. And to tell the truth, I don't know which is harder to know."

The boat pitched side to side on monster waves. The sea was angry today. Maybe because the selkies were. *Because they lost a brother to the land today*, I hoped with every fiber of my being. I squeezed my eyes shut, so sick of the sight of the gray-green water.

He had to be in Galway. He had to be. Absently, one finger twisted my Claddagh ring around and around. My chest ached with the regular pulsing of my heart, and though I fell asleep each night with the words drifting through my head—*Fana liom; fan liom; fan liom*—I knew I wouldn't have the strength to fight Rosie. Our flight home was tomorrow. We would be going home tomorrow.

Whether Rory came back or not.

Finally, I pulled out Mrs. O'Leary's diary, found July 5, 1972, and read.

Deatach agus Lasracha
SMOKE AND FLAMES

5 July, 1972

I still feel as though I can't breathe. You'll never know, little book, you'll never know what it feels like to breathe and breathe, putting nothing into your lungs but smoke.

I was at home alone while Seamus went out with the lads to celebrate the Fourth. I wasn't feeling well, and I'd just curled up in the living room with a big book of fairies, the windows open to the sea breeze, when I heard the yells from outside.

"Witch!"

"Marriage wrecker!"

"Murderer!"

And more words too awful to write.

I knew they didn't like me, leabhar beag, but I never thought to fear the fireworks. Fire isn't something a selkie is taught to fear.

When an object sailed through the open window, I started, but it wasn't until the loud pop that I thought to run. It pop, pop, popped all over the living room, and there were flames on the carpet in seconds. Where do you run when the floor is on fire?

Oh, how I wished I could swim away!

The smell was horrific, and each breath was more difficult than the last, and I was sure this was drowning out of water. The smoke filled my nostrils, my lungs, my eyes, my heart, and I wanted to die. To stop breathing. To float away on the wind like a selkie on a wave. I should never have left.

I was going to die with my lungs full of smoke, never to see my boys again.

Instead, I passed out. I woke in the hospital.

Seamus says I could have died. Of course I knew that already. I saw it all, in my mind's eye. The doctor says everything is okay, but it was a close call. Seamus was quite shaken and angrier than I've seen him in some time. I couldn't tell who it was who yelled those mean things outside the window, but Seamus says the police have arrested Frank Nolan and his friends. I should think Laura put him up to it. But the police say they didn't mean me real harm, only a holiday prank. But the police didn't hear the things they yelled.

I do not think anymore that it is a skin that tells people what you are. That's somewhere else. Somewhere they can never know. Unless they try.

And they won't try. Which means as long as I wear this skin, I shall smell that smell and breathe that smoke.

I can't stay here.

I know I promised Seamus, but I can't stay here. I see flames in my dreams, waking and asleep. It makes me doubly glad I didn't condemn my boys to this life of hatred just because of a foolish decision I once made.

The smoke, the smell, the fear—I don't want to feel like that again, and my boys never will. It hurts my heart to think of Seamus, alone here, but then I remember the last time I felt this bad. After I learned Seamus was in the hospital. I'd never felt so wretched. And that's how I know that I can return to the sea content, as long as I know that Seamus is alive and well. Seamus and our children. For Seamus, that is the land. For our children, it is the sea.

And for me, it is the sea. I know I promised Seamus, but you can't burn underwater, and I don't want to burn. Besides, what are broken promises but words that have stopped being true?

Love always,

Lia

Seal na hOíche
GRAVEYARD SHIFT

S HE'D BEEN AFRAID FOR HER LIFE. THAT'S WHY she'd done everything she did. And Seamus had forgiven her. They'd both done things I didn't know if I would ever be able to forgive, yet they loved anyway. I wanted a love like that, but I wanted something more. Seamus and Lia had taught me that a love didn't have to last to be real and true and memorable. But I didn't want the memories alone. I wanted a love that would last.

I didn't want our story to end the way Seamus and Lia's had.

When the bus neared its stop in Galway, I was the first to jump to my feet.

"Cora?" Rosie yelped, jostled away from her nap as I darted down the aisle, my backpack slung over one arm.

"Stay seated 'til the bus comes to a stop!" the driver snapped, but I didn't budge, my Claddagh ring clinking against the railing as I grabbed on for balance and the bus pulled to a stop. As soon as the doors opened, I ran.

Bumping into people was unavoidable as I stumbled down Shop Street, but their indignant comments bounced off me. Martin Freeley the "lynch" expert was waltzing with an invisible partner near a busker playing oldies, but I didn't return his wave. Near the bottom of Shop Street, the crowd thinned, and I ran flat-out.

The river was high, and gulls hollered overhead as I crossed the bridge and made for the boat graveyard. It was just as I remembered it, and that felt wrong. The world had changed, I had changed. Everything else should have changed, too. I darted between the decrepit boats, looking in each one.

But boat after boat was empty—or filled with ancient fishing gear and lobster pots.

Across the Corrib, the old orange boat caught my eye—our boat. The one Rory and I had been caught trespassing on one night. It had been repainted and cleaned up, probably by new owners.

I looked helplessly around me. He wasn't there.

Rosie caught up eventually and simply looked around and came to the same conclusion. "Let's check the apartment," she said gently, taking my hand and tugging me back toward bustling Shop Street.

Rosie let us inside, and we both paused near the front door, listening. It didn't sound like anyone was home. I followed Rosie to the sitting room—empty but for Rex who pricked his ears at us—then made a beeline for Rory's room.

It was exactly as we'd left it. Empty.

Behind me, Rosie peeked into Niall's room, and then Niamh's. When she turned around, she saw me standing helplessly in the doorway.

"I'm sorry," she said softly. "But there are still a few hours left."

I nodded. "I can't stay cooped up in here."

She nodded. "I'll get us some food and meet you down at the boat graveyard."

A little green boat with a hard wooden crossbar for a seat made the perfect lookout in its place at the edge of the graveyard, looking out over Galway Bay. I sat bundled in Rory's hoodie, my hands pulled into the sleeves. Watching. Listening. Thinking.

My thoughts were so jumbled, I didn't even know what I was hoping for anymore. I wanted Rory back, of course. What if something had happened? Gone wrong? I was worried. But what if he hadn't found Aidan yet? He might need another two weeks. Or what if … what if he liked it? Loved it? What if he felt the sea in his veins the way Lia had written about in her diary?

What if Rory never came back? And what if it was by choice?

It was selfish, but I couldn't get on that plane not knowing the answers.

After a while, Rosie plopped down beside me on the little seat of the boat and dropped a hamburger in my lap. Like the good friend she was, she munched away quietly, communing in my silence, and when the food was gone, she disappeared with the trash before coming back and leaning against me. She was solid and real, and if it turned out that nothing else this last year was as tangible as her friendship, at least I had that.

The noises of happy drunk people in town spilled through the medieval streets, making the wide open expanse of the graveyard on the banks of the river feel emptier than usual. Even with Rosie's head leaning against my shoulder, huddled up against me for warmth, I felt alone.

At long, long last, Rosie shifted, rocking the boat, setting the rocks sliding beneath its hull, and she whispered, "Midnight, Cor."

She gave me another half hour before she laid a hand on the sleeve of Rory's hoodie. I could feel her cold fingers through the fabric. She'd done enough for me. It was time I stopped waiting around. Seamus was right. I nodded and let her pull me out of the boat.

Though I'd walked it over and over since arriving in Galway, Shop Street felt foreign to me now. People laughed and joked and chattered and danced in the street in the way I'd come to associate with this beautiful city.

In the apartment, Rosie sat down on the couch and patted the space beside her for me to join her. But she immediately succumbed to a huge yawn and toppled sideways onto the couch as her eyelids began sliding closed. I tiptoed to Rory's room.

It was cold. I stood two steps over the threshold and thought, *It doesn't smell like him anymore.* Rushing to his dresser, I grabbed his aftershave and sprayed the air. Again and again, until I was nearly choking on it. Outside the big windows, seagulls raced down Shop Street. The seagull highway. How I wished I was still lying in bed with Rory watching the gulls race toward the sea.

Hugging Rory's hoodie tightly around me, I crawled into his bed and laid my head on his pillow slowly, almost reverently. *Heartbroken*, I thought. *Heart. Broken.* The word made more sense than I'd ever realized. There was no other word to explain the feeling in my chest—a pile of rubble weighing heavy on my breastbone.

And as I lay there surrounded by his stuff, the reality of the situation hit me: *What am I going to tell Mr. and Mrs. O'Brien?* I'd have to go to Oyster Beach with Seamus and explain all of this. By then, another spring tide would have passed. If Rory still wasn't back… There was no way to continue this lie. They would live in fear and confusion forever. Searching, always searching.

Like Mrs. O'Leary.

No, they needed to know the truth. How on earth would we tell them this truth?

Tears leaked from my eyes. I couldn't bear this burden, it was too great. Too unbelievable. And now I knew how Rory had felt for all those years. The tears came harder and I wiped my nose on the sleeve of the hoodie. How would I ever find the words to describe to Mr. and Mrs. O'Brien who their children were? *What* they were? Where they'd gone? Everything I'd learned?

Sobs wracked my body, and I let them come. There was no point trying to keep them at bay—a pressure was building inside me and I feared the breaking point.

Saol Eile
ANOTHER LIFE

M Y HEAD FELT LIKE A BALLOON, CERTAINLY the effect of crying oneself to sleep. I blinked into the dark room—straight at a dark silhouette moving toward me.

I screamed for dear life.

"Shh!" A hand came toward my face, spiking the terror in me. But it didn't go to cover my mouth—it cupped my cheek. "Cora, *mise atá ann!*"

I scrambled upright, and the scent of salt assaulted my nostrils.

The light on the bedside table flipped on, and there sat Rory, chest heaving, on the edge of the bed.

"Rory?" Blinking painfully into the bright light, I tried to steady my arms, but my heart was beating too fast as his face split into the widest grin I'd ever seen on him.

"Forget me already?" he asked.

A strangled laugh erupted like a sob and I launched

myself at him. His laugh was full and happy but muffled in my hair as I squeezed him to me, my hands hanging onto his firm back for dear life.

"And here I was afraid you wouldn't be happy to see me," he whispered.

"What was it like?"

"You waited," he said.

"Tell me everything."

"You waited for me."

His clothes were damp beneath my hands, and his hair smelled vaguely of seaweed. My hands roamed, feeling his firm shoulders, his arms, his neck, his face. Everything seemed okay. I pulled back to better examine his face.

He was a bit pale, but his soft lips were there, and his deep brown eyes, and the little crease between his eyebrows that he always got when he was contemplating me. It was the face that had been my first kiss. The face that had first loved me. The face that had written a song for me and sung it in front of a bar full of people. "You're okay," I whispered.

"I'm okay." He shook his head, looking confused, then nodded and tucked a lock of my hair behind my ear.

"Rory," I whispered, glancing at the doorway. "Where's Aidan?"

I must have known before he replied, for the sadness had already settled in my chest by the time Rory shook his head.

My breath stuttered.

"*Tá sé ceart go leor*," Rory said quickly, then shook his head again. "It's okay. I promise. He's okay."

"You found him?"

Rory nodded. After a thoughtful pause, he said, "Come here."

As he pulled away, I saw the seal skin in his lap. He set it on the bedside table, stood, and held his hand out to me. I looked from the seal skin, lying there, discarded, so lifelessly, to Rory's outstretched hand. Outstretched to me.

I took it and let him haul me out of bed. "You're barefoot!" I said in surprise.

"I had to raid a clothesline," he said, gesturing to his clothes, which I saw now were too big for him and remarkably befitting an old man. "Unfortunately, they don't put shoes on clotheslines." He gave me a weak grin. "I was trying to get close to Galway—the boat graveyard, I thought that's where you might be—"

"I was!" I said, tears springing to my eyes. "But when you didn't come at midnight, I thought … I didn't think you were coming back."

Rory kissed me on the forehead. "*Tá brón orm.* I'm sorry. I overshot it and ended up way down the coast in Connemara. It took me forever to find clothes and get back here."

When I blinked, my eyes overflowed. "That's the second time you've walked barefoot across the city for me."

He smirked and as it faded away, he kissed my forehead again and whispered, "I'd walk a lot farther than Connemara without shoes to get back to you, Cora."

I swallowed against the lump in my throat, but he didn't give me time to form any words.

"Now come on. Put on *do bhróga*—your shoes, hoodie thief." Pulling playfully at the strings of his hoodie, he turned and slipped into his own tennis shoes.

"Where are we going?" I asked, dashing after him as he headed for the front door.

Rory smiled. "Wait for it."

I grabbed his arm. "A smart person once told me a life with a selkie is a life of waiting."

Rory leaned over and kissed me. When he pulled away, I was quite breathless. "I promise this is the last of it."

The taxi let us out several miles outside the city, beneath an ancient archway with a square tower on each side, and I wondered that the driver didn't question our destination. With Rory's hand firmly guiding mine, I wasn't scared of the dark lane that led past several sprawling houses, a canopy of trees blocking the light of the moon and stars. The road ended at a long metal gate, but Rory didn't pause.

"Up and over," he said, already scaling it. The bars were slick with dew, but when I slipped, Rory was there to steady me.

The dew soaked my shoes as we hiked across a wide field, and as the trees at the edges cleared, there came into view a hulking ruin covered in green foliage as thick as paint.

"What is this place?" I asked as we passed into its shadow.

"Menlo Castle," Rory said. "An *eastát*—sorry. An estate that burned down ages ago."

"It's…stunning." The young moon gave just enough light to cast the ruins in sharp relief as we walked a worn path bordered on the other side by a squat, crumbling structure that still resembled what it had obviously once been—the barn.

And then the grass opened up again, and I turned to look back at the enchanting façade of the old house, trying to image what it once looked like, but Rory pulled me onward.

When I turned around, I saw that the grass ended abruptly, the sound of lapping water meeting my ears. It wasn't like the sea, this movement, and I couldn't help but marvel—marvel at how I'd gone in one year from being unable to swim to being so familiar with the water, I knew its sounds, its smells, its creatures.

"The River Corrib," Rory said, stopping at the edge of the grass. After only a moment, his grip on my hand tightened. "*Ansin.* There."

I followed his pointed finger to a spot upstream, where a glistening orb floated in the river like a reflection of the moon.

My breath hitched. "Is that…"

"I thought he'd still be here."

"Rory, is that…Aidan?"

"We came up here a lot to be alone. Most seals don't venture this far from the bay."

The silvery head dunked under the water and reappeared a few feet closer, close enough for me to make out two huge, glowing eyes staring right at us. "He's…beautiful," I said softly.

"He likes to explore the river—the open ocean still scares him a bit. But he'll get used to it."

"Used to it," I repeated in a strangled whisper.

Rory squeezed my hand. "He's not coming back, Cora. Not yet."

I nodded and watched Aidan duck back under the water, leaving us staring at nothing but the rippling water. "You're okay with that?"

"Yes," Rory said. "We talked a lot. Not talked, but… I'll explain it all to you sometime. But it was incredible, Cora." He turned away from the river to face me. "It was like being asleep and being more awake than you've ever been before at the very same time. I know it's weird, and not something anyone else could understand, but…it felt like home."

"You once told me home is not always where we expect it to be."

Rory gave me half a grin and cupped my face. "But it wasn't for me. There were things calling me back to land." He pulled me to him, and I sank against his chest. "Still, I can understand why he would want to stay. It's not an opportunity many get. And Aidan, he's had a difficult time with his illness, and with his diagnosis, there are no promises for his future. Seeing him out there, he was just… He wasn't sick, he wasn't tired, he wasn't scared.

"Before, I thought he was giving up. But this…" He nodded toward the water, and I followed his gaze to the water's edge. Aidan was bobbing there, his great eyes shining with moonlight. It was the strangest feeling, but those eyes, they seemed to be smiling. "It's not *this* life," Rory whispered, "it's a very different kind of life. But it *is* a life."

Without taking my arms from around his waist, I rested my head in the crook of his neck. "Will you tell me all about it?"

"Everything."

Aidan disappeared and then reappeared above the water with a great splash that sent sprinkles our way, before diving back down. I giggled.

"He's showing off," Rory murmured into my hair.

Surfacing once again with a splash, Aidan dove backward, came to the surface, and dove repeatedly in a series of somersaults. He finally came up and sat bobbing, staring at us, all the while smiling with those immense eyes.

Stepping out of Rory's embrace, I kneeled at the edge of the water and reached out. Aidan swam to my hand and ducked beneath it, letting my fingers glide across his head.

"I miss you," I said.

He twisted away from me and dove backward, sending a spray of water at me.

Covering my face, I tumbled backward onto my butt, laughing outright. "As annoying as ever, I see!"

Rory kneeled beside me as Aidan surfaced out in the middle of the river. He blinked at us for a moment before ducking under, and I lost sight of him. Seconds later, he was ten yards farther downstream. He blinked at us once more, then turned, and sunk back beneath the water.

My throat felt tight with tears. "Where's he going?"

"Back to the sea." Rory chuckled softly. "He's always hungry."

We watched, waiting, until the droplets on my skin began to raise goose bumps on my arms, and Rory took my hand, pulling me to my feet.

"He's happy, Cora. I promise you that. And that's the most important thing to me."

I swallowed. "And your parents?"

Rory's Adam's apple bobbed. "I have to tell them."

"Seamus wants to help," I said.

"I don't need his help," Rory replied quickly, and I suddenly remembered all the things I'd learned that Rory didn't know. Not least of all the existence of his little sister. It seemed too monumental to approach alone, and I suddenly wished I had Seamus there at that very moment.

"He's a good man, Rory. And he wants the best for you. Please trust me." I gave his hands a reassuring squeeze, but Rory was silent.

Finally, after gazing into the dark water for minutes on end, he said, "The whole time I was out there, I was scared. Scared you wouldn't want to see me after the things I said to you, and leaving like that… I'm so sorry, Cora. I'm sorry for the stuff I said about your sister. At the time, after Aidan going off, I thought I understood some small inkling of how you felt, having lost your sister like that. But I was wrong. About so much. And my brother's still out there, and I want to be there for you, to try to really understand you and your family and your past as much as you've tried to understand mine, and… I'm just sorry."

"It's okay," I whispered. "If there's one thing I've learned from Seamus while you were gone, it's how to forgive."

He gave me a weak smile. "You really think he cares about us—me and Aidan?

"More than you know."

Rory sighed. "I guess it would help to have him along to explain everything to Mum and Dad. But…will you come, too?"

"Of course." I gulped. "But first, I have so much I need to tell you."

Deartháir Mór
BIG BROTHER

I 'M SORRY, I'M SO, SO SORRY," I HEARD RORY saying into the phone the next morning. "I'll explain everything, I promise you, but I have to be there in person, Mum." I paused in the hall outside his room, not wanting to interrupt. His voice sounded so hurt. "I'm coming home. I promise I'll be there on the next flight."

Turning back down the hall, I dodged our packed bags lined up against the wall and padded to the sitting room, where Rosie was again curled up with Rex on the couch. She'd walked into Rory's room this morning to find not just me, but the selkie himself, and so I figured she'd earned this nap. I quietly went to the windows and sat down on the sill to stare down at Shop Street.

It was crowded with buskers and shoppers, and I saw Martin Freeley strolling past shop windows, his hands behind his back, as if truly interested in the fashionable clothing and souvenirs. Just below me, a stationary Oscar

Wilde conversed with another statue, oblivious to the strangers sitting between them.

"Good-bye, Ireland," I said to the window. "Don't be a stranger."

Rosie snuffled in her sleep—or maybe it was Rex. Either way, I shut my mouth, not wanting to wake either of them.

Rory and I had talked all night. As much as I wanted to hear about his adventure and everything he'd seen and learned, I knew it was more important for him to hear everything that *I'd* learned. And he'd listened, letting me turn to pages of the diary to back up all the unbelievable things I was telling him.

He didn't say much. Just sat there, his eyes glistening, as I whisper-talked in his room until the sun came up and Rosie walked in and promptly erupted into a scream that brought Niamh and Niall running.

We'd spent the better part of the morning explaining things to Rosie and then planning. There was so much to be done. I turned my ear toward the hall, listening. Sure enough, Rory's voice was still murmuring in his room. The conversation he was currently having with his parents had to be the most difficult they'd ever had. But the things he needed to tell them weren't things he could say over the phone.

Turning back to the window, I pressed my face against the cool glass. The gulls raced past the windows, and I remembered what Rory had said: his and Aidan's lives, they were an opportunity not many had. As was mine. Knowing a selkie—or three—and coming to love one. A smile tugged at my lips as the music of a tin whistle floated up, and the gray clouds pressed down, threatening the kind of gentle rain that makes you want to go outside and dance in it.

"You all ready to go?" Rosie asked, and I turned. Yawning, she stretched and sat up on the couch, simultaneously dislodging Rex, who gave a petulant groan.

"Almost," I said, biting my lip as I twisted back to the windows. "We have one more thing to do."

Rory walked slowly down Shop Street, and I matched his pace, not wanting to rush him. His hand was warm in mine, but the day blew chilly and brisk around us. By the time we reached the fork in Shop Street, I was convinced I could actually "feel" his nervous vibes. The little pub squished between a jewelry store and a bank wasn't all that busy, but as I headed for the door under the gold letters spelling Tig Cóilí, Rory pulled his hand out of mine. He stepped away from me, up to the windows and looked inside.

Stepping up beside him, I took his hand back into mine and peered inside with him. Deirdre and Patrick already sat at one of the few tables, Róisín looking tiny and afraid between them. Seamus was standing near the wall, leaning against a ledge that ran along it like a bar and seemingly staring into space. Kieran was returning from the bar with a beer and what looked like MiWadi. He set that down in front of Róisín, the beer for himself, and took a seat beside his son.

"Are you ready?" I asked Rory softly.

He swallowed and nodded. Giving his hand a squeeze, I led him inside.

Deirdre saw him first, and I saw in her eyes something between fear and regret. For the first time, I thought about what she'd done when she took in Róisín and how she might feel now. She nudged Patrick, who looked up, saw us, and looked desperately to Kieran.

For once in our acquaintance, Kieran didn't glare at me or throw out some bitter words. Instead, he turned to Seamus.

"Róisín," Seamus said, stepping up to the table just as we did and placing a gentle hand on Róisín's shoulder. The little girl looked up, her face open and optimistic, but her hands twisting on the table. "This is your half-brother."

"Rory," he said quickly, before Seamus could introduce him as anything else. "I'm Rory."

She looked at me, and I nodded encouragingly. "I-I'm Róisín," she said in a shaking voice.

"I've heard a lot about you, Róisín," Rory said. As he pulled out a chair and sat across from his little sister, pride welled up in me. He'd been through so much yet was facing still more with an open heart. "It's so nice to finally meet you."

Róisín blushed a bit and looked up at her mother, who put an arm around her daughter's shoulders and forced a smile. "Rory," she said, "Róisín would like to tell you about her school."

"I'm in fifth class," Róisín said eagerly, the nerves already melting away. "Are you in a class?"

Their words faded as I silently slipped away to the bar to order a Coke. Seamus joined me there, and we watched, silent observers, as a brother and sister came to each other, years after they should have. I knew their words would turn to selkies—maybe not now, with everyone listening, but someday—and for the first time, I thought maybe Rory would be okay with it.

"You've been good to him," Seamus said, letting his tired body crumple onto a stool at the bar.

"So have you," I said.

They were the only words we exchanged in the thirty minutes we sat, side by side, me drinking my Coke, Seamus a Guinness, each of us lost in a world of thought. His deep sigh is what made me look up and then follow his gaze to the door, where a newcomer stood, sweeping a hand through his snow-white hair, hat in hand.

Colm.

Colm's mouth fell open as his gaze landed on the table where Róisín sat, still talking to Rory, and his eyes welled up. I knew at once that they'd already told him why they needed to see him. Kieran looked up, and his face was struck dumb with fear. Seamus wore a mask of grim resignation as he heaved another sigh, slipped off his stool, and strode forward, apparently at peace with the part he'd played in this and willing to make it right.

I went to the table, putting a hand on Rory's arm. He turned and followed my gaze to the door. He swallowed. "We should go."

I nodded.

"Róisín," Rory said gently, in that gentle voice people reserve for children—and now his sister. "We have to go, but we'll talk again soon. When I get back from America, okay?"

Róisín's face fell just a fraction before she nodded, then stood and rounded the table. She flung her arms around Rory's middle.

He stood awkwardly, arms raised, for a moment before a smile curved up his lips and he dropped his hands to his little sister's back. He patted her gently. "See you real soon, kiddo."

"Bye, Rory. Bye, Cora." She graced me with a decidedly less passionate hug as Deirdre and Patrick stood nervously, their eyes over our heads. I grabbed Rory's hand, and we stepped aside. Rory hurried to the door, but I couldn't resist stopping to look over my shoulder.

Colm stood before the table, staring at Róisín, his whole body crumpled forward.

Róisín stared back, her eyes wide.

"Colm," Seamus said, shattering the frozen silence. "This is your daughter, Róisín. When she was born, Lia called her Áine."

A lump grew in my throat, and I turned to see if Rory was listening.

I was alone. Through the glass of the door, I could see Rory in the middle of Shop Street, shoppers streaming around him, as he stood furiously wiping tears off his face.

Athaontú
REUNION

T HE AIRPORT WAS BUSY WITH SUMMER TOURISTS that evening. I stood among them, a weird sort of tourist myself, as Rosie checked out in a small shop. Rory and Seamus sat near the gate, been deep in conversation since I'd stepped away from them to get snacks and call my mom before the flight. And as the phone rang, I watched the two men, so different and yet so alike in their movements, I realized, as I saw them side by side. I wanted to know what they were talking about more than anything. Could it be that they were going to overcome everything that had happened? That Rory could let go of his anger and hurt, and Seamus could make up for carving out this strange life for his sons?

"Cora?"

I snapped back to attention. "Mom, hi," I said into the phone.

"What are you doing calling at noon? Don't you

know I'm hungover from the Kreiser benefit last night?"

"I did not know, but I'm sorry," I said, a small smile playing at my lips, because my mother and I having a joking relationship was a relatively new phenomenon. "Our flight is this evening. I just wanted to let you know I need to stop in Oyster Beach before coming home."

"Oh?" Mom said. "What's there for you in Oyster Beach?"

More than you could ever know.

"It has to do with Rory," I said, hesitating. After years of bad communication, my first instinct was not to tell my mother anything. But I decided my relationship with my mother had evolved enough since that day I took her to see Mrs. O'Leary that it now warranted some version of the truth. "He needs to have a difficult conversation with his parents, and I want to be there for him."

"I see." Mom was quiet a moment, and I thought it was silent disapproval, that we were moving backward, but she finally said, "Would it be all right if I met you there? After the difficult conversation? I'd like to meet this boy of yours again, if he's up for it, and we don't have any renters lined up at the Pink Palace. And…I miss you."

"Um, yeah. That would be…that would be nice," I said. And I meant it. My mom would always be my mom. And Rory wasn't going anywhere, either, because I was determined our story wouldn't end like Seamus and Lia's.

"Okay," Mom said, surprised. "I'll give you some time with his parents. Meet you there in a few days?"

"That sounds perfect," I said.

"Cora, they called our boarding number!" Rosie shouted at me from down the hall. I hadn't even noticed her walking off. When did she become the responsible one? I grinned and told my mom I had to go.

"See you soon, honey. I love you."

"I love you too, Mom."

"Cora, come on!"

I dashed toward Rosie and joined her back at our seats to scoop up my backpack, which was packed full of carefully wrapped Belleek china for Joan. Seamus and Rory were already in line, Rory looking over his shoulder for me. I smiled. That boy was looking for *me*.

There was a long twisting corridor to get from the gate to the plane, and I walked behind Seamus, my hand in Rory's. When we reached the end of it, Seamus stopped, and I worried it had been too much walking for him.

"You okay?" I asked softly.

He took a deep breath and nodded. "I just never thought I'd be leaving Ireland again."

My heart twisted. He had come back here to live the rest of his days. He had come back to die here. Amid all the stories and memories, I'd forgotten that Mr. O'Leary was an old man. An old man who had pined for his Ireland long before Mrs. O'Leary pined after the sea. They weren't so different after all, were they?

Before I could say anything reassuring, Rory stepped forward, and put a hand on Seamus's arm. "Thank you for doing this. For me."

Seamus looked down at his hand, his eyes gleaming, like it was a sight he'd never expected to see. And he probably hadn't.

He put his own weathered hand on top of Rory's and patted it twice before raising his head, taking a deep breath, and stepping onto the plane.

Seamus and Rory were seated among strangers since they'd bought their tickets so late. But because Rosie is the best friend a girl could ask for, she switched places with Rory. Though I do think the attractive young guy next to Rory's seat might have had something to do with it. Regardless, I settled happily down in my spot and then turned to Rory.

"Tell me everything,"

He laughed. "Okay. *Lig cead dom*—damnit."

"What is that?" I said. "You keep doing that."

"I know, it's like I can't control it, Irish just keeps slipping out, ever since I got back from…you know."

Oh, I knew. And I had so many questions. "Did it hurt?"

"Hold on," Rory said, then he turned to the man next to him and said something I couldn't hear. A moment later, Rory stood, much to the stewardess's chagrin, and disappeared down the aisle. The guy next to him got up and followed.

Almost immediately, Rory came back and sat down, Seamus at his heels.

"So, where was I? Hurt. No, it didn't hurt," Rory said, continuing as though this were the most normal thing in the world. Seamus buckled his seatbelt and leaned in to listen.

The picture of them, sitting beside each other, son telling father of things most people wouldn't dream of, it made tears prick at the backs of my eyes.

"I just wrapped myself in the coat and sank into the water," Rory went on. "Underwater, it doesn't hurt—not like that time in my room,

Cora. It just feels a bit uncomfortable, kind of like a rug burn, and then suddenly…everything went a little clearer under the water, it didn't hurt my eyes, and I felt like I could swim just by thinking it. And it was like…like I didn't need air. For like, five minutes, I could just swim without needing to surface. And when I did surface, it was like, like everything was muted except the sea and the sky and… It was incredible."

Seamus smiled at him.

"I thought it would be cold," Rory said, his head swiveling between the two of us, "but it was warm. So warm. Like my skin was made for life under there. I could communicate with them—the others…the-the *seals*. Just by thinking it. I mean, I guess I was speaking, I don't know. And I went to Galway, and when I saw Aidan I just…I *knew*. Like I could smell him or something." Rory laughed. "I don't know. Sounds made up, huh?"

"A little," I admitted.

He reached over and took my hand. "I wish you could see it, Cora."

I smiled back. "Me too."

Seamus stood on the boardwalk, completely still, solid as a tree in the flurry of wind and sea and beachgoers around him. His gaze didn't waver from the little yellow house. It looked more pristine and perfect than before, and even though I knew the O'Briens had done some work on it, the sight still felt foreign.

Even as we watched, the front door opened, and my heart

stumbled, eager to see her face. The old, weathered face that had kindly called me up from the boardwalk into this wild world of selkies and my very first love.

Instead, a young couple looked back at us, a bit alarmed.

Of course. The O'Briens were renting out the place. Rory had told me that.

Seamus snapped out of his trance, gave the spooked couple a quick smile, and moved on down the boardwalk toward the resort. I followed, walking quickly to where Rory stood a few feet away, waiting for us. I slipped my hand into his and we moved off after Seamus.

"Hey," I said softly, putting my free hand on Rory's arm. "I was thinking maybe I should take off now. Let you guys talk alone."

He looked at me in alarm. "No," he said quickly, squeezing my hand. "Please. I need you."

I squeezed back. "Okay. I'm here."

We hurried to meet Seamus where he stood outside the resort, gazing up at the sign that read *O'Brien Resort*. Rory stepped forward and placed his hand on the door.

"I wish Phillip were here," Seamus murmured.

And despite how things had started out between me and Mr. Hall last summer, I found myself wishing the same. Mrs. O'Leary's diary had painted a portrait of quite a different man than the gruff old man who spoke in riddles.

There was no time for me to say anything to Seamus, however, because the door to the resort was open, and a relieved cry pierced the air.

"Hey, Mum," Rory said, his voice choked.

Taking his hand, I followed him inside.

Mr. O'Brien was a tall, thin man whose face was far too haggard for his age—but that was probably due to the circumstances. He stood behind his wife as she hugged Rory fiercely. He looked over my shoulder just as his wife did, and they both froze in shock.

"Holy mother of God," Mr. O'Brien said at long last. "Seamus, you're…alive!"

Seamus still stood in front of the door, his weather-beaten face curled with the slightest smile. "Yes, Daniel, I am. But in a few moments you're going to wish I weren't."

"Where is he?" Mrs. O'Brien demanded, recovering from the shock of seeing Seamus alive and well years after his disappearance. "Where's Aidan?"

"Mum, Dad," Rory said, his voice shaking, "I know you're worried about him, but I just have to beg you not to be. He's okay. And what I have to tell you…it's pretty huge."

Seamus strode into the room and put a hand on Rory's shoulder. "We best go to the kitchen. All life's surprises are best revealed over a cuppa."

An Todhchaí
THE FUTURE

INNER WITH MY PARENTS THE NEXT EVENING was a decidedly less dramatic affair. My dad and Princess showing up with my mom was the biggest surprise of the night—except for maybe how attentive both my parents were to Rory. It seemed that, at long last, they'd accepted him. Of course, we didn't test the boundaries of that acceptance by telling them he was a selkie.

His own parents had taken it well enough. Seamus had first revealed that he was the boys' father, and Mr. O'Brien had surprised us all by revealing that they'd known as much. Or at least suspected it. After all, half the town had been gossiping about Seamus having fathered the boys out of wedlock. The fact that Lia O'Leary was their mother was a little more of a surprise.

And after that, Seamus had stated, "The boys were born fifty-plus years ago. Lia was a selkie. That means the boys have it in them, too. And she chose that life for them, sending them to the sea when they were mere infants. It was many years of my searching for them before I succeeded, and when I did, I wanted a good home for them, a home where they could lead normal lives. *Your* home."

Needless to say, that required a bit more explanation. Several hours' worth.

Both Mr. and Mrs. O'Brien had heard the myth, but it took some coaxing to convince them to believe it no myth at all. I don't think anyone but Seamus O'Leary himself, in his soft, firm voice that held more strength than if he'd yelled, could have convinced them. It also helped that so many pieces fell into place with that explanation—the rumors of Mrs. O'Leary killing her babies, her "death" the previous year, Seamus's disappearance, Rory's affinity for the water—and now Aidan's disappearance.

Both parents were devastated to learn that Aidan had had a relapse and kept the test results from them. But Rory held his mother while she cried and assured her Aidan was happy and that she would see him again. He even told them all about Áine, and how her existence today was hope that Aidan's crazy plan would work. That the sea just might heal him so that he could come back some day. Mr. and Mrs. O'Brien were also alarmed to learn Rory had attempted it—going back to the sea—while in Ireland, but when he assured them he was just fine, they asked him to tell them everything.

At that point, I decided they deserved some time alone with their son, and Seamus must have agreed, for he excused himself just as I thought to do the same. They set each of us up in our own cabin at the resort that night, but Rory sneaked into mine when his parents finally fell asleep. He spent the next day with his parents, and I hung on the periphery, helping where needed and holding hands when necessary. After all that had happened, everything that I'd learned, it felt good to just be. Just be in Oyster Beach and hold Rory's hand. To know we'd reached the end of the secrets and lies. At long last, they'd run out.

And now it was time to move forward.

"Your parents don't hate me anymore," Rory said brightly.

We'd had a laidback dinner of takeout at the Pink Palace, where seeing my parents had made me a tiny bit excited to go home. Maybe things had changed because of my dad's lawsuit, but if I'd learned anything this summer, it was that change didn't have to be bad.

Now Rory and I stood leaning on the railing on the balcony off my room, Princess between us. The wind whipped around us, promising a storm in the night.

I shrugged playfully. "I guess he doesn't want to go through life hating the guy his daughter loves."

Rory made a pretend surprised face and pointed at his chest. "Me? Is that guy me?"

Shoving him playfully, I teased, "That remains to be seen."

He grabbed my shoving arms and pulled me to him, squishing Princess between our legs. She didn't move. "Does that mean whatever you imagine as your future has me in it?"

I nodded. "At least the scenario where I *don't* become a famous actress. That version of the future has Daniel Radcliffe in it."

Rory pretended to think about it. "Fair enough. So in this other version, I'm the leading man?"

"I'm all yours."

He closed the tiny distance between us and kissed me softly. "How do I make sure we're on the road to that version?"

I sighed. "Well, I need to go home for my last year of community college."

Rory nodded. "And I need to stay here for a bit, make sure my parents are okay. Maybe take them to Ireland when we can."

"And then…" I swallowed. "Seamus mentioned a program in Galway about the Irish language and culture. I was thinking I could apply there."

Rory grinned. "How fortunate that you know one or two people in Galway."

"Yeah, and there's this singer there who I'm, like, in love with."

Laughing, he kissed me again, and instead of pulling away, he rested his forehead against mine. For all my worrying that things would never be the same when Rory got back, I'd finally realized that maybe that was okay. In order to move forward, things couldn't stay the same. Rory had taken the biggest risk of his life this year in order to deal with his past, and we'd come out the stronger for it.

"Are you okay, Rory?" I asked softly, scared of ruining this moment.

He sighed and took my hand into his. "Yes," he said, twisting the Claddagh ring around my finger. "I'm surprised to say it, but…I am."

"Good," I said, sliding my arm around his neck. "*Grá mo chroí thú.*"

Rory smiled. "Where did you learn that?"

"I learned a thing or two while you were gone."

"Oh yeah?" He pulled me in closer. "*Níl mé inan fanacht ar an lá atá amach anseo in éineacht leat, mo grá.*"

"Okay, I didn't learn that," I admitted.

"I said I can't wait for the future with you."

I smiled. "Even with a mere mortal like myself?"

He kissed me lightly. "I guess I have a thing for humans. What about you? Do you think you could love a selkie?"

"Oh, I already do."

Séamus + Lia
SEAMUS + LIA

T HAT NIGHT, I COULDN'T SLEEP, NESTLED AWAY in my room in the Pink Palace, far away from Rory for the first time since we'd gotten here. And as I lay awake, my thoughts racing, they kept returning to one thing again and again: *I wonder how difficult being here is for Seamus.*

My mind repeatedly returned to the entry in Mrs. O'Leary's diary where she spoke of Seamus carving their names into the jetty: *Seamus + Lia.* How in love they must have been. After a few hours, I gave up on sleep and went to my balcony. From there, I could just see the jetty. From this distance, I couldn't quite tell, but it looked almost like someone was standing on it.

Rory?

Without thinking, I rushed back into my room, pulled on sweatpants and shoes, and headed for the door. The boardwalk was nearly empty at this time of night, but I reveled in it. It made me feel closer, more intimate with the sea, and since I was no selkie, this was likely as close as I was ever going to get. I couldn't wait to hold Rory and maybe hunt for the carving in the wood of the jetty. It was pretty decrepit, so there was a chance the piece holding their name and their love had been swept away, but we'd have fun hunting.

As I traipsed across the sand toward the jetty, something moved to my right, and I saw that whoever had been on the jetty had moved to the beach just beyond it. A cloud moved aside, letting the moon cast its light on the form, and I paused, confused, before crouching in the shadows at the land end of the jetty.

It wasn't Rory.

It was Seamus.

Ankle-deep in the waves, he was facing the sea, his eyes fixed on a point somewhere farther out. I watched, wondering what he was doing, for nearly a minute before something disrupted the waves a few feet in front of him. He took an unsteady step forward, the waves darkening his pants, as a figure rose out of the water before him.

My hand flew to my mouth as I attempted to strangle my gasp.

Lia O'Leary moved slowly forward, her bent, fragile body wrapped in the dark fabric that I knew was her seal coat.

From this angle, I could see the smile on her face, but nothing of Seamus's expression. Whatever his feelings, he stepped forward, and they stopped just a foot apart, the waves above their knees. For the longest moment of my life, they stared at each other, and then Lia stumbled forward and wrapped her arms around him. He hugged her back fiercely.

Their embrace was battered by the waves, and as they moved, I saw, thanks to illumination from the star-studded sky, the expression on Seamus's face. He was happy.

Lia pulled away, speaking rapidly. I only just barely caught the name "Fionn" in a barrage of Irish words.

"He's okay," Seamus said in Irish, and it was only because the emotion slowed his words that I could understand him. "He's okay." After a moment, he added, "He's gone to Ireland."

The ocean was too loud for me to hear Mrs. O'Leary's reply, but a moment later, Seamus said, "And Áine…"

Mrs. O'Leary's large, round eyes stared at him, her mouth agape.

"She's alive, Lia, and she's healthy and happy."

"How?" Mrs. O'Leary asked, followed by a rush of Irish. Seamus responded tenderly, but the ocean was loud and their words foreign— what little I could hear was Irish I didn't know.

Finally, Seamus said, "Everything is okay."

"Everything is okay," Mrs. O'Leary repeated, as if she couldn't believe it, and her words seemed to hit Seamus hard. He wiped a hand across his eyes.

"*Tá brón orm*," he said, words he'd uttered at various times during our lessons. My scant grasp of Irish was just enough to translate: I'm sorry. "*Tá brón orm*, Lia."

She nodded and whispered something that I took to be an apology.

"It's my fault," he said desperately, and she shook her head, putting a hand to his arm. "It is," he insisted. "*Ní fhanann trá le fear mall.* An ebb tide does not wait for the slow man. I'm sorry."

She shook her head gently, and Seamus cupped a hand around her cheek, his eyes glistening in the light of the moon. At long last, he leaned forward and kissed her. She grasped his forearms, and when he pulled away, she was smiling wider than I'd ever known her to.

Lia asked a question then, the only bit of which I understood was the Irish word for "happy."

Seamus nodded slowly and asked, "*An bhfuil tú?*" *Are you?*

Lia smiled and nodded. The wind carried her next words loud and clear, and they were words I recognized. Simple words. Strong words. "*Tá me i nGrá leat.*"

I love you.

Seamus smiled. "*Táim i nGrá leatsa chomh maith.*"

They drifted apart, almost as if it was the will of the waves themselves, and Lia walked until the water reached her waist. She turned and waved to Seamus, a sad smile on her lips. Then she slowly ducked under the waves and disappeared.

DEIREADH

the end

ABOUT THE AUTHOR

A short, dog-obsessed, ketchup-loving romantic from the middle of the U.S., Annie Cosby spent three years living in Galway, Ireland, which gave her mono, set her soul on fire, and introduced her to her husband.

She is the author of the USA Today-recommended *Hearts Out of Water* and *Souls Out of Ireland* series, the Amazon-chart-soaring *Humming Song Saga*, and countless other tales seeped in Celtic lore.

She now lives in St. Louis, Missouri, with a Rottweiler mix named Lucy and her favorite Irishman.

Sign up for her Readers Club and find more bookish fun at AnnieCosby.com.

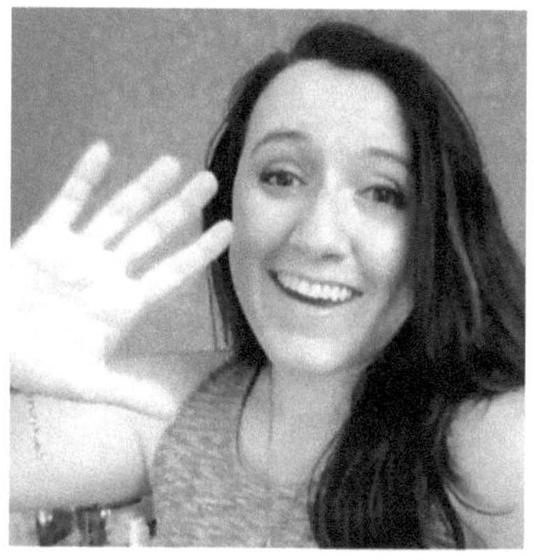

BOOKS BY ANNIE COSBY

HEARTS OUT OF WATER

All the Tales We Tell

Lifespan of a Memory

The Last Secret

Fadó, Fadó: Selkies, Kelpies and Other Celtic Creatures

(A Companion Collection to *Hearts Out of Water*)

SOULS OUT OF IRELAND

The Daughters of Morrigan

THE HUMMING SONG SAGA

Daughter of the Diamond King

www.ingramcontent.com/pod-product-compliance
Lightning Source LLC
Chambersburg PA
CBHW051627180726
48284CB00006B/1634